THE MOUSE WHO WOULDN'T PLAY BALL

Everard Hope was dead. Of that there was no doubt. The old man had fallen down the stairs and broken his neck. And there were no mourners, for as a wealthy old miser of unprepossessing habits Everard Hope had been singularly un-beloved. Instead of mourners there was a crowd of needy relatives all eager for the pickings: suspects aplenty if Everard Hope's untimely end had been no acci-dent. It was a case which took all of Arthur Crook's rude ingenuity to unravel.

THE MOUSE WHO WOULDN'T PLAY BALL

ANTHONY GILBERT

CHIVERS PRESS
BATH

First published in the United Kingdom 1943
by
Collins
This Large Print edition published by
Chivers Press
by arrangement with the copyright holder
at the request of
The London & Home Counties Branch
of
The Library Association
1980

ISBN 0 85997 482 0

British Library Cataloguing in Publication Data

Gilbert, Anthony
    The mouse who wouldn't play ball. –
    Large print ed.
    I. Title
    823'.9'1F   PR6025.A438M/

    ISBN 0–85997–482–0

Photoset, printed and bound
in Great Britain by
REDWOOD BURN LIMITED
Trowbridge & Esher

THE MOUSE WHO WOULDN'T PLAY BALL

CHAPTER ONE

I

IN THE ICY long-dark house someone waited for zero hour. Time passed so slowly you could almost hear the shuffle of his feet. A watch ticked. One-two, one-two. A loosened shutter flapped in the wind. Behind the crumbling wainscot a mouse nibbled industriously.

The bedroom door a few inches ajar the listener waited, knowing, like an actor, that everything depended on perfect timing. Somewhere at the end of the corridor a foot sounded, a door closed softly. Silence came down again, silence impressive as a shriek. Still the watch ticked, one-two, one-two. The loosened shutter flapped on. Behind the crumbling wainscot the mouse, alarmed by something, was motionless.

Out of the heart of that black silence the terrible cry rose.

Fire! Fire!

The great barn of a house took the words and sent them rolling into the impenetrable shadows of the upper floors, battered them against the walls, flung down the echoes into the well of the mighty staircase. Doors opened, feet sounded, voices called. One, clear as a bell, cried, 'Come back! Come back! There's no light...' That was part of the horror. The old man was so mean he had the electricity switched off at ten o'clock, and thereafter his guests must make shift with candle-ends, or the torches they brought with them.

The great main stairway was a chasm of darkness. At its head the wall curved inwards; here, until the treacherous light betrayed the secret, a figure could hide—hide and watch and wait for the moment of doom. The murderer's heart beat like a drum. The imperious will demanded, 'Quickly. Come quickly before it's too late.' And again that cry of fear went pealing through the dark.

'Where is the damned fire?' asked a man's voice.

'One of the other rooms, I suppose,' came the answer. 'Not mine.'

At last light appeared on the scene, a flickering beam from a candle-end held high. The murderer muttered, heart black with disappointed rage. Too soon, too soon. But before the light could do its work the bearer stumbled—it was easy to stumble on those ragged carpets, for the old man's meanness was not confined to the use of electricity— and the candle fell over the carved bannisters

2

into the distant hall and was extinguished in its flight.

'No need to start another fire,' said a woman's abrupt voice. They were all barging into one another by this time. The would-be slayer waited, sick with fury. If this should fail!

'No,' cried the furious heart. 'Not this.'

Death! Such a small word, meaning so much. The end of threats, the end of humiliations, the years-old debt settled at last. Then, when hope seemed at an end, the moment came. One figure dislodged itself from the rest, came in a quick familiar movement by the stair-head. Now! One well-timed thrust with the old man's stick and the deed was done. You could fancy the figure falling, down, down, grotesque, helpless, into the black hall. Not much hope for any soft human creature who had made that journey!

An instant too late the light flared again.

II

No one was quite sure how soon after the second cry of Fire! the crash occurred, though every one heard the gurgling scream that accompanied it and the sickening sound of something falling, bumping and falling again. The pandemonium on the upper landing grew. Voices clashed with one another.

'Who is it?'

'Who called?'

'Who fell?'

A large woman, no longer young, came past the shivering group at the head of the stairs, carrying a warden's torch that flung its beam on the tattered carpets and the feet arrested by that cry and its horrible sequel. The light descended rapidly, just a beam apparently going down, down by itself. The woman who carried it remained in shadow. One of the men held a candle high above his head. The monstrous shadows danced on the painted wall.

'Take care!' said a woman's deep voice. 'Candle-grease.'

'You couldn't do much harm to these carpets,' retorted the man on a high note.

Another man pushed past. 'Must see what's happened. Was that Lilias who went down? Chris!'

'I'm here,' said Christopher Lacey in reply to his brother's summons. 'Lord, what a staircase!'

'Take care you don't catch your foot, too.'

The voices all had the peculiar anonymity of voices heard in semi-darkness.

From the hall came the voice of the woman, Lilias Tempest. 'Is that Garth? Oh, Christopher, it's you. It's Cousin Everard. I

4

think he's broken his neck.'

Christopher Lacey said in dry tones: 'It wouldn't be surprising if he'd smashed every bone in his body, falling from that height.'

Upstairs a slim figure came running along the corridor. 'What's happened? Where's the fire?'

In the candle-light she was revealed fair and trim, with an ageless face that even the stuff she put on it at night could not rob of a kind of hard beauty.

Cecil Tempest, who held the candle, said between chattering teeth: 'God! I'd forgotten about the fire. Julia...'

'He has these turns sometimes,' said the woman with the abrupt voice. 'A kind of nightmare.'

'It's a nightmare all right.' Cecil clung to the head of the stairway with his free hand. 'Lilias!'

'Don't come down, not for a minute,' called Lilias clearly. 'We're just moving him. How about a doctor? Where's Julia?'

'I'm coming,' said the one they called Julia. She had been the old man's companion-housekeeper for fifteen years, ever since he inherited his dead brother's house and money. She came marching down the stairs. It was like a macabre kind of ballet, all of them weaving in and out with

5

only that candle-end to light the scene.

The steps went down and down. Suddenly there was a low cry.

'God!' cried Cecil from the stairhead. 'Not another accident?'

'Tripped over something,' said Julia in her abrupt way. She stooped and groped on the stairs. 'Oh!'

Christopher Lacey, who was standing by the piece of human wreckage on the hall floor, called up: 'What is it?'

'His teeth,' said Julia grimly. 'Lower set, that is. Must have fallen out when he—crashed. Unless he was carrying them.'

'The other half's in his mouth,' said Lilias. Cecil didn't know how she could be so calm. It was all he could do not to be sick.

'A doctor?' murmured Hugh.

'I don't suppose he can do anything,' said Lilias, 'but I think we'd better get him.'

'I am getting him,' said Julia, and they heard the faint tinkle of the telephone bell.

'It's a wonder Cousin Everard ever had the telephone in,' said Garth Hope abruptly.

'That was my doing,' shouted Julia. 'Hallo. Yes, I want Dr. Musgrave. Took me two years,' she added.

The two left at the head of the staircase insensibly moved a little closer.

'I loathe the sight of blood,' confided Cecil

shamefacedly.

'There are plenty of them without us,' returned Lucille Hope. 'Is that your stick?'

Cecil stooped. 'No. It's one of old Everard's. I suppose he brought it up to bed.'

'I shouldn't be surprised,' agreed Lucille. 'He was always lamer when there were people about than when he was alone.'

'I don't smell any fire,' said Cecil.

'I don't suppose there was one. Just his imagination. He was a dreadful old man. How Julia has stood him for fifteen years I can't imagine.'

'I expect she had her reasons,' returned Cecil grimly.

'You mean the money?'

'No one would guess he was a rich man.' Cecil leaned over the bannister. 'You know, I think we ought to go down now. They've moved him out of the hall to judge by all those footsteps.'

'All right,' agreed Lucille reluctantly. 'Though there can't be anything we can do.'

The group below had indeed lifted the smashed body in its shabby blue dressing-gown a tramp would hardly have valued, girt round the emaciated body with a ragged cord, and laid it on a sofa, with a cushion under the head. Hugh, the younger of the Lacey brothers, had spread a handkerchief

7

over the dreadful face. At the foot of the couch stood Garth Hope, one of those heavily-built men with sombre expressions that seem to proclaim a natural hostility to all mankind. Garth knew human nature was up to no good, and his experience as a lawyer confirmed his original suspicion. There was no pity in his eyes as he looked at the little crumpled figure under the rug. It had been a mean little face, all bones. Great bony nose, protruding forehead, the bones bulging through the skin, lean cheeks, long chin, scarcely as much flesh as would have covered a good-sized bird. Ah, but for all the disadvantage of age he'd kept his secrets well. Only death could wrest them from him. His thin miser's hands were crossed above the rug someone had laid over him.

Christopher Lacey, large, blond, forty-one, looking as if he couldn't conceivably be related to the dead man, asked slowly: 'Does any one know how it happened?'

'I suppose he heard the cry of Fire like the rest of us and came out of his room,' said Lilias, a little uncomfortably.

'Who gave the alarm?' asked Garth in an impersonal voice. No one answered him.

He looked round the little circle. Cecil Tempest told him uneasily: 'Julia says he may have done it in his sleep.'

'The police won't like that,' said Garth.

'The police?' Lucille at his elbow sounded staggered.

'Do you imagine we can keep them out?'

Christopher said slowly: 'Damned awkward if we get them in. Rich old gentlemen shouldn't die by mysterious accidents when all their relations are on the premises. Poor taste!'

'I don't know that that remark's in the best possible taste,' said Garth coldly.

But Christopher was not discountenanced. 'Truth seldom is,' he observed.

Julia, done with telephoning, came to join them. 'Dr. Musgrave's coming at once,' she said. 'What are we going to say?'

Garth noticed that she not only took a realist's view of the situation, but was prepared to admit it. The lawyer in him applauded her.

His wife, Lucille, who had had the wit to stay behind in her room and collect her jewels and handbag when the alarm was given, said coolly: 'Surely if we say what happened, won't that do?'

'If any one knows what did happen,' said Julia. She looked thoughtfully at the cousins and their wives. No one spoke.

'Isn't it obvious?' demanded Cecil after a silence that seemed endless. 'He must have caught his foot in a hole in the carpet. It's

9

surprising really no one's broken his neck that way before now.'

'He must have thought the fire was his end of the house,' said Julia. 'Otherwise he'd have gone down by the little stair near his room instead of hobbling all along the corridor to the main staircase.'

'Probably heard all of us here,' suggested Christopher, 'and came to see what was up. Obviously we'd all make for this staircase, as being the nearest.'

'No one here gave the alarm?' demanded Julia, her eyes turning from face to face.

'No one admits it,' said Garth. 'Personally I was in bed . . .'

'So was I,' put in Lucille quickly.

'I was reading,' said Hugh in his leisurely way.

'I was in the bathroom,' said Cecil.

'Too bad,' said Hugh. 'I mean, if you'd been in your own room, you and Lilias would have been one another's alibis.'

'You didn't?' said Julia to Christopher, and he shook his head. In a grim fashion he was amused to see her taking so high a hand, though, actually, it was only what you'd expect. Julia had been taking a high hand with the household at The Brakes for fifteen years. She was the only person who could make the dead man shell out half-a-crown.

10

Cecil, shivering in his skimpy dressing-gown, thought: 'Only a few hours ago I was talking to him. Only a few hours ago he was jeering at me. A thousand pounds, he said. That's a lot of money, my boy. Where do you suppose I could find a thousand pounds?' He shivered again. Lilias said: 'You'll catch cold, Cecil. Your overcoat's in the hall, you'd better get that.' And he hurried away, thankful to be released from the battery of inquisitive eyes. He wondered how much Lilias knew. Everything, perhaps, but she'd never give herself away.

Lucille had shut her eyes. Her body was very rigid. She couldn't bear to look at the dead man. She wondered if it would be possible to go upstairs now. 'Who gets the money?' she wondered. 'Garth was always sure—Garth's generally right. But something's happened lately, though he won't tell us. But I'll find out.'

Christopher glanced at Hugh. Damned fools we must be looking, the brothers thought. Only Lilias stood calm, yet certainly not unmoved, by the sofa. A strange woman, Lilias. One wondered what on earth she'd seen in Cecil. Hugh brought out a cigarette-case but Christopher shook his head. Not yet, it wouldn't be decent. Garth looked as though he were carved in stone.

11

'That doctor's taking his time,' he said.

'He has to cycle. His car will be garaged at this hour,' returned Julia. Her face told you about as much as a shop-window with the blinds drawn.

Cecil came back, the overcoat clumsily pulled over the thin dressing-gown. He thought they looked like a group at Madame Tussauds, one of the historical murder scenes. He choked back an hysterical laugh. Garth put his hands in his pockets, Christopher walked restlessly to the shrouded window. Hugh looked away. A shame to stare at the other fellow when he was so defenceless. Odd to think that sometime they'd all come to it. He blew his nose.

The tension was frightful.

*   *   *

Julia, throwing up her head that was tied in a scarf, exclaimed: 'We ought to phone Mr. Midleton. He'll have to come down.'

Garth said impatiently: 'You can't rouse a lawyer in the middle of the night.'

'He was coming on Friday,' said Julia. 'It'll only mean making it one day earlier.'

'Coming here?' exclaimed Garth.

'Yes. Didn't you know?'

'How should I know?'

'Mr. Hope said he'd told every one.'

'He didn't tell me,' said Cecil quickly.

'He said it was a good joke,' continued Julia. 'Every one minding their p's and q's, he said.'

Christopher glanced at his brother. 'Did you know?'

Hugh shook his head. 'It doesn't matter. Hallo, that'll be the doctor at last.' Julia went to let him in.

'Do you think he could have committed suicide?' questioned Cecil abruptly.

'Be your age,' said Christopher. 'When did Cousin Everard ever give away anything?'

Garth made a movement of disgust, but his cousin remained unmoved.

The doctor came in, blinking with weariness, looking unshaved and blue. He shot a rapid glance at the oddly-garbed gathering, Christopher's luxurious dressing-gown held his attention for a moment, but the calm handsome face above it told him nothing; Lilias wore her hair in a net and had dragged on a flowered wrapper; Lucille looked neat and unmoved, but there was a general air of nervous exhaustion about them all.

He wasted little time asking questions. The position was too obvious. He gave his opinion brusquely.

'He must have been nearly eighty,'

13

exclaimed Lucille Hope, fancying that his eye rested on her.

The doctor looked at her as though she were a new kind of human being he hadn't met before.

'It's never been my experience that men part with life any more readily at eighty than they do at eighteen,' he observed.

Julia, who had slipped away unnoticed, returned to the room. 'There's a huge tear in the carpet on the top stair,' she said. 'I suppose he tore it worse when he caught his foot. I've put a bit of brown paper over it and fastened it down with drawing-pins. We don't want a second death on the premises to-night.'

Cecil said in an abrupt tone: 'In the midst of life we are in death.'

Christopher's hand closed over his arm. 'Pull yourself together, man,' he adjured him.

'There'll be an inquest, of course,' said the doctor, stepping back and replacing the handkerchief over the battered face. 'There shouldn't be any trouble. Shock alone would have done for him.'

Julia came forward with offers of whisky and the doctor accompanied her into the next room.

The party he had left looked at one

14

another. Garth was the first to speak.

'This means we shall have to stay till after the funeral,' he observed.

'Someone,' said Cecil, in his high, unnatural voice, 'will have to close the house.'

'Unless the lucky heir decides to live in it,' contributed Christopher. It was like a game at which every one had to make a remark.

'No one could possibly want to,' said Lucille quickly. 'I mean, it's an unlucky house. First, Cousin William...' She paused and they thought of William who had fallen from a window on the second floor nearly sixteen years ago.

'I wonder what would happen to a third occupant,' Hugh suggested.

'I know I wouldn't live here,' repeated Lucille.

'You haven't got the chance yet,' snapped her husband.

'But you said...' Lucille began. And stopped.

Outside the doctor gulped down his whisky and remarked: 'Queer batch, what?'

'I expect all relations hoping to come into a bit are the same,' said Julia coolly.

'Do you know who gets it?' asked the doctor.

'Someone who wouldn't have got it if he'd lived another week,' returned Julia grimly.

'Oh, they're all saying now they didn't know Mr. Midleton was coming down. Well, perhaps he was playing a game. He was fond of games.'

Musgrave shook his head in an odd gesture, as though he were shaking something out of his eyes. Yes, he knew Everard Hope, the little furtive, twisting mind, the jealousy he'd had to swallow as he watched his spendthrift brother squandering a fortune that, in the absence of legitimate issue, must eventually come to himself. His games hadn't been nice ones. It wasn't likely anyone would mourn for him. All the same, he couldn't help wondering which of them was going to be the richer by reason of the accident. He looked round him at the dilapidated hall, the spreading cracks in the ceiling, the blackened condition of the walls

'The place practically wants rebuilding,' he said. 'It's falling down foot by foot.'

'If you told him that he'd only laugh and say it would last his time. He moved his bedroom three times in the last five years. When the rain began to drip through the ceiling he'd think it time to make a change.'

'Jolly for his guests,' said the doctor, 'but I suppose it was a case of the shorter the sweeter where their visits were concerned.' He picked up his bag. 'The verdict will be death by misadventure,' he prophesied. 'I'll try and get the inquest fixed for this afternoon.'

'Good thing this isn't the Judgment day,' said Julia, passing his hat and gloves. 'Secrets of all hearts being revealed—might be a bit uncomfortable.'

'Like hell it might,' thought the doctor, but he'd learned long ago that ignorance, if not bliss, often saves a good deal of time, and he said nothing.

CHAPTER TWO

I

ON THE WAY back he stopped the shabby little green car when he saw his friend, Sergeant Bliss, crossing the street towards the local station.

'Bringing another soul into the world?' asked Bliss. The doctor had delivered both his children.

The doctor shook his head. 'Arrived just too late to see one shove off. Old Everard Hope.'

The policeman nodded thoughtfully. 'So he's gone, has he? Wonder how much good all his money is to him now.'

'If it's no more good to his heirs he might as well have it buried with him,' said the doctor.

'Heart?' murmured the sergeant.

'A fall down the stairs,' said the doctor.

'At this time of night?' The sergeant sounded suspicious.

'Had an idea there was a fire on the premises.'

'He was bats about fire,' said the sergeant. 'Everyone knew that.'

'So they did,' said the doctor dryly.

'Think it was foul play?' inquired Bliss.

The doctor shrugged weary shoulders. 'What's the good? Suppose I say yes? You go up there and turn 'em all inside out. The press has a good time, and whoever gets the money's roasted for the rest of his days and very likely isn't the guilty one—if any of 'em's guilty.'

'Not sure, are you?' said the sergeant.

'Ever heard of the proverb about sleeping dogs?' asked the doctor.

'I didn't like it,' said Bliss.

'If you start a stink you'll only get your behind kicked by the press,' warned the doctor inelegantly. 'You won't be able to prove a thing. Why, they aren't even accusing one another. They're all in too weak a situation.'

'Wonder who gets the money,' ruminated the sergeant.

'So do they,' said the doctor.

'And in the end he may have left it to a cripples' home.'

'I wouldn't be a bit surprised,' said the doctor. 'There'll be an inquest, of course, as to cause of death.' He looked hard at the sergeant.

'Falling downstairs at this hour of the night,' repeated Bliss. 'I don't like it.'

'Have to swallow it,' said the doctor. He

19

wound up the window of the car and drove on. 'One of 'em did it, of course,' he told himself, 'but we shall never know which, so what the hell?'

He had realised long ago that a man can't tackle more than one job at a time. He was there to defeat death on all possible occasions, but if death stepped in before he did, then he shrugged his shoulders and went on to the next visit on his list—in cases like this, that is, where no professional end was to be served by stirring up mud.

II

There being no reason for staying up, the relatives of the dead man made their way back to their respective rooms.

'I wonder which of us he suspects,' said Hugh to his brother.

'If he's a wise man he won't suspect any one till he knows what's in the will,' returned Christopher cynically. 'And he won't suspect him even then, because suspecting rich men doesn't get you anywhere.'

'I shan't mind sleeping somewhere else tomorrow night,' Hugh acknowledged. 'This place is all death-watch beetles and damp.'

'I could do with some of what he's left,' added Christopher, 'but he's just the sort of cove to make it a condition that the lucky heir has to live on the premises. I suppose we'll all be called as witnesses,' he added.

'A chap I know told me the best thing is to know nothing,' Hugh warned him.

'That ought to be pretty easy in this case.' He fished out a cigarette-case and a lighter. 'I wonder how much Julia knows.'

'It isn't what she knows but what she's going to tell the coroner that counts. After all, she's got her future to consider like the rest of us. Women without private means can't afford to be tactless. Thanks!' Hugh helped himself to a cigarette. 'I've been parched for that for the past half-hour. Oh well, nothing to wait up for, I suppose.'

As he shed his dressing-gown and got into bed he could hear the rise and fall of voices in the next room where Cecil and Lilias were accommodated. Cecil seemed still a little hysterical.

'Don't know anything,' Hugh reminded himself resolutely, and blew out his candle.

III

'You may as well come to bed, Cecil,' observed Lilias sensibly. 'There's no sense standing by the window. There's nothing to be seen with the black-out up.'

Cecil turned, his thin sensitive face quivering. 'That chap didn't believe us,' he said.

'He believes it's murder.'

'The doctor? He didn't say so.'

'Not to us. He will to the police.'

'Even so,' said Lilias, steadily, 'that won't affect us, will it? We don't know anything.'

'No,' cried Cecil. 'But—did you see the look Julia gave me? I know she holds me responsible.'

'Julia isn't the coroner,' Lilias pointed out.

'It's not true, Lilias,' her husband cried. 'I swear it isn't true. I know it may look strange...'

Lilias silenced him. 'If it were true no one could prove it. That's something worth remembering.'

'You mean, you don't think it was an accident, either?'

'Well!' Lilias looked at him consideringly. 'What do you think yourself? No, don't tell me. We don't know anything and we don't want to know anything. Well, there's one thing to be said for Cousin Everard's meanness in the way of lights.'

Cecil found a cigarette and took a box of vestas from his dressing-gown pocket.

'I don't understand you.'

'Suppose we'd been able to switch on the lights the moment we heard the cry? That would have been inconvenient, if you like. Any of us might have seen something we'd

22

rather not. As it is, what can we say but that, so far as we know, Cousin Everard caught his foot in a rent and pitched down the stairs.'

'I wish I knew why he came to those stairs. Lilias, suppose he didn't? Suppose he was carried there?'

'It's much better not to know,' said Lilias. 'Take care of that cigarette. You don't want to start a real fire. That would be anti-climax, if you like.'

IV

'Garth,' said Lucille, carefully replacing her jewel-case under her pillow, 'do you know who shouted Fire to-night?'

'No,' said Garth colourlessly.

'Do you think it might have been Cousin Everard himself?'

'Just remember at the inquest you won't be asked for suggestions, only for facts. And even if I knew who it was,' he added deliberately, 'I shouldn't speak. I couldn't prove it and I should only attract attention to myself.'

He went through the door into the communicating room where he slept. He wondered how long they'd have to wait before they knew how the money had been bequeathed.

V

When the rest of the household was abed

23

Julia Carbery stole quietly along the passage to the dead man's room. The body had been left downstairs. No one relished carrying that ghastly burden up the long flight of steps, and in the morning they'd come and fetch him away. It was a great ghostly apartment, with enormous cupboards, three of them, each big enough to house a man. The candle she carried, the beam carefully shaded, spread shadows in the corners. She looked at the smooth bed where he would never lie again, at the chill orderliness of the room. He'd pulled on his trousers, but the rest of his things trailed on a chair by the wall. She didn't stay long. There was nothing she could do. Everard Hope would make no further demands of her.

But of all the dwellers under that roof that night she alone was certain who had shouted Fire in those desperate tones, and she alone knew why.

VI

The next day dawned pale and cool. The family, with the exception of Lucille who asked for coffee in her room, came down betimes. Garth reported his wife was feeling the shock.

'I suppose that madam thinks this is an hotel,' observed Maggie, the only maid who

24

lived in. Everard Hope didn't approve of paying wages. It was a miracle that Julia could get him to engage a daily woman to help the elderly Maggie in this big inconvenient house.

'Don't feel like facing all them others if you ask me,' said Mrs. 'Arris, the daily in question. 'What did 'appen last night, Mrs. Martin?'

'And that's another thing,' said Maggie in aggrieved tones. 'You know I sleep downstairs. Well, at my age you can't go traipsing up and down stairs half the night. Wouldn't you have thought, with a death on the premises, one of them would have come and told me? But no. That's gentry all over. Keep the best of everything for themselves.'

'I do call it a shame,' agreed Mrs. 'Arris warmly. 'Did they tell you this morning.'

'I know what they said,' returned Maggie, like a sour oracle. ''E thought the house was afire and fell downstairs. Likely, ain't it?'

'Convenient,' agreed Mrs. 'Arris. 'Very. What's the police goin' to say?'

'Ah!' said Maggie. 'Now you're asking. One thing, I shan't be sorry to get away from this 'ouse.'

'Can't think 'ow you've stood it so long,' said Mrs. 'Arris.

'I was sorry for Miss Carbery. Not much

fun for 'er, you know, and she's not as young as she was.'

'Wonder she stayed,' said Mrs. 'Arris.

'P'raps she didn't have no choice,' suggested Maggie. 'You know, Mrs. 'Arris, I have wondered sometimes if she could have been one of Mr. William's ladies once upon a time. Oh, I know she was just housekeeper when he died, but—say what you like—she wouldn't be the first or the last.'

''E must 'ave fancied a funny shape,' said Mrs. 'Arris bluntly.

'She'd ha' bin a bit younger twenty years ago' argued Mrs. Martin. (Fortunately Julia never realised that her character was being thus suspected; fortunately, too, William Hope didn't guess it either. He would have turned in his grave with horror, having been a man of discernment where his enthusiasms were involved.) 'Besides, she could make the skinflint buy a new pot now and again. Though, if he could, he'd have let her and me buy everything we needed.'

'D'you think 'e's left anything to 'er?' breathed Mrs. 'Arris.

Maggie Martin shook her head. 'There's no knowing. Only it'll be a surprise, whatever it is. Mr. 'Ope was like that.'

'Don't see why you shouldn't get it as much as any of them,' opined Mrs. 'Arris.

'You done a lot for 'im.'

Maggie's reaction was instantaneous. 'I'm sure I've always been respectable, Mrs. 'Arris,' she said. 'And I don't want no gentleman's money.'

'You must be the only one in the 'ouse that doesn't, then,' returned Mrs. 'Arris sturdily.

'The crows can have it for me,' said Maggie. 'Law, there they are. Now we'll learn something.'

VII

Mr. Midleton, summoned by the indefatigable Julia, arrived late for lunch. The inquest was to be held at 2.30. He was a small prim man with a small grey moustache and the tightness of bearing of a Victorian spinster, as the Georgians imagine them. He betrayed no emotion of any kind on hearing of his client's death or the manner of it. He sat like an automaton through the inquest, which was brief and to the point. Everard Hope was known to be an eccentric, and Dr. Musgrave's evidence helped the jury to come to a decision that pleased everyone, except Sergeant Bliss. The coroner agreed with the verdict, tendered extremely formal sympathy to the bereaved and said the funeral could be proceeded with forthwith. Mr Midleton shook all the cousins chillily by the hand and caught the 4.27 to London. Later he telephoned that the funeral would take place on Saturday afternoon at 2.30.

'That means staying over the week-end,' said Garth. 'All this time wasted...'

'Garth ought to live in Soviet Russia,' said Hugh. 'He obviously approves of a seven-day week.'

'He's quite right,' said Cecil. 'It is inconvenient. You know what the Sunday trains are like, and those of us who have to report early on Monday morning...'

Hugh shuddered and moved away. He had been through Dunkirk and now had an appointment of sorts at the War Office. He worked as hard as Cecil did, but he wouldn't have had it known. Cecil was employed by the Youth Ethical Press, the conception of a grand old man called Thomas Whaley, who published quantities of books for the young, youth being in his view a matter of outlook rather than birth certificates. Cecil wrote some of the books and a good many of the articles in the Press's two papers. He was, in short, a general dogsbody. He felt very nervous about ringing up Mr. Whaley, but to his surprise his employer was most affable.

'Naturally, I understand,' he purred over the wires. 'Naturally you feel you must stay and do all you can. I understand perfectly.'

28

And so indeed he did. Cecil had spoken more than once with what Julia would have recognised as unfounded optimism of his own prospects in the event of Everard Hope's death.

'If he comes in for a bit, as he's always led us to suspect,' said Mr. Whaley, to his partner, Mr. Sim, 'he might be persuaded to invest part of it in the Press. The offer of a junior partnership might attract him. We need funds for expansion.'

'Excellent idea,' approved Mr. Sim who, like Mr. Whaley, had put most of his capital into armament firms before the war, and didn't feel he ought to withdraw it before victory was achieved.

'Men like ourselves,' he and his partner agreed, 'men who can't fight ourselves and have no sons to send to fight for us, must be contented with the second best. We must send our money. That must be our weapon.'

And so it was, and it captured a good many prisoners in the shape of dividends for Mr. Whaley and Mr. Sim.

Garth, of course, as senior partner in a legal firm, had simply to telegraph the news of his unavoidable absence. Christopher sent a telegram too. In 1938 his profession had been that of Clubman, but when war broke out he tried for something more virile. The

Services wouldn't look at him. The Services had been very exclusive at the beginning of the war. There was civil defence, but he didn't see himself either as a fireman or a warden, and he applied for the Secret Service. They put him at once into the Ministry of Information, and he sent a message to headquarters to say he was detained on official business and it didn't occur to them to question the statement. Information comes from so many sources, and if Holland, Belgium, Germany, Norway, Yugoslavia and the United States, why not Fox Norton in the county of Hornshire.

He and Hugh walked into the nearest town to choose a suitable wreath and argued about what they should write on the card. Across the road they saw Cecil at an inferior florist buying a sheaf, that cost 12/6 as against 25/−. Garth selected a pretentious and quite inappropriate affair of laurel and rose. Julia's sense of humour impelled her to order a cross.

Rather to the family's surprise the entire village turned out for the start of the funeral procession and, near the graveyard, tailed off to the bar of the Dog and Lizard. Maggie and Mrs. 'Arris were among the first to arrive. Normally Maggie would not have associated with a cleaner, but it was understood that

Mrs. 'Arris had come down in the world owing to marriage and similar misfortunes, so they settled themselves to comfortable glasses of stout and beer mixed and talked about the funeral.

'Very nice class,' said Maggie with satisfaction as the mixture gurgled smoothly down their throats. 'I always think a cross gives tone to a funeral.'

'Bit of an 'int if you ask me,' said Mrs. 'Arris. 'Wonder what 'e'd 'ave thought.'

''E wouldn't have approved of any of it,' said Maggie decisively. 'Not falling down the stairs nor nothing.'

Mrs. 'Arris lifted an exultant face. 'Mrs. Martin, you're never going to tell me . . .'

'I'm not going to tell you nothing,' said Maggie, 'because I don't know nothing, see. And what's more I don't want to know nothing. But I will say for the gentry they do know 'ow to cover things up. If it 'ad bin you or me and our old man had come a cropper things would ha' bin very different. But you can take it from me that gentlemen that never drink anything stronger than milk don't go falling downstairs of their own accord. But there, least said soonest mended, and they've been a funny family by all accounts.'

She drained her glass and said in refined tones: 'You'll have one with me, I 'ope,' and

31

Mrs. 'Arris said she didn't mind if she did.

A stout man in a brown suit who had been seated at the bar when the two ladies arrived found himself so much fascinated by their conversation and so much in agreement with their conclusions, that he contrived to insinuate himself into their good books, and was soon learning a good deal more about the late Everard Hope than either lady realised she knew. He discovered that the dead man was an unpopular miserly sort of chap, surrounded by sycophantic relatives, all of whom had been in the house at the time of the death that had taken place in the dark. Although she had been employed at The Brakes for upwards of eighteen years no one had thought of telling Maggie what had happened till the next morning. Easy to see she thought that worse than committing a crime.

'You take care,' he told them in friendly fashion. 'You don't want to get saying too much. Just you remember coroners are like customers, they're always right.'

Mrs. 'Arris, London-born, independent, said truculently: 'A body's got a right to think. Even 'Itler can't stop people from thinking.'

'He might stop you from thinking out loud,' said Crook.

Maggie nudged her. 'Police,' said that

nudge. 'Up to every kind of dirty trick.' She stood up. 'I'm afraid we'll have to be going,' she said. 'They'll be back from the funeral any minute now.'

'One more before you go,' suggested Crook. 'Just to show there's no hard feelings.'

He smiled at them in what he intended to be an ingratiating manner. Bill always said it reminded him of the Alligator House. But it served its purpose.

'Perhaps we'll be seeing you again,' said the barman hopefully glancing at the clock.

'It could be,' said Mr. Crook, enthusiastically. 'It could be.'

And he grinned.

VIII

The funeral party returned shortly before four and having dispatched tea got down to business.

Mr. Midleton, by common consent, was given the best chair. He drew a long sealed envelope out of his pocket and looked gravely at the gathering.

'It's—er—quite a short document,' he said. 'And all his relatives are mentioned by name. Perhaps I had better read it as it stands.'

Everard Hope's will was as peculiar as his

life had been. His legacies staggered every-one, having, on the whole, no value in law. He said that Garth, being a lawyer obviously knew how to line his pockets and would need no outside assistance. That disposed of Garth. With regard to Cecil, he said he had read some of the products of the Youth Ethi-cal Press and noticed that poverty was always highly praised. In fact, any characters who did achieve wealth simultaneously achieved moral ruin. In these circumstances, he con-sidered that his cousin would be insulted by the offer of a fortune. That disposed of Cecil. Of the Lacey brothers he said that they appeared to live a great deal more comfort-ably on nothing a year than he himself on a considerable income. He, therefore, had no intention of upsetting their balance. Of Julia he said that she had so frequently assured him she would not be in his shoes that he would not do her the disservice of bequeath-ing them to her. But as a token of his regard he gave her the set of water-colour paintings of the Holy Land made by his Aunt Rachel in her youth and now hanging in various offices about the house.

His entire fortune, when death and other legal expenses had been met, went to his kinswoman, Dorothea Capper of London, on one definite condition. Should she not comply with that condition, the money would go to his nearest relation in law. He left it to the law and the relations concerned to decide which that should be.

After the reading of the will there was a period of appalled silence, so pregnant of coming storm that Julia Carbery lifted her head in anticipation of the roll of thunder and burst of rain.

It was Hugh who spoke first. 'Has any one ever seen the Capper woman?' he inquired.

'Never so much as heard of her,' said Garth. 'I suppose she's another of these remote cousins that afflict every family.'

'Damned rummy condition to make,' commented Christopher.

'Of course,' Garth's voice rose in fury, 'I shall contest the will. It's infamous.'

Mr. Midleton's voice, cold as a pebble, fell like icy rain on the heat of the speaker's mood.

'On what grounds, Mr. Hope?'

'Incapacity,' snapped Garth. 'Senile decay.'

'Dating from . . .?'

'He'd been as crazy as a loon for a long time past,' said Garth recklessly. 'Look at the way he counted ha'pence, putting out those grubby little candle-ends in tin sticks in a row in the hall for what he called night-birds.'

Lucille leaned forward. 'Yes. And tying the only box of matches to a fastener in the wall, in case someone should take them.'

'And look at his clothes,' continued Garth. 'Oh, there's not a doubt about it. He wasn't balanced.'

Mr. Midleton leaned forward. 'One month previous to making this will,' he said, 'he made another leaving everything to yourself. Is it your contention that insanity set in during that particular month?'

'This woman must have had some hold over him,' suggested Garth.

'I believe he had not seen her since childhood,' was Mr. Midleton's cold reply.

'Then—Good God, you're not going to tell us she's his illegitimate child.'

Mr. Midleton looked outraged. 'Certainly not.' He put his papers together and prepared to rise.

'In any case,' continued Garth, 'I shall contest the will.' Mr. Midleton shrugged.

The debate continued.

It was adjourned by the married couples in the early hours of Sunday morning. The bachelors had shown far less staying-power, and had, in fact, removed themselves, bag and baggage, with Mr. Midleton, to the Cock Pheasant at Wolf Norton, a few miles up the line. They were surprised, when they reached the inn, to find they had been preceded by Miss Carbery.

'What's she doing here?' demanded Christopher.

'A very proper spirit,' said Mr. Midleton. 'She is no longer in Mr. Hope's employ, and she has received no invitation from the present owner to remain.'

'Well, but damn it all, Garth hasn't had an invitation either,' protested Hugh.

'He regards himself as the house's spiritual owner,' observed Mr. Midleton with a frosty smile.

'And naturally Cecil isn't going to leave Garth in possession of the field,' Hugh continued. 'Well, there's one thing. We shall never be asked to spend a night in that damned house again.'

Miss Carbery tactfully had dinner in her room, and by the time the brothers came down next morning they heard that she had left on the 9.4.

'How women love to make life uncomfortable!' groaned Christopher.

Hugh began to laugh.

'Gosh, what a game!'

'What on earth . . .?'

'Don't you get it? Good old Julia! I say, how mad Garth will be!'

Light broke over Christopher. 'You don't

37

mean you think she . . .'

Well, isn't it obvious?'

Oblivious to Mr. Midleton's chill surprise they had a neck and neck race to the telephone, each hoping to be the first to warn Garth that their cousin's late secretary had stolen a march on all of them, and was probably at this very moment travelling Londonwards to be first in the field with the new heiress.

CHAPTER THREE

I

MISS DOROTHEA (GIFT OF GOD) CAPPER was laying out a pair of clean suede-finish gloves for wear at Morning Service when her telephone bell rang. She was as startled and almost as delighted as if she had heard church bells ringing in the peace.

In a quiet life, whose quietude, had she but known it, was practically at an end, the telephone stood to Miss Capper for adventure and the Unknown. All her hopes of change, her dreams of a rich unimagined existence, were knit up with the black instrument now ringing with a peculiar hiccoughing sound, due to its having been dropped one dark night when she scurried in to answer one of her numerous wrong numbers, and not since repaired on the ground that there was a war on. Dropping the gloves she tore into the living-room and clutched at the receiver. A psychologist would have thought her pathetic, this prematurely faded spinster of thirty-eight, who drew her consolation from the knowledge that she had been a good daughter to her invalid mother, a good niece to crippled Aunt Amy and was now a faithful and devoted member of the Reverend Clifton Bryce's congregation at St. Sebastian, The Bush, W.37.

It will be Georgie, Dorothea told herself, lifting the receiver and saying, as directed, 'This is Bush 4141.' She always likes to ring up when I am setting out for church to see if I can resist the temptation to talk to her and so be late.

Georgie was Miss Trent, Miss Capper's one real friend. She did not attend Divine Service, saying she could worship her Maker better in a daffodil field.

But what about the seasons when there are no daffodils? Dorothea had asked seriously. To which Miss Trent replied that there were always daffodils in one's heart.

'Hold on, Bush,' said a voice. 'I have a call for you.'

Miss Capper's heart began to beat faster. This wouldn't be Georgie. Georgie had her own telephone and made her own connections.

The operator came through again, saying: 'You're through Moorhen' (at least, that was what Miss Capper made of it) and then a man's voice said clearly: 'Bush 4141? Is Miss Carbery there?'

Dorothea's hopes drooped like flowers no one has watered. She might have guessed. A wrong number or at best a mistake. She largely maintained her telephone for the benefit of wrong numbers.

'I'm afraid not,' she said.

'Is that Miss Capper speaking?'

That did startle her. 'Yes, it is, but...'

'And you say Miss Carbery hasn't arrived. That's strange.'

'Not really,' said Dorothea. 'I'm not expecting any Miss Carbery.'

'That won't make any difference,' said the voice.

'I don't even know who she is,' Dorothea protested.

'You soon will. She'll explain. Only it won't do to accept everything she tells you as gospel. There's a good romantic novelist lost in Julia Carbery. The best thing to do is say nothing till you've seen one of us.'

'I've nothing to say,' protested Dorothea, in desperation.

There were three little pings and the operator said 'Three minutes,' and whoever was on the other end instantly rang off. After a staggered moment Dorothea did likewise. She looked vaguely round the room. It was, miraculously, the same as usual, the chairs that had belonged to her mother, the octagonal rosewood table that had belonged to Aunt Amy, the old-fashioned china cupboards, the hanging brackets, the Japanese prints. Over the little bookcase hung an embroidered text. 'Heaven is my Home.' When he came to bless the flat the Vicar had noticed that and approved it. A very good motto, he had said. Life was no more than a boarding-house where one stayed too short a time to bother much if the hot water system didn't work very well or the beds were lumpy. He worked it into his sermon the following Sunday. Dorothea cherished that thought. It made tepid water and lumpy beds comparatively unimportant.

The clock on the white mantelpiece, that had been given to dear Aunt Amy's dear husband to mark five-and-twenty years of faithful stewardship at St. Stanislaus, Upper Norwood, chimed eleven. This week it was set to Westminister Chime. Next week she would change it to Eight Bells. In Lent it was put to Silent, to mark a period of penance and withdrawal. Dorothea stood up, still feeling dazed. Unless she hurried she was going to be late for church. People who were late were conspicuous. To be conspicuous was to be vulgar. To be vulgar was to be unworthy of Mamma's daughter. (Never, she noted subconsciously, Papa's daughter. But there were reasons for that.)

The gospel spoke very appropriately of

faith and the power of prayer. Faith—and the power of prayer—could remove mountains as easily as she (Dorothea) could lift a saucepan off the stove. Faith could turn a call from a stranger into something thrilling and momentous. Faith could do a good deal, but it couldn't put back the clock, couldn't make her less than an elderly thirty-eight—unless, of course, it could turn her into a young thirty-eight. But even faith, thought the trembling Miss Capper, would have its work cut out to do that. Her hand strayed to her mouse-coloured hair under the brim of last year's straw hat.

She felt a pang of hope as she saw the Vicar mount the pulpit, a feeling she shared with practically ever woman in the congregation. Perhaps, she thought, he will give me a lead.

The Vicar leaned forward and announced his text. '12th chapter of St. Luke and the 20th verse,' he said.

The Campion girls (twins of 57), who occupied the pew behind Miss Capper, hastily turned the leaves of their Bible in the hope of discovering the text before the Vicar gave it out. They did this every Sunday and every Sunday the Vicar beat them to it.

'Thou fool,' he thundered, 'this night shall thy soul be required of thee.'

Miss Capper sighed. It wasn't a promising

beginning, she thought nervously. Rather a rude sort of text in fact. She settled herself to listen.

The Vicar delivered his sermon in a series of verbal bumps.

Thud! Thud! Thud! Feet on the stairs. Feet moving slowly. Why do they move so slowly? They are carrying a coffin. (No one present apparently thought this statement peculiar.) Whose coffin? Your coffin, dear friend. . . .

In the midst of life we are in death. . . . Which of us knows when his last hour cometh?

The sermon had this in common with the play of *Hamlet*, that it was full of quotations.

It was obvious that the congregation on the whole was not enjoying itself. Women who are mainly poor and obscure and not very young have nothing but their lives to treasure. Other people have fame or money or at least the expectation of these. They can afford to be a little prodigal. When you've nothing but your life you set an inordinate value on it, which is presumably why the virtuous (who don't think they ought to have any of the luxuries of this world) are so loth to let life itself go. Just as only children may be deformed or deficient but are still dear to their mothers, so the meanest life is precious

44

to its owner. Miss Capper's was as plain as a war-time cake, but, like a wartime cake, she doled it out slice by economical slice to make it last as long as possible.

The Reverend Clifton Bryce was warming up to his subject, leaning over the pulpit-edge in a manner that made a small boy in the audience hold his breath with excitement in the hope that he would fall out altogether, perhaps even break his neck. But the kindest of Vicars is seldom so accommodating as this.

That knock on the door, exulted the Vicar, that ring at the bell—how can you be sure it is not the messenger of death coming for you before the ending of the day?

How indeed, the terrified Miss Capper asked herself. He hadn't actually said that mysterious telephone call, but naturally that was implied. And if strange men in the street were dangerous, strange men on a telephone, who couldn't even be recognised, were worse. And who was the mysterious Miss Carbery? Her mother had always warned her against strange women. Don't have anything to do with them, she said. Even if they're fainting in the street and want you to go home with them, don't do it. Call a policeman instead.

Death on the doorstep, reflected Dorothea, and nearly fainted herself.

45

The sermon came to its triumphant conclusion and they all rose to sing a hymn while the collection was taken up:

Days and moments quickly flying,
Join the living with the dead;
Soon will you and I be lying,
Each within our narrow bed.

Dorothea dropped in her customary sixpence and thought about Miss Carbery. It was disappointing that she shouldn't have received a message from the sermon. During the prayer for the Church Militant it occurred to her that perhaps she had. Perhaps she had been warned. But the next moment a familiar confusion assailed her. The strange man had rung up to warn her against the unknown woman. But what if it were the man who was the danger? What if Julia Carbery were one of his victims, flying to Dorothea Capper for aid? It was typical of Dorothea's mental reactions that she shouldn't wonder how the poor thing had ever heard Miss Capper's name. A nobler emotion overwhelmed her. This woman, this girl most likely, was being threatened by the sinister owner of the anonymous voice. She was seeking sanctuary and it lay in Dorothea's power to rescue her or to deliver her to her oppressor. All this chimed precisely in tune with the little books published by a well-known religious society that had been popular in Miss Capper's youth.

There was a song, reflected Dorothea, rising to her feet with the rest of the congregation, that the Vicar sang at the Parish Party.

Life gives us all one chance, they say,
She gave me mine that November day,
She gave me mine and I threw it away.

It wasn't November, of course, but April wouldn't scan so well.

Miss Capper came out of her haze in time to see the Vicar disappearing into the vestry. She dropped hurriedly on to her knees. It was odd to find the church unchanged while she felt she had undergone a complete metamorphosis. She was no longer timid Dorothea Capper, anxious to placate a probably hostile world, she was part of an army terrible with banners, and she was going to fight the unknown man for the sake of a woman she'd never set eyes on but who was probably at that very instant travelling towards her flat.

She picked up her gloves and other impediments, forgetting in her excitement the Vicar's humorous injunction to his congregation in the January number of the Parish Magazine:

> When you've risen from your knees
> Make quite sure you've got your book,
> Gasmask, gloves, umbrella, keys,
> We don't want the care of these,
> We are busy, too, and—PLEASE—
> Hang your hassock on the hook.

Miss Capper marched up Blakesley Avenue, her latch-key in her hand stabbing the air like St. George stabbing at the dragon. By the time she reached her own doorstep Julia—no longer Miss Carbery but Mrs. Someone Else—was holding an infant in her arms and saying: 'We shall call her Dorothea, because we owe her to you,' a biological conclusion that Miss Capper's mind could accept with no difficulty at all.

II

The telephone was ringing furiously as she came in. She sped along to the instrument, filled with exultation.

'Yes,' she cried valorously.

'I have a telegram here for Bush 4141,' said the operator's pert voice. 'Will you take it, please?' And as though it didn't mean anything at all she read out: 'Do nothing without advice, Tempest. Will you read it back to me

48

please?'

'Do nothing without advice, Tempest,' repeated Dorothea. 'But it doesn't make sense.'

'That's the message,' said the girl briskly, and rang off. Dorothea, after a moment during which she waited for an angel to explain what it was all about, did the same. Presently it occurred to her that Tempest might be the name of the man who had rung up earlier in the day. It was all most confusing. Definitely Miss Capper wanted advice. She would dearly have liked to ask the Vicar what he thought about it, but, except in cases of sudden death, Vicars must not be disturbed on Sundays. And even on a weekday Dorothea would have hesitated a long time. Anyway, the Vicar being out of the question, there was no one left but Georgie. Miss Trent might be winsome over daffodils, but she had a forthright personality all the same. She often told Dorothea she had allowed life to roll her out flat. Georgie could deal with half a dozen mysterious men before breakfast, and like it.

She dialled a number and instantly Miss Trent's exuberant voice said, 'Hullo-ullo-ullo!'

'Oh Georgie,' breathed Miss Capper. 'The most extraordinary thing has happened. I don't know what to do.'

49

'Don't tell me the Vicar's asked you to tea,' said Georgie, who believed this to be humorous. And if humour lies in the improbable, so it was.

'Of course not. I—I've had a telephone call.'

'Cheers!' said Georgie, who appeared to be in excellent spirits.

'The extraordinary thing is it wasn't really for me.'

'More extraordinary if it had been,' boomed Georgie.

'It's for somebody called Carbery, who doesn't live here.'

'It was a wrong number,' Georgie pointed out kindly.

'It was for Bush 4141, but...'

'Then he'd got hold of the wrong number.'

'I don't think he had, because, you see, there was a telegram as well.'

'Pull yourself together, Dottie,' said Miss Trent. 'This is one of the days you're living up to your name.'

That was another of her jokes. She made it pretty often, laughing to show Dorothea, who was thin-skinned on occasions, that it was all girlish fun.

'Must go now,' said Georgie breezily. 'The boy-friend's waiting.'

The boy-friend was an old gentleman who

50

had known Georgie's mother and who sometimes took his old friend's daughter out to
lunch on Sundays. Georgie, who was a true-
blue Briton in the sense that she never knew
when she was defeated, hoped that one of
these days he'd propose.

'I shall beat you to the altar yet,' she would
assure a shrinking Dorothea. Mr. Protheroe
was over seventy and had four grown-up children, but that didn't deter Miss Trent. In a
war, she said, if you couldn't have pre-war
standards you must do the best with the sub-
stitutes that were available. Anyway, Georgie
herself was no chicken. She hadn't even had
to register yet.

Dorothea heard the too-familiar click of
the receiver—she was never the first to ring
off—and went to collect her lunch of cold
pressed galantine, bought off the ration, and
a cornflour rice shape. She had the kind of
meals that would have won a medal for valour
if the Ministry of Food had thought of insti-
tuting any, but, of course, men don't think of
inventing medals that only women would
win. She was piling the plates in the sink
when the telephone rang again.

'Miss Carbery arrived yet? Sure? She
couldn't have slipped in when you weren't
looking?'

Dorothea looked wildly round her. Unless

51

Miss Carbery had popped into the ottoman, which was unlikely, there wasn't a sign of her.

'Are you Tempest?' she asked desperately, and the voice said at once: 'You want to steer clear of that connection. Might have guessed they'd try to get in touch.'

'Then who are you?' persisted Dorothea.

'One of your cousins,' said the voice. 'Look here, whatever you do, sign nothing till you've seen Midleton.'

'I shouldn't dream . . .' began Dorothea, but the voice interrupted brusquely: 'You've no notion what you're up against. You won't know you have signed anything until it's too late, unless you're on your guard.'

Dorothea felt the time had come to assert herself. 'I feel I should warn you,' she said, 'that I intend to do everything possible to help her.'

'In that case,' said the voice smoothly, 'you may as well make your will at once.'

'I don't understand,' began poor Miss Capper, but all the voice said was, 'You wait' and then the little bell pinged imperiously and once again the receiver was replaced.

Silence came down on the flat until 3.30 when a wrong number coincided with an awfully jolly Russian play on the B.B.C. After that there was nothing to do but wait. It says a good deal for Miss Capper's sense of responsibility that she stayed away from Evensong for the first time since she had influenza two years ago.

III

It was, in point of fact, quite late when Miss Carbery actually arrived. Dorothea was wondering whether it wouldn't be more sensible to have supper and treat the telephone calls and telegram as a practical joke, when the front door bell pealed.

'It may be Georgie,' Miss Capper reminded herself, opening the flat door and running down the stairs to the hall. 'Nothing to be excited about. But, of course, if it should be Julia Carbery, which is most unlikely, she must spend the night here. I must make her realise she's safe. She's simply got to stay.'

Even if she hadn't arrived at this decision it would have made no difference, since Miss Carbery had planned to stay in any case.

On the other side of the door Miss Carbery waited, listening for the sound of descending feet. A tiring railway journey, involving two changes and a missed connection, had done little to impair her energy. She had, indeed, considered telephoning Miss Capper's flat, but wisdom urged that one of the lessons of the war was that surprise attacks are generally

53

the most successful and more likely to scupper the enemy amidships, as she put it.

'Pity she isn't younger,' she reflected. 'Thirty-eight is generally pigheaded. Still, if I tell her I don't know a soul in London and the hotels are all full, that ought to do the trick. If she doesn't ask me, I must just stay.'

It was true about the hotels. London was filling up again. It was actually a choice of evils. Come to London and chance bombing. Stay in the country and chance invasion. On the whole London was more amusing, so to London people came.

The door opened at last and before Dorothea could recover from her shock Miss Carbery bounced into the hall.

'I am Julia Carbery,' she said.

Dorothea pulled herself together. 'I've been expecting you for some time,' she said, faintly. 'At least...' But she couldn't find words to explain that she had been expecting a girl like an April evening, all blue and gold, not this mannish, preposterous figure with a red glengarry pulled firmly down over ginger curls, and a spreading red and green mixture tweed suit, with hands like hams and feet like beetle-crushers, who marched into the hall like Hitler marching into one of the occupied countries, without stopping to find out if he would be welcome.

'Expecting me?' demanded Miss Carbery. She sounded suspicious, even hostile. Dorothea realised she could be very hostile indeed. You could see her making wax figures and sticking pins into them with such fervour that the victims really did pine away. Dorothea didn't think Julia's victims would dare do anything else.

She shivered.

'Cold?' inquired Miss Carbery briskly. 'Well, it's not too bad here. You should have had my journey. Two changes and a missed connection owing to the intolerable organisation of the railway company. I spoke to a guard about it, though, of course, it isn't really his fault. It's the men at the top...' She squinted up the stairs. 'How far?'

'The—the top,' repeated Dorothea, hypnotised by the odd little figure and thinking: 'No wonder they wanted to know where she was. She's probably escaped from somewhere.'

'Then let's go on up.' She picked up the big suitcase and staggered to the foot of the stairs. Dorothea, like someone under a spell, took it from her and meekly led the way.

'Say you knew I was coming?' rapped out Miss Carbery. 'Who warned you?'

Warned you. An odd expression.

'I only know his name,' she confessed. 'It

was Tempest. At least, one of them. I can't imagine how he knew me.'

Miss Carbery uttered a brief snort, indicating amusement. 'More people know Tom Fool than Tom Fool knows,' she announced. 'You'll learn. Another flight?'

'The top,' repeated Dorothea apologetically. 'I'm sorry there's no lift.'

'Soon change all that,' said Julia.

Dorothea had no notion what she meant; most likely Julia hadn't either, she reflected.

'You want to watch out,' the extraordinary visitor continued. 'They'll all milk you if you give them the chance. That's why I'm here. To look after you.'

They reached the top step and Dorothea fumbled for her latch-key. (It was one of the house's disadvantages that the main front door was kept locked throughout the day and you had to go down every time there was a bell.)

'Milk me?' repeated Dorothea, blushing. 'Who will?'

'The whole crowd.' Miss Carbery thrust her way into the little hall. 'You can put that bag down now. It's heavy. I know. Been carrying it all day. No porters and no chivalry, and if you say anything they tell you there's a war on. Of course they all hate you. That's only to be expected. And they've all

56

got their different methods of approach. One will appeal to your better feelings and another to the law. Don't listen to any of 'em. It's your only hope. You've your rights the same as the rest of the world, and you stick up for 'em.'

Dorothea, who had never been aware of possessing any rights and who, indeed, was inclined to regard free air to breathe as a favour on which it wasn't really safe to count, was dumbfounded. Miss Carbery, having looked at the uninteresting hall, turned to examine her involuntary host. She saw what would indubitably be described as a nice woman, with a pale neat face, surrounded by pale hair arranged in an uninteresting and inexpensive fashion. Her eyes were a rather uninteresting pale blue. In fact, uninteresting seemed the obvious adjective.

Harmless, deprecatory, shy—oh, definitely uninteresting. Julia Carbery's mental reaction was characteristic.

'Looks a fool,' she thought. 'She'll do.'

Dorothea for her part saw a skin like a Brussels carpet, a nose like a cape and a mouth like the Straits of Dover. Green eyes set deep under thick sandy brows expressed liveliness and a complete absence of scruple.

'Don't you have anything to do with any of them till you've seen your own lawyer,' Miss

Carbery told the shrinking Dorothea.

'I haven't one,' Miss Capper whispered.

'Wise woman,' commented her astounding guest, who didn't appear to be troubled with consistency. 'Much better let me look after things for you. Know why legal documents are so complicated? So that women shan't understand them. If they did, they'd never sign them.'

She laughed, nodding her head till the scarlet glengary bobbed like a boat in a storm.

'I've never heard of any of them,' said poor Dorothea, meaning relatives.

'You're going to hear plenty in the future,' prophesied Miss Carbery. 'That room let?' She nodded towards Dorothea's cosy sitting-room.

'Let? I . . .'

'Don't say you don't understand in that dazed fashion or I shall think they've let you out for the day,' continued Miss Carbery, looking ferocious. 'I mean, have you got a lodger?'

Dorothea said faintly no, of course she hadn't.

'Then what are we standing here for?' demanded Miss Carbery sensibly. 'It's all right for you, I dare say. Had a nice snooze during the sermon and being lying up ever since. But

58

I've been on my feet since early morning and all on your account. Let's go in and sit down.'

She walked into the sitting-room. There was a divan covered with a brown and yellow Liberty spread against one wall. The visitor seated herself.

'You don't sleep on this?' she suggested. 'No, I expect you have a Buty-Rest in the other room. But I've slept on worse. Mind you, if any of them offer to come round, you have a previous engagement. I wouldn't put it past Cecil Tempest to put steel filings in your coffee—or any of them for that matter, if they thought they could do it without being found out.'

'I wish you wouldn't keep saying they,' exploded Dorothea, 'without adding who they are.'

Julia leaned forward. She assumed a seraphic expression; her thumbs revolved innocently.

'Your loving relations,' she said, 'all wanting to be the first to wish you luck.'

Dorothea knew then that she was bats. She wondered whom you telephoned—doctor or police. Common sense said police. The police have their own doctor included in the rates, whereas if you ring one up on your own account you're expected to foot the bill, even if it isn't for you.

59

Because she hadn't any relations, none, at least, that her mother had cared to acknowledge. So, of course, Dorothea couldn't acknowledge them either, because it would look as though she thought her mother was wrong. In Dorothea's childhood mothers were never wrong.

'I have no relations,' she said quietly. 'That is, no near ones.'

'They're a whole lot nearer than they were this time last week,' returned Julia vigorously. 'And they'll be nearer still in the next twenty-four hours. Don't tell me you never heard of Everard Hope?'

Dorothea stiffened. She said that she believed he was a distant relative and he had once or twice written to her mother, in connection with money, she thought. Gertrude Capper had been generous according to her lights, but she hadn't felt disposed to open up negotiations with Everard Hope.

'Well, he's more generous than she was,' said Miss Carbery in her downright way. 'Or, of course, it may just have been that he wanted to get the laugh of the others.'

'My mother didn't approve of him,' said Dorothea icily. Miss Carbery stared. 'What's that got to do with it? And anyway, what damned cheek. You have to be somebody, you know, to disapprove of rich relations.'

60

'I didn't know he was rich,' countered Dorothea feebly.

'You'll soon find out.' Miss Carbery chuckled again.

'Not that that would have made any difference to Mother,' added Dorothea hastily.

A born fool, thought Julia Carbery. Like mother, like daughter. Never mind, it would simplify things for her.

'Oh well,' she said, 'it's all right if you can afford to be proud. I never could. My father didn't leave a penny.'

'Nor did mine,' said Dorothea quickly. 'At least, not to my mother or me. We just managed on her little portion.'

'Like that?' said Miss Carbery. 'I call it an infernal shame. If I were in Parliament the first thing I'd do would be to pass a bill to force men to leave something to their wives and let the doxies look after themselves.'

The shock of hearing this word and the private conviction that nothing was further from reality than Miss Carbery in Parliament kept Dorothea dumb for a moment. At last she said: 'Anyway, we didn't want his money, wouldn't have taken money from any one...' She sounded very cold and proud but Miss Carbery made short work of that attitude.

'Oh, you wouldn't, would you? And who

do you think you are to go round dictating to Providence? If Providence chooses to leave you a hundred thousand pounds...'

Dorothea knew now beyond all doubt that her guest was raving. She was stringing off lists of names, Garth and Christopher and Lucille and Cecil and Hugh. Dorothea thought it unfortunate that she had seated herself next to the telephone. One could only hope that, after a long journey, she might want a few minutes' privacy, which would give her hostess her chance. All this talk of relations!

'I don't expect to be seeing any of them,' she observed.

Miss Carbery laughed uproariously and a calendar fell off the wall.

'And even if I do,' continued Dorothea in desperation, 'it's ridiculous to talk about steel filings in coffee. And dangerous,' she added, with a sudden spurt of courage.

'Of course it's dangerous,' said Miss Carbery. 'That's what I'm telling you. And another thing. Don't go for a walk with any of them near the edge of a cliff either.'

'There aren't any cliffs in the Bush,' Dorothea pointed out.

'You're not likely to be staying here long,' Miss Carbery reminded her.

Dorothea, who had sometimes deplored

the limitations of her little flat, immediately felt it was preferable to Buckingham Palace, or would be if she could get Miss Carbery out of it.

'I have the flat for another year,' she pointed out.

'Let it, my dear girl. Or, if you can't, and I daresay there wouldn't be a lot of competition, let it rip. What do you care? The important thing is not to let any of them slip the blinkers over you. There are a good many, remember, and they're like foreign armies, they attack from all sides at once. And they won't waste any time either,' she added, silencing Dorothea who was trying to slip in a word. 'Garth's a lawyer, he knows all the ropes. His wife was probably a vulture in another incarnation. Cecil—but I have told you about Cecil. Christopher and Hugh are unmarried. Laceys they are. A bad strain. But nice coverings. Very nice coverings. Cecil, by the way, will ask if you're fond of children, and when he finds you haven't any—I take it you haven't? (Dorothea blindly shook her head)—he'll tell you how expensive school bills are. If he or Garth asks you to go for a walk in Kensington High Street, you remember that advertisement about the cat. I have nine lives but you have not. And, take it from me, even a cat wouldn't last long with

63

Garth.'

Dorothea put one hand to her head, that she felt was bursting.

'I think I'm going mad,' she said simply.

'They might even try that gag,' Julia warned her. 'When you're with any of them you remember that silence is golden, and even if the country's gone off the Gold Standard, there's no reason why you should. And you've only to read the papers to see the accidents that happen that no one but a coroner would accept.

> Green Line Coach,
> Miss D.C.
> Gentle shove,
> R.I.P.

Got there?'

Dorothea felt as though she'd got into the Zoo out of hours, when all the cage doors were unlocked.

Miss Carbery, to show that she now felt herself at home, removed the glengarry, unhooked what looked like a piece of fried haddock from her throat, and deposited both on the divan beside her.

'Can't bear to feel my brain's prisoned,' she announced. 'Well, I'm warning you. We all know the procedure. Driver exonerated.

Suggestion that perhaps the lady was intoxicated made by the defence. Coroner offers sincere sympathy to the bereaved. Half the bereaved to my mind were crocodiles in a previous existence.'

Dorothea sat down, defeated at last. 'And you think that because Cousin Everard, as you call him, may have left me some money...'

'May have? Has. A hundred thousand pounds, less debts and they're not likely to amount to more than half a crown. I ought to know. Oh, it may not sound very much to you. Wouldn't keep the war going much more than ten minutes, but even that's something. Think of it. All the factories at work, the men in the mines, the men in the air, the men on the sea, the army and the navy, the air force, civil defence, civil service—why, just think that for ten minutes you can support all that and pay Mr. Churchill's salary and the whole of the War Cabinet—though if it were me some of them would lose that ten minutes—well, if that doesn't bring it home to you, nothing will.'

It was obvious that at last Miss Carbery had hit the bullseye. Dorothea sat stunned. She, the meek, the unobtrusive, one of the congregation of St. Sebastian who say Good-morning hopefully to the Vicar but never dream of asking for private interviews, she could do all that. Why, during those few minutes Peace might be signed. She might have bought the moment of peace single-handed. She nearly swooned.

'Getting there?' inquired Miss Carbery cheerfully. 'How do you like the notion?'

Dorothea leaned forward. 'It's really true?'

'As far as it goes,' said Miss Carbery soberly. 'Whether it becomes actual fact depends on yourself.'

'So there is a condition?'

'Yes. That's why I'm here. To explain it to you.'

'It's very kind . . .' murmured Dorothea.

'Not a bit,' contradicted Julia. 'Self-preservation, that's all. I've got myself to think of, haven't I? I'm a poor relation, too. Been acting as housekeeper for Mr. Hope for the past fifteen years. That's why they're all warning you against me. You see, I know too much.'

'Too much about what?'

'All of them. I know their little ways. I know how they'll come sneaking up to you. And they know I know it. That's why they want to keep us apart. Just as I knew all about him and his little secrets that some of them never guessed at. Why, they even thought he might leave his money to me. Or

66

to a Home for Destitute Virgins.' She looked at Dorothea thoughtfully. If Everard Hope had left his money that way she might have eventually benefited. She had a rather destitute look, decided Julia, and she would certainly fit the rest of the bill.

'And instead he's left it to me?' Dorothea came back once more to this astounding starting-point.

'If you're very careful.'

'You did say something about a condition,' Miss Capper murmured.

Julia began to chuckle. 'They all said he had no sense of humour. They weren't right. He had plenty only it was the kind other people didn't appreciate. I dare say you won't either.'

'What is the condition?' almost screamed Dorothea.

'You must be alive to claim your inheritance thirty days after the reading of the will.'

CHAPTER FOUR

I

SOMEONE LAUGHED.

That, thought Dorothea, more shocked than ever, must be Miss Carbery. She was definitely queer. That laugh alone proved it. Only a woman who was a bit mad would dream of laughing at such a moment. For it was a fearful moment. There was no doubt about that. It meant that she, Dorothea Capper, really was in danger. She was convinced of it at last. And she imagined the impish delight Cousin Everard must have taken in making that condition.

'Pull yourself together,' said Miss Carbery sharply. 'This is no laughing matter.'

So it was she who had laughed, which meant they must both of them be mad. She was sober on the instant.

'When did all this happen?' she whispered.

Julia told her. 'You weren't sent for because none of us knew you existed. Mr. Midleton—one D., remember. He'll charge you extra if you put in two—come down to read the will. You'll pay his expenses, of course, if you inherit, and if you don't inherit one of the others will. Mr. Midleton won't.

Lawyers never do.'

Dorothea clung to the word lawyer. If a lawyer was involved then it was serious. Lawyers were intensely serious people. Why, they got six-and-eightpence for every letter they wrote, whereas ordinary people were simply twopence-half-penny down on the stamp. Perhaps this Mr. Midleton would write to her. It might seem more real if she saw it in black and white. Of course, he'd want his share of the hundred thousand pounds, and then there was the Government. A rich man had just said that rich people paid 19s. 6d. in the £ for taxes, which only left sixpence.

Her glazed eyes met Miss Carbery. 'A hundred thousand sixpences,' she said, 'only it won't really be so much, because I shan't get a hundred thousand. Say eighty thousand. Forty sixpences to the pound, four hundred to ten pounds, four thousand to . . .'

'Are you subject to epileptic fits?' inquired Miss Carbery abruptly.

Dorothea, equally abruptly, said No, of course not.

'All right,' said Julia. 'I just wondered.'

Dorothea, remembering her manners, said again how kind it was of Julia to come.

'I didn't do it because I'm a good citizen,' said Miss Carbery cheerfully. 'No one's such a good citizen as that, not unless he gets a good salary for it. No, I had a little proposition to put to you.'

Dorothea felt this was too much. 'Perhaps in the morning,' she said. 'That is, if you'll tell me where you're staying . . .' But she knew it was a forlorn hope even as she spoke. Any one could see where Miss Carbery intended to spend the night.

'I'm staying here,' she said simply, 'and you thank your lucky stars I am. If I didn't, there mightn't be any morning for you. Ever hear of the Spider? He used to drop through a trap-door—I noticed you had one outside—with a long Chinese knife. Ever hear of the gang that used the Infected Centipede? You might be asleep when it came under the crack, crawling up on to your bed . . .'

Dorothea pulled herself together. 'How would it get into my flat?'

'Under the door,' said Miss Carbery promptly. 'Noticed there was a crack.'

'How could you be sure it would come to my bed and not yours?' demanded Dorothea.

'They won't send any centipede so long as I'm here. Now then, I'll put all my cards on the table.' She stretched out her arms and Dorothea almost expected to see a flood of aces fall out of the sleeves. 'Now, the old man's death leaves me in a spot. I'm out of a

70

job. Mind you, I'm not sponging. This is my experiment as much as yours and there's no reason why you should pay for it. Of course, Mr. Hope paid for my services, but I shouldn't expect that of you. I've got my little bit put by. I was taught early to look after Number One. In fact, if you're a bit pushed for the ready...' But Dorothea, looking shocked, said she wasn't. She thought owing money a refined form of stealing.

'Well,' said Miss Carbery. 'I think I might be useful to you and later on you could be useful to me. How about it?'

Dorothea in a daze said she generally had a cup of tea at this hour and how about that?

'Breakfast, lunch, tea and dinner, that's what I'm counting on,' said Julia robustly. 'Don't tell me you haven't a room. This day-bed affair will do for me. I'm not fussy.' She smote the emaciated springs with a will and they groaned in defeat.

'If I don't agree to see any of my cousins I don't think I'm in much danger,' suggested Dorothea, but without conviction.

'How about the post?' demanded Julia. 'How about the poisoned handshake? How about gasmen coming to read the meter? How about billeting officers? How about callers from the Board of Trade, wasting paper by getting you to fill up forms about clothing coupons? Why, my dear girl, the war's given the most glorious chance of their lives to house-to-house criminals. The Englishman's home isn't his castle any more. It's a bit of the front line the Government might feel inclined to take over at any minute. You haven't a chance unless you're guarded. That's been the great lesson of the war to date. Bombers simply can't make it if they haven't got fighters in tow. You're the bomber,' she chuckled, 'the hundred thousand pound bomber, but I'm the fighter and—don't forget—the fighter's essential.'

'But this is sheer melodrama,' cried Dorothea, fighting down a desire to scream, to bite the tablecloth, to roll on the floor, to dissolve into hysterics.

'Life, you mean,' exclaimed her companion. 'Look at this.' She shook out the brightest of all the Sunday papers before Dorothea's fasinated gaze. 'Woman's Body found in Bear-Pit. Secret of an Oven. Body two weeks in lift shaft. And there are more on the next page. If you're not careful, there'll be a similar column about you in the next thirty days. Why, how was it, do you suppose, your cousin lived so long? They'd have been singing "Now the labourer's task is o'er" over him years ago if it hadn't been for me.'

'But people don't commit murder so casually,' exclaimed Dorothea. 'Not people one knows, I mean.'

'That's just the point. You don't know that. And it's happened before.'

'But not—...'

'Oh yes,' said Miss Carbery calmly. 'Only the other day. You don't really imagine that Cousin Everard fell down a flight of his own stairs and broke his neck by accident, do you? Because I can tell you, he didn't do anything of the kind.'

II

Dorothea tottered off and put the kettle on for tea. She made it very strong and she sweetened her cup with plenty of sugar. Miss Carbery said she didn't take sugar. 'I do,' said Dorothea. Wildly. Anything to keep off the subject of murder. 'Lots and lots of sugar. Sugar makes energy.'

'It makes fat,' said Julia.

'Not on me it doesn't,' said Dorothea with obvious truth. 'If ever I go out for a coffee with Georgie or—or—well, for a coffee with Georgie—I always take two extra lumps with me in a little blue tin Georgie gave me for Christmas.' She produced the little tin. It had a picture of three lumps of sugar and My Ration in white lettering on the lid. 'So convenient,' babbled Dorothea, almost expecting to see Miss Carbery turn into an infected centipede under her eyes. 'Of course if you don't take sugar in your tea you're very, very lucky. Oh, please pour yourself out another cup.'

If she talked fast enough she might wake up and find it all a dream.

'Not in someone's else's house,' returned Miss Carbery grimly. 'Don't you know what happens if you do? You have twins within the year. Well, if I did, I should hold you responsible.'

'Oh, but I don't think—I mean, I couldn't—that is, I'm sure it wouldn't happen.'

Miss Carbery chuckled lewdly. 'I'm sure it wouldn't either,' she agreed. She whirled into the hall and snapped open the clasp of her shabby suitcase and whirled out a pair of heavily flowered pyjamas.

'Bought them at the jumble,' she said. 'One shilling and no coupons. Know where they came from, too. Well, it must make a change for them getting into bed with me every night. Now, where do you keep your sheets? No, don't bother. You've had a bit of a shock. I'll find everything. Just tell me where you keep your towels. I've brought my own soap.

74

She was rapidly disarranging Miss Capper's neat sitting-room into a sort of old clothes shop, but a tank could hardly have stopped her. She even stood up and began to undress, talking all the time.

'I've sometimes thought of writing my reminiscences,' she said cheerfully. 'Something to bring in a little money, you know. But then, I've always found it paid me better not to write them.'

'I don't understand,' murmured Dorothea, for about the hundredth time.

'People will sometimes pay you more not to write than publishers for putting the facts on to paper,' observed Miss Carbery obscurely.

She pulled a green patterned slip over her head.

'And now,' she demanded, her grotesque red head entangled in its folds, 'are you and me going to play ball?'

Dorothea stared and wriggled a little farther away.

'You look like a little mouse,' said Miss Carbery, 'a little scared grey mouse. Come, come, you mustn't be frightened of me. We're going to get along very well together, I'm sure.'

There was a new note in her voice that roused the dazed Dorothea's protective sense.

She said desperately: 'Yes, of course, but . . .'

'No buts,' said Miss Carbery. 'I'll tell you what I thought. I thought you'd give me some little agreement—say, ten per cent of the gross—I think that's how they put it—and I'll see you through.'

The words of the mysterious telegram flashed into Dorothea's mind. Sign nothing without advice.

'I think perhaps I ought to see Mr. Midleton before I do anything,' she faltered.

'Midleton's an old woman. He won't be any good to you. It's nothing to him who gets the money. Actually, of course, it's nothing to me either, unless I stand to make something.' She looked at Dorothea meaningly. 'You won't stand a chance against the others. You see, if you lose the next-of-kin inherits.'

'And who's that?'

'No one knows, but they'll all try and prove it's them,' returned Julia ungrammatically, 'so it's to the advantage of every one of them to start saving for your wreath. And—don't forget—one of them has already killed Everard Hope.'

She began to unfasten her suspenders. Dorothea went quickly away and sat in the kitchen. She thought perhaps the Vicar had been prophetic. She had died since the morn-

76

ing service, and this was the ante-room of
hell.

III

It wasn't Miss Carbery who lay awake that
night, although Dorothea, an honest woman,
must have admitted that the daybed wasn't
any one's idea of comfort. Still, Miss Carbery
either had a clear conscience or no conscience
at all. Dorothea's conscience was clear
enough, but it didn't seem much help in her
present situation. The questions she couldn't
ask her visitor came flooding over her as she
lay sleepless and feverish in the dark.

How did Miss Carbery know that Everard
Hope hadn't died by accident?

Why hadn't she gone to the police?

What had she meant by its being more
profitable sometimes to refrain from publication?

What would really happen to her
(Dorothea) if, in Miss Carbery's execrable
phraseology, she refused to play ball? Would
there then be a second funeral to be paid for
out of Everard Hope's estate? Only, of course
it wouldn't come out of his estate. It would
come out of Miss Capper's. There wasn't
much, but there would be enough for that,
even enough to provide the mourners with
black, unless of course they said no mourning

by request, request of the survivors, not of the deceased. Miss Capper felt like a mouse treading rapidly round a pail of water, feeling its strength failing, knowing it couldn't last much longer. And then the worst thought of all came to torment her. What if they were all in it together, Julia and Garth and Cecil and the rest, all seven of them? What if the telegram and the telephone call were part of an elaborate plot to bandage her eyes? After all, if it wasn't prearranged, how had they been so sure where Miss Carbery was to be found? And hadn't they all been just a little over-emphatic in their warnings? Garth was a lawyer, and lawyers were supposed to be men of discretion. (Mr. Crook could have told her that there are several ways of spelling discretion and not all lawyers spell it alike, but at this juncture she hadn't met Mr. Crook.) The more she thought, the more probable it seemed. Say what you liked, no one was quite sure who would get the money in the event of the original heir not surviving long enough to inherit, but even a seventh of a hundred thousand pounds, even after Mr. Midleton and the Government had taken their share, was not to be sneezed at. British history, thought Dorothea, turning wearily over in the bed that seemed to-night to be stuffed with turnips, was full of victories against fear-

78

ful odds, but even so, seven to one was right off the board. Seven practised murderers—for they already had poor Cousin Everard to their credit—against a little woman like a mouse who'd never wanted a hundred thousand pounds and probably wasn't going to get them anyway—the odds were too great. Even Mr. Churchill, the gambler of his generation, would have refused to play ball.

She no longer doubted that Everard had met his death by foul play. It isn't natural for a rich man to die by accident in a house full of relations. If that has to happen, the dead man should have nothing but goodwill to leave.

Shooting out a nervous hand, unable any longer to bear the impenetrable darkness, she knocked over the bedside lamp. By the tinkle of glass she knew the bulb was broken. Now, thought she, Miss Carbery will come through the door. She saw the fantastic figure, ginger curls, flowered pyjamas and all—armed with her (Dorothea's) breadknife. Probably at this very instant... Distraught with terror she fell out of bed and dashed at the door. As she approached it it opened a crack. Dorothea hurled herself against it. There was no opposition and she turned the key with a sense of crazy relief. Then she switched on the ceiling light. The pier-glass showed her a panting dishevelled woman in a tumbled nightgown of flowered fergonese, home-made, waiting for attack. But the attack didn't materialise. Only, after a moment, a mighty rumble surged through the flat. It began like the noise of a distant train, becoming louder and louder and finally exploding in a tumult of sound that staggered the terrified listener. Could it be the bombers coming over? And how grand if they demolished Miss Carbery and left her (Dorothea) unharmed. Only bombs are seldom as tactful as that.

Suddenly her heart reassured her by going back to its normal beat. She sat on the edge of the bed and began to laugh. She laughed and laughed. The noise almost drowned the other noise that seemed to deafen the flat. Because it wasn't an air-raid warning, it wasn't planes overhead, it wasn't the prelude to an unspeakable crime.

It was simply Julia Carbery enjoying her sleep.

IV

Julia Carbery's precipitate action in installing herself in Miss Capper's household was not without its effect on the rest of the late Mr. Hope's relatives. Originally intending to remain at Fox Norton until Monday and catch the comparatively comfortable 10.2 to town, both married couples resolved, at

80

whatever sacrifice, to travel up on Sunday afternoon. This involved so many changes, so much waiting and such packed trains, including becoming involved with a touring company who hotly disputed their right to the seats they had with difficulty secured, that none of the four had much energy left for anything but sleep when at length they arrived. It was in any case well after ten p.m. and none of them wanted to start wrong with the heiress by telephoning when she would, presumably, be in bed. They therefore agreed that they had been welshed, cheesed, and led up the garden by the old man, and something must be done about it, but by mutual consent waited till next morning to do anything.

By eight a.m., however, all four were so pleasantly refreshed that they were prepared to start discussion anew. In their Kensington house Cecil Tempest, who might put steel filings into Dorothea's coffee, said restively: 'One wonders what precise hold this Capper woman had over him.'

Lilias, tranquil as usual in the wrong clothes, observed innocently: 'That's simple enough. He hadn't got anything against her.'

'I wonder if there was anything between him and her mother,' continued Cecil, who, as Pansy Bright, wrote serials for the Youth

Ethical Press and knew that romance rings the bell every time.

'Well, darling,' said Lilias, temperately, 'from what I've seen of your Cousin Everard I shouldn't have said he felt any obligations towards a woman he can't have seen for years and years, if ever.'

'He might have had pangs of conscience,' insisted Cecil, for in his serial, *The Hand of Fate*, all was put right in the last chapter by the sudden discovery of a conscience on the part of the villain, who a little bewilderingly changed places with the hero and breasted the tape to the accompaniment of wedding bells.

'Only in books,' said Lilias firmly. 'You know in real life it never happens. People who're mean over money—and how mean he was!—don't suddenly make generous gestures. Your Mr. Whaley doesn't...'

She got no further than that for Cecil made a generous gesture on his own account and the coffee spread all over the table.

'Women are different,' he said. He had been keeping a roof over his head, though not perhaps a very sound one, for fifteen years by his adherence to this gospel. In all his stories the women were different—different from what they would have been in real life, Lilias explained. 'It might be a good thing to invite

82

her here for a little. She's probably lonely.'

Lilias didn't write novels, but she knew a good deal about life, too much to turn out saleable fiction, she told her husband. 'No one who's expecting to inherit a hundred thousand pounds is ever lonely,' she said in firm tones.

'It would be a friendly gesture,' Cecil insisted.

'And I don't know whose bed you were proposing she could sleep in,' continued Lilias, with a flash of that coarseness that made Cecil wonder sometimes why he'd fallen in love with her.

'There's the camp bed,' he said sharply.

'Not awfully suitable for an heiress.'

'She'll know we're not millionaires.'

'Oh, she'll know that all right,' Lilias agreed. 'You don't think she may find it odd we should so suddenly realise her existence?'

'How could we realise it before, when we'd never heard of it?'

'That's true,' agreed Lilias. 'Of course, from our commercial point of view, she's only just born.'

Cecil, who had his own warped sense of humour, wondered how it was he got away with a romantic serial every nine months and heaven only knew how many romantic stories a year, when you remembered what marriage really was. He supposed his reading public was practically composed of spinsters.

'You might send her a line in any case,' he said.

But Lilias looked doubtful. 'Even if you get her here,' she said, 'how are you going to persuade her to part? Because I take it that's your idea. Casting our bread and rations on the waters in the hopes of getting it back in due course.'

Cecil, touchy like most writers, chose to take offence. 'You talk as though we were starving and I was trying to rob her,' he exclaimed. 'After all, I have been bringing home the bacon for a good many years.'

'Yes,' agreed Lilias, 'but—don't be cross—never more than just enough for a rasher apiece for breakfast and not always the best cuts. Think what it must feel like to have a whole side in the house at once.'

Cecil let that go. It was too like a wife to be worthy of comment.

'It's an iniquitous will,' he said fiercely. 'I'm sure Miss Capper will see that for herself if it's put to her.'

'You've more faith in human nature than I have,' said his wife candidly. 'No one ever sees anything unjust about inheriting money.'

'A hundred thousand pounds for a woman

in her position is preposterous.'

'Ah, but she'll soon change her position.'

'In any case, you might make an effort for the children's sake. Having none of her own . . .'

'There's time,' said Lilias. 'She's only thirty-eight.' (For they had unearthed a surprising amount of information about her, between them.)

'She's never had any before,' Cecil snapped.

'She's never had a hundred thousand pounds before.'

'And she hasn't got it yet,' Cecil reminded his wife grimly.

Lilias was looking troubled. 'I'm sure it would be wiser to let her alone till after she'd got it,' she said. 'Suppose we ask her here to stay and she comes? Suppose she gets appendicitis? Suppose she dies of it? Suppose she's the poetical type that likes leaning out of windows and watching sunsets? And suppose she leans too far? You're a novelist and I'm not, but even I can guess what Garth and the others would say.'

Cecil stood up. 'I've asked you to write and there's an end of it,' he said. 'If you won't, you won't. If you don't care about your children's future . . . My God, Lilias, look at the time. I ought to have gone five minutes ago, and since you don't intend to help me with Miss Capper, it's more important than ever I shouldn't be late for work. You know,' he folded his paper clumsily, 'no one can call me a jealous man, but the thought of that woman's luck is almost more than I can endure.'

'I wouldn't be in her shoes,' said Lilias, beginning to pile the plates together.

'Well, of course you wouldn't, agreed Cecil stiffly. 'Naturally not. All the same, one does ask oneself—Can a woman of her experience appreciate such an enormous sum?'

'And one asks oneself even more urgently—Is she going to have the chance? Don't gape so, Cecil. Any one would think you had goitre.'

Cecil got up and walked sulkily out of the room. Heaven knew he was a good husband, but even the best of them like occasionally to get the last word. And somehow Lilias must be persuaded to write to Miss Capper. Cecil thought of the letter he had had the day they went down to Fox Norton for the old man's annual party, and the second that had come on this morning's post. Luckily he had met the postman and so Lilias hadn't seen the envelope. Yet didn't she know? Wives don't need to see envelopes to realise their husbands were in difficulties. Granted he'd been mad. Gambling was always madness, and to gamble when you knew nothing, because a sudden dream unfolded itself, because a man said it was a dead snip and you were tired of lying awake at night wondering what would happen to your wife and children if anything happened to you ... He'd taken giant risks and they hadn't come off. If Mr. Whaley found out that he owed a bookmaker nearly a thousand pounds he'd lose his job; and though his serials were very suitable for the Youth Ethical Press they wouldn't find a market anywhere else. Cecil knew, because he'd tried. And there was actually a clause in his contract that betting was not permitted to employees of the Press. Somehow, therefore, Mr. Ben must be squared and at once. But how? He'd thought at first that Cousin Everard might be the solution, but he'd failed there. Now here was Dorothea offering him a second chance. This time he didn't dare fail. At worst he'd get a percentage of the hundred thousand, he told himself, since the cousins must all be equally related. Probably Everard had only put the clause in to put temptation in as many paths as possible. It was a typical Everard pleasantry. Cecil found himself unable to concentrate on the new instalment of: Poppy. A Country Blossom. He could think of nothing but that wretched thousand pounds.

He hadn't been long at his desk when Mr. Whaley marched in, carrying much before him.

'Ah, good-morning, Tempest,' said he suavely. 'Glad to see you back. Very sad about your cousin. Sad in every sense of the word.'

'Very sudden,' gulped Cecil, thinking it was only sad from one angle and that scarcely the one Mr. Whaley had in mind.

'And I'm afraid—speaking purely as a man of the world, you'll understand—it was disappointing for you—the will, I mean. I gather you always expected to be remembered.'

Cecil gulped again. 'As a matter of fact, it was rather a staggerer for all of us. I mean, my cousin seems to have told more than one of his relations that he'd benefit under the will and naturally—one doesn't care to speculate, but...'

'Naturally,' said Mr. Whaley, inclining his head.

'As for Miss Capper, we none of us knew of her existence.' He gulped once more. 'It's even possible she didn't know of his.'

'Most probable,' agreed Mr. Whaley, gently massaging his stomach with his palms. And indeed in his experience it verged on the incredible that any one should possess a wealthy relative and consistently ignore him for years.

'My cousin certainly spoke on more than one occasion about providing for the next generation,' Cecil continued desperately. He felt he owed Mr. Whaley an apology for not inheriting the money. Mr. Whaley had that effect on a good many poorish people.

'I take it this lady is the next generation,' said Mr. Whaley smoothly. 'Well, well, Tempest, we know the promise. In the world ye shall have tribulation.' He walked to the door where he turned. 'But it's disappointing,' he added, 'very disappointing indeed.'

Cecil sat motionless at his desk after he found himself alone, staring miserably at the closed door.

'What the devil did he mean by that?' he wondered.

He knew Mr. Whaley had a favourite nephew who according to his uncle, was dying to come into the firm. He was at present in the Army but he suffered from gastric disturbances and it seemed probable that he wouldn't be in the Army much longer. Oh, for a bomb to destroy the nephew before he could get his discharge, thought Cecil.

'If I lose this job I'm done,' he told himself, getting up and walking feverishly up and down his office, 'and it looks to me uncommonly as if I am to lose it. Still—there's still one chance and I shall have to take it.'

He came back to the desk and picked up his pen.

'She came into the dim room, dusty with age and grief, looking like a little red rose on an ancient grey wall.'

CHAPTER FIVE

I

AT WESTMOUNT, Rochester Row, W.1. the home of the Garth Hopes, Lucille Hope looked curiously through her husband's post while he took a telephone call in the library. There had been, thought Lucille, who answered the telephone in the first instance, something a little odd about the voice at the other end of the line. But nothing like so odd as Garth's face when presently he came in. Lucille stared at him.

'Garth! What is it?'

'What's what?'

'You look as though you were going to faint.'

'How absurd you are, Lucille. Pour me some coffee.'

'Who was that on the phone?' asked Lucille.

'The office,' said Garth promptly. 'I've got to go early.'

'Did they say anything about the will?' inquired Lucille.

'It doesn't affect them. Why should they?' But his lips weren't quite steady as he spoke.

He took up the *Times* and began to read the

middle sheet.

'There's a nice bit about Cousin Everard in my paper,' offered Lucille, spreading honey on strips of toast.

Garth dashed his own newspaper aside. 'Already? My God, what vultures. What do they say?'

'Just Recluse's Curious Will. I wonder they haven't found out that the Capper's Cousin Everard's illegit. Oh well,' she handed the paper across the table, 'it's more notice than you or I would get, though he was such a horrible old man.'

As she spoke, it was as though something froze her face into hatred. She was a very smart beautifully-dressed woman in the early thirties. Hair, nails, complexion, everything about her was perfect. She was like a cover drawing for *Vogue*, and, like the drawing, all her heart was on the surface. She could never forgive life for arranging that, with all her gifts and looks, she should not have progressed beyond the second-rate in her chosen profession. She had seen herself in leading roles, her name in electric lights, and touring companies and ladies-maids in London was all she had ever achieved. If she had been more successful she wouldn't have married Garth.

'Oh, I don't know,' said Garth, suddenly

as bitter as she. 'I fancy, at the moment, if all were known, I might rate as much space as our departed cousin.'

Lucille's eyes widened. for a moment she seemed almost human. 'Garth, what are you saying?'

'What do you think I'm saying?'

'Not that—that—'

'Not what?'

'That you know how Cousin Everard died.'

'We all know how Cousin Everard died. He fell downstairs. And I, for one, don't want to know any more.'

'So long as no one knows any more,' agreed Lucille. 'But I don't trust Julia.'

Garth put his hands in his pockets. 'What do you suppose Julia knows that might be dangerous?'

'I didn't say she knew anything, but I did just wonder . . .'

'Well?'

'If she flew to London to protect the heiress.'

He thrust forward his lower lip. 'Against what?'

'Don't the police say that a man who commits one murder often commits a second, and usually in the same way? Isn't it possible that whoever—eliminated—Cousin Everard may be planning to eliminate Dorothea Capper too?'

'You're very sure someone did eliminate Cousin Everard.'

'There was a good deal of motive, wasn't there?'

'What exactly do you mean by that?'

'I know Cecil wanted money, and I daresay all the others are in the same boat. You are, aren't you, Garth?'

His face was suddenly grey. 'Why do you say that?'

'There was a message last week from a man called Morris.'

His lips drew back from his teeth. 'You didn't tell me.'

'He said he was going to ring you up at the office.'

'I believe he did.'

'I thought he would.'

'I don't know why you should deduce from that . . .'

Lucille shook her lovely head. 'It's no good, Garth. I got his number and rang it later and I found out he was a moneylender.'

'Suppose he is?' said Garth, brazening it out.

'On a considerable scale.'

'When did you know me deal with little men?'

'You owe him a good deal, don't you?'

Even Garth's lips were white now. He looked rather horrible, that big swarthy man, whitened by fear, his large square hands holding on to the table as though it were a human throat. She thought, What powerful hands he has. No one, certainly not an old man, would have a chance against them.

'It's new for you to take an interest in my affairs, isn't it?'

She said clearly: 'I'm prepared to call it quits.'

He looked at her sharply. 'What does that mean?'

'I'll forget anything I know about your concerns, if you'll be equally obliging.'

He understood her then. That damned gigolo she was going round with. She'd always liked to trail a man at her fashionable skirts, but this time it was getting beyond a joke. His eyes met hers that were grey as steel and as unyielding.

He shrugged his shoulders. 'As for mine,' he said 'there's nothing much to forget. The whole affair will be cleared up in a very few days. I shall see to that.'

'With Cousin Dorothea's money?' asked Lucille.

'It'll never be her money,' said Garth in his dryest tone. Of Dorothea herself he refused to think. He couldn't afford to be sorry for

95

Dorothea. Pity's expensive. Besides, it was his life against her, and on all counts he was obviously the more worth retaining.

II

Reaching his office Garth put through a telephone call to Mr. Morris and made an appointment for that afternoon. At three o'clock he sent in his name, and was at once admitted to Mr. Morris's presence. The moneylender was a quiet Scottish-looking gentleman with a pleasant manner and an attractive smile.

'Ah, Mr. Hope, glad to see you. I expect you've got good news for us.'

'If you've seen this morning's paper, as I don't doubt you have,' said Garth grimly, 'you'll know I've nothing of the sort.' It hadn't needed this incident to prove to the lawyer that so long as your creditors believe you to be the heir of a wealthy man they will give you any amount of licence, but so soon as they realise you've only yourself to depend on, they close in like wolves. 'I can't at the moment see my way to meet your demands.'

Mr. Morris's eyebrows lifted. It seemed he was surprised at the news. 'You must surely realise, Mr. Hope, we can't allow you any appreciable extension of the time. The loan's been running for a considerable period now,

96

and if you can't oblige us we shall have no choice but to bring action.'

'That won't help you,' said Garth coolly, disguising the fact that it would spell absolute ruin for himself. An action now must reveal the truth that Garth had foolishly added himself to the list of solicitors who speculate with clients' funds with unfortunate results. Still, give him a month, said Garth.

Mr. Morris considered. He had a shrewd suspicion that it would do him little service to press for immediate payment. He thought it probable that Garth was telling the truth when he said he intended to contest the will. Should he prove successful it would not be in Mr. Morris's interests to quarrel with his client. After a short pause he made up his mind.

'A lawyer yourself, Mr. Hope, you will appreciate that though the mills of justice may grind exceeding small they also grind exceeding slow. Frankly, we cannot afford to be out of our money for very much longer. On the other hand we have no wish to embarrass you, if it can be avoided. We will, therefore, give you another thirty days' grace. A good deal, Mr. Hope, may happen in thirty days.'

The phrase rang in Garth's head as he walked back to his office. It linked itself with another memory.

'. . . . I do give and bequeath to my kins-woman, Dorothea Capper, provided she is alive, to claim my estate thirty days after the reading of this will.'

III

The brothers Lacey breakfasted later than the other members of their family. They also breakfasted more luxuriously. But they had this in common with their cousins, that their post consisted mainly of bills.

'I'm disappointed in Hurley,' announced Christopher, opening his first envelope and tossing the enclosed note on to the table. 'I shouldn't have expected such vulgarity from a man with such an eye for line.'

Hugh picked up the letter and glanced at it. 'Hurley seems to be a bit disappointed in you,' he announced, 'and more than a bit dis-appointed in Cousin Everard. It's your con-founded optimism, Chris.'

'It's my confounded optimism as you call it that's made it possible for me to dangle Hurley on a line for nearly four years without a penny. If I'd been a realist I'd have been dressing at the Sixty-Five Shilling Tailors long ago. I say, I suppose no one, bar Julia, has yet set eyes on the heiress?'

'I shouldn't expect too much,' Hugh warned him. 'Women who get left a hundred thousand pounds look more like Mrs. Fairchild than Marlene Dietrich.'

Christopher shuddered. 'A really good woman.'

'I've been telling you for years that a good woman might make all the difference,' said Hugh.

Christopher, most unfortunately tangled with a lady who couldn't by any standards be so described, frowned darkly. Hurley's bill was a small matter but the demand for two thousand pounds at present reposing in his waistcoat pocket was urgent. If he didn't find the two thousand pounds, the injured husband proposed to bring a petition for divorce. The fact that he didn't care two straws about his wife and was leaping at the chance of making two thousand pounds off her didn't affect the case. What really mattered was that Christopher was as inwardly ambitious as he was outwardly lethargic. He didn't intend to pass the rest of the war at the M.O.I. waiting for his share of the I. to be dished out to him. He had set his heart on an appointment that would offer him real scope. But, since the English persist in confounding morality with ability, he knew he didn't stand a chance if his name was being bandied about in the Divorce Court. The lady wasn't worth two thousand pounds or a tenth of that sum, but he hadn't realised that at the outset. He thought it most probable that she and her precious husband were in a plot together to milk him of two thousand pounds, but he was, he told himself fiercely, prepared to commit murder, if necessary. It was useless to try money-lenders as Garth had done, for he had only the security that goes with a Government appointment, and anyone who has ever had dealings with moneylenders knows how far that will get you. He said abruptly: 'I've got to see a man at eleven and I haven't shaved yet,' and went out.

Hugh waited till he heard the front door close behind him and then pulled the tele-phone towards himself and dialled Bush 4141.

IV

Rather to her surprise Miss Capper woke to find herself all in one piece. Lying in bed, thinking, I mustn't get up too early, in case I disturb Miss Carbery, she came to a decision. She would ring up the Vicar and get advice. She had never done anything so drastic before. Normally she wouldn't expect him to be able to spare any of his valuable time for her, but circumstances now warranted a change of outlook.

'Of course,' Miss Capper assured herself,

'it will not make the least difference. I know, naturally, that he won't be remotely influenced by financial considerations, but equally naturally he has to think of his work.' In brief, there was no getting away from the fact that a parishioner with £100,000, Even if only in prospect, is more deserving of the Vicar's time than one living on the Old Age Pension and the family hat.

She had just reached this conclusion and had decided to get up forthwith, in order to catch the vicar before he set out on the day's ploys, when someone bumped vigorously on the door.

'Hey!' yelled Miss Carbery. 'What's going on in here?'

Nervously Dorothea turned the key. 'Brought you your breakfast,' said Miss Carbery, staggering in with a tray. 'Oh, no trouble, I assure you. I always used to encourage Mr. Hope to have breakfast in bed. Kept him out of the way of the household.' Which might, reflected Dorothea, have been all right for Cousin Everard, but wasn't quite the same thing for Miss Capper in her own flat. However, she was already beginning to suspect it was going to be 'our flat' pretty soon if it wasn't that already.

'You shouldn't have troubled,' she said, aware of hair in rubber curlers and an unpowdered nose, but Miss Carbery said: 'No trouble at all. That's what you've got me for. Julia Carbery. The Useful Woman in the Home. Never absent, never late. Cheaper than a rest cure, no travelling, no passport difficulties. No forbidden areas...' She dumped the tray on the bed. 'I couldn't find any cereals in your cupboard, so I've brought you some of my regularity rusks. Best on the market. I've had 'em for years and look at me.

Fortunately for Miss Capper, who seemed about to have an apoplectic fit, at this instant the telephone bell rang. Miss Carbery flew to answer it. Dorothea glanced at her watch and was horrified to discover it said 7.30, as it had done a long time ago.

She heard her handy woman's brisk voice in the next room, and then a click as the receiver was hung up.

'Someone called Trent,' announced Julia, returning. 'And—no, you don't have to get up yet.'

'What time is it?' inquired Dorothea.

'Nine-thirty. A bit late, but I thought I'd let you sleep.'

'I wasn't sleeping,' Dorothea protested, but Miss Carbery wagged a warning finger.

'Now, now,' she said. 'I listened at the keyhole.'

Dorothea let that insult pass. 'Was that a wrong number?' she inquired. 'Oh no, you said it was Miss Trent. You—you didn't ring her off?'

'Certainly I rang her off. You're having your breakfast, aren't you?'

'You rang Georgie off? You rang GEORGIE off?'

'How was I to know who it was? It might have been one of your cousins speaking in a disguised voice. Hadn't thought of that, had you? That's what you've got to be on your guard against. That's why I'm here.'

Dorothea struggled for dignity. 'I prefer to take my own calls,' she announced.

'When you're dressed,' said Miss Carberry smoothly, 'you can ring her yourself. Then you can find out if it was her just now.'

'But no one can do me any harm over the telephone,' protested Dorothea.

Miss Carbery poured some milk over the regularity rusks. 'Never heard of blowing germs over the line, I suppose?'

But Dorothea said you had to get hold of germs first, and germs weren't like goldfish, you couldn't buy them at the Army and Navy Stores.

'Can't buy goldfish either, so I'm told,' retorted Julia, with the air of scoring a point. 'All wanted for the national emergency.' She walked out of the room leaving Dorothea to the unpalatable worm-like substances in the soup-plate. Dorothea struggled with them for a moment, then flared up into revolt. It was too much. For thirty-eight years she had lived a life of drab virtue, and where had it landed her? In this unromantic flat with a few, oh so unromantic, friends, the consolations of conscience, and the prospect, if she lived long enough, of one day being the oldest parishioner. Talk about danger, thought Dorothea, throwing the rusks aside and thinking they looked like mealworms that have been sunbathing. At least let danger wear an attractive mien. Let it come as a wolf if it must, and let her be the St. Francis of a new day taming and subduing it. As she threw on her clothes she remembered the Vicar on the last feast of St. Francis in October.

'He preached to the wild birds of Heaven,' he announced, 'whereas I preach to the old hens.'

For years, said Dorothea, picking up a hairbrush, I have been an old hen, a tough, stringy, prematurely aged hen. Now I will be a wild bird of heaven. The mirror somewhat daunted her ambitions, but she buoyed them up with her best brown æolian dress with a coffee-coloured frill, her long brown spring coat, her varnished brown straw hat, her nice brown cavalier shoes with gilt buckles. The mirror reflected a perfect lady. You would be looking at an eagle a long time before you thought of Dorothea Capper, but her heart fluttered as though it contained a whole nest of eaglets. She had just finished dressing when she heard the preliminary hiccough of the telephone. By divine dispensation Miss Carbery was in the bathroom and Dorothea got there first.

'Miss Capper?' said a cheerful male voice. 'Or should I say Dorothea? This is your envious if congratulatory Cousin Hugh.'

Dorothea felt staggered but flattered. There wasn't a doubt about it she was on a tough spot, but an old hen never got out of the run of it all. This was the first time in her life a man had rung her up who wasn't a builder or a plumber or, as the Vicar liked to say jocosely, of that ilk.

'I suppose dear Julia's with you?' the voice went on.

Dorothea said: 'Yes. In the bathroom.'

'Take my tip and keep her there,' said Cousin Hugh. 'Did she say why she came?'

'To warn me,' said Dorothea crudely. 'At least, that is . . .'

'Don't apologise,' said Hugh. 'She's quite right. You want to steer clear of the whole boiling of us. That's why I'm ringing you up.'

'I don't think I understand,' whispered Dorothea.

'Come to lunch with me and I'll explain,' Hugh suggested. 'I don't say Julia's any more dangerous than the rest of us, but she is the wolf in sheep's clothing, whereas we are honest wolves.'

There it was—wolves again. Mentally Miss Capper invoked the spirit of St. Francis.

'She has offered to act as a chaperon,' she went on, 'but I don't think a woman of my age requires one.'

'Not you,' Hugh explained. 'Your hundred thousand pounds. That really ought to have a convoy. She's mortally afraid you may not get it, but if you do, then she wants to be in at the death.' He seemed to realise that was an unfortunate phrase and added hurriedly: 'Would the Magnificent Grill to-day, one fifteen, suit you? I'll wear a green handkerchief Pan-fashion,' and without waiting for her reply rang off.

'He's very experienced with women,' thought Dorothea with reluctant admiration. 'He knew I wouldn't be able to resist the Magnificent.'

But what Hugh had really known was that she wouldn't be able to resist the vision of him waiting for her at the Magnificent, wearing a green handkerchief, Pan-fashion, whatever that might mean.

The door opened and Miss Carbery stormed in. She said nothing but stood staring at Dorothea until the latter said a little uncomfortably: 'I'm afraid I have to go out to lunch.'

'Don't mind me,' said Miss Carbery grimly.

Dorothea did, but not for the reason Miss Carbery supposed. She hated the idea of that small human corkscrew worming its way among her things. She was quite sure she would have no scruples about reading letters not addressed to her. It didn't occur to Dorothea that you could have read all her letters in front of the Royal Exchange and no one would have stopped to listen for thirty seconds.

'Which of them was that?' demanded Miss Carbery, who didn't suffer from false modesty, 'and don't tell me it was the Trent woman because she said she goes queueing from nine-thirty to ten-thirty, so she can't be back yet.'

'It was Cousin Hugh,' said Dorothea desperately.

'H'm. You take my tip and lunch at home. These beautiful young men are up to no good.'

'And I have to do some shopping first,' continued Dorothea.

'I'll come and carry the basket,' offered Miss Capper.

'It isn't that sort of shopping,' said Dorothea.

'That means you're going to buy pretties. You know, you're madder than I thought if you're going to spend the money before you get it. You take my advice and let me make you a macaroni cheese. If you don't, you may live to regret it. Or, on the other hand, you may not.'

Dorothea, however, having made up her mulish mind, stuck to her guns. Brushing out her dull fair hair over a pencil to make it curl over the ears, she came to a momentous decision. She would mark her first lunch at the Magnificent, her first lunch anywhere with a beautiful young man, with a new frock. Possibly a new hat. But certainly a frock. She counted her coupons. Yes, she could just do it. She fetched out her best bag, made of pleated black silk and decorated with two black malachite dogs. It had originally belonged to Georgie and had cost two guineas, but Georgie had decided the dogs didn't suit her temperament and had passed it on. She carried it into the living-room and began to

108

tumble out the contents of her big sensible brown leather everyday bag, counting them aloud as she did so. Money, keys, handkerchief, identity card, sugar-box (must refill the sugar-box; she went to the kitchen cupboard and brought out two more lumps), clothing card, wireless licence, pocket-comb . . .

'Anyone can see you aren't accustomed to lunching out,' said Miss Carbery in a God-pity-you-poor-little-thing voice, and then the telephone rang again and this time it was Georgie.

'Hallo,' said Georgie, 'you are in the news. Haven't wasted much time either, have you? This is Miss Capper's secretary.' She mimicked Julia's stentorian tones. 'Vicar called yet? Oh, but he will. Probably bring a little bunch of daisies with him. When you're a millionaire, don't forget your old friends.'

Dorothea said breathlessly: 'I haven't got it yet, but when I do, I'm going to have a little cottage in the country and a donkey-cart.'

'Put the donkey-cart out of your mind,' said Georgie sensibly. 'Concentrate on the Rolls-Royce. I was going to suggest we should try that British restaurant in Queen Elizabeth Street, but I suppose you're too grand now.'

Dorothea was conscious of embarrassment. She was convinced that Julia was listening with all ears, but by turning her back and speaking confidentially into the mouthpiece she tried to establish some appearance of privacy.

'I'm terribly sorry,' she said, 'but as a matter of fact I (she tried to restrain herself but human nature was too much for her)— I'm lunching at the Magnificent. Really, I ought to fly.'

'Your friend lunches early, doesn't he?' suggested Georgie, in mild surprise. 'It's only just gone half-past ten. Or is he only standing you coffee?'

Dorothea blushing furiously, said she had some shopping to do and Georgie said: 'Well, don't look too bridal, not if it's the first time he's lunching you. I know you have to help men nine-tenths of the way, but *you* can afford to let him make some of the running, all things considered.'

Dorothea hung up, saying quite superfluously: 'That was Miss Trent.'

'I should think every one in the borough could hear her,' was Miss Carbery's acid retort. 'If you're really going to get a new outfit you've no time to lose. I only hope,' she added, passing Dorothea her bag, 'I shall recognise you when you get back.'

After Dorothea had hurried off, with a final polish to her nose, Miss Carbery watched her from the window.

'Oh well,' she said with a shrug, turning back to the disordered room. 'I warned her. I wonder how long she'll last.'

CHAPTER SIX

I

DOROTHEA'S normal notion of shopping was to visit a large Oxford Street store and try on a number of dresses, finally selecting the one that fitted her most nearly at the highest price she could afford. It wasn't the worst possible way of getting covered but it had its disadvantages that were obvious to Dorothea's friends, if not to Dorothea, as soon as she put the new garment on. As a rule, she sidled into the department, glancing nervously this way and that, terrified of being accosted by an assistant, muttering hurriedly, if so attacked, that she was just walking through, waiting for a lady, or even asking prices for the same non-existent lady. None of these pathetic devices deceived the assistants for a moment. They were employed by impecunious would-be customers every hour of the day, and the skilful saleswoman's task was to pin the unfortunate firmly down to buying something, not as a rule what she wanted, because that usually proved to be beyond her purse, but at all events something. They could then record a sale. To-day, however, Miss Capper didn't steal up to a model and, under pretence of examining neck-line or hem clutch at the little white ticket that gave the price. She marched in, looking round as though she expected someone to salute, and said firmly: 'I want a dress, please, or perhaps a dress and a coat. Something to go out to lunch in.'

'What colour, madam?' the assistant inquired, and Miss Capper surprised them both by saying: 'Well, what colour would you suggest?'

The assistant, intrigued out of her professional boredom, said they had a sweet model in black and yellow.

'Black!' Miss Capper sounded doubtful.

'You're so fair, madam, you could wear black, and of course the yellow dress does lighten it.'

She produced the model that consisted of a light woollen model, exceptionally well-cut, and a black edge-to-edge lightweight coat.

'Won't that be rather warm?' murmured Dorothea, who had envisaged something dashing in floral art. silk, with perhaps a green georgette coat to tone.

'The coat's collarless, madam, and it's so well-cut you won't feel the weight.'

She coerced the hesitant Dorothea into a fitting-room. For form's sake she slung a few more dresses over her arm, but as she closed the door she said: 'I know you're going to adore the black and yellow ensemble, madam. I've been looking for a customer fair enough to wear it.'

Dorothea scrambled out of the brown dress and stood revealed in a perfectly straight imitation silk slip. The assistant put on the yellow frock, fastened the rather fascinating belt, very narrow and original, adjusted the close-fitting buttoned sleeves and stood back to observe the effect. Dorothea observed it also, and looked surprised. The frock was so very plain she had been going to suggest a nice embroidered collar or a little nosegay pinned on the left breast, but even she realised that it was better as it was.

'Of course,' said the tactful assistant, 'Madam must change her make-up a little. You need a more orange tone with such a gown.'

Dorothea, who had never experimented with a lipstick in her life beyond one sixpenny sample surreptitiously bought and only put on to be instantly wiped off again, said meekly, Yes, she thought so, too. She was secretly staggered by the difference in her appearance. You couldn't say she looked young, but she looked as though she had a figure, a fact no one had ever noticed before. The assistant slipped on the black coat, pointing out its virtues. It had no belt, but was cut to the figure, fastening with a single hook at the waist, and a tiny yellow button at the throat.

'It's rather short,' demurred Dorothea.

'Not for you, madam,' said the resourceful assistant. 'Some ladies can't afford to show their legs, and I wouldn't dream of offering them this gown. Naturally, you'd want black slippers and a black hat.'

Without consulting her customer, who she realised was drugged by contemplation of her own effigy in the long mirror, she dispatched a junior to the millinery. A grey-haired lady, addressed as Miss Jasper, appeared with two hats, both of modern design and as unlike Miss Capper's large boater-shaped brown straw as possible. One hat was a coarse light straw with a black ribbon artfully tied to suggest subtlety, the other a varnished black model with a daring bunch of buttercups on the saucy brim.

'This is Madam's hat,' said Miss Jasper firmly, tossing down the light straw as though it wasn't priced at three guineas, and fitting on the black hat at an appalling angle over Dorothea's meek brow.

If she couldn't agree it was precisely the hat for her, it was unquestionably the hat for the suit, Dorothea recognised. Both the women seemed to take it for granted that she intended to buy the black hat, and mingled shyness and a delirious excitement at the astonishing vision the glass revealed made Dorothea accept the preposterous price of sixty-nine-and-sixpence in her stride.

'It's a model,' explained Miss Jasper, who might have been showing a new-born babe to its mother, 'and will reshape beautifully next year. Besides, it's a hat you'll never get tired of.'

Dorothea pretended to consider. 'Of course, I could take off the buttercups and get a bit of ribbon and wear it with my wine-coloured marocain,' she told what was left of her conscience that disapproved of hats at this price in a world where so many people hadn't enough to eat. But fortunately she did not make this observation aloud. Both assistants would certainly have fainted if she had.

'I want to wear everything for lunch,' said Dorothea firmly.

'You have an account, madam?'

Fortunately Dorothea had. It was a very small one, but it sufficed. An hour later she found herself emerging from the store's Beauty Shop, after a facial massage and make-up, a hurried re-set of the fair curls in a fashion somewhat dismaying to their possessor, wearing apricot powder and a sunkist orange lipstick. Gloves, shoes, even a little pair of ear-rings—she had fallen for the whole transformation.

By this time it was 12.45, and she hailed a taxi and was driven to the Magnificent, feeling not a day over 30 and secretly thinking that a good many people might take her for 25.

A number of people might, but Hugh Lacey was not among them. His experienced eye took her in at once, the brilliant newness of her clothes, her eager anticipation masking unsureness of her surroundings. His spirit sank a little. He had anticipated a coat and skirt bought off the hook and rayon stockings, and perhaps even one of those strips of fur that women without much bosom like to wear like some Order across their chests, but nothing quite so conspicuous, so glaring as this.

'All bought for the occasion,' he told himself, 'and all quite unforgettable.'

He decided that most people would probably think he was dining with his aunt up from the country for the day. Then he reminded himself that this was probably quite an occasion for her. To him the Magnificent was just a place where you met your friends and ate and drank, all of which you had to do somewhere. It didn't excite him any more than the Corner House would have

117

excited Dorothea, but he saw at once that to her it was an adventure.

'Cousin Dorothea?' he exclaimed, coming forward with a really charming smile.

'How clever of you to know me!' said Dorothea, who had been tormenting herself with the dread that she wouldn't be recognised and might be asked what she wanted. Like most women of her age and experience she would sooner have tackled a parachutist than a waiter. But here was Hugh, in uniform, looking so smart, so young, taking her hand and holding it a minute and saying with a smile: 'I live by my wits, you know, these days. I'm in the War Office. What's yours?'

She began to explain that she lived in the Bush—a place I don't suppose you've ever heard of, Captain Lacey—all this with a modish little flourish of the hands and shake of the shoulders intended to convey sophistication . . .

'How fearfully interesting!' murmured Hugh, attracting the attention of a waiter. 'Two Grand Guignols.'

The waiter said Yes, sir, and Dorothea's flow of words dried up at once. He didn't want to know where she lived, he meant what would she have to drink, and she, who had meant to appear so at home in the Magnificent, live up to her appearance, as it were, had missed her very first cue. She felt like an amateur actress who has made the wrong entrance and isn't skilled enough to recover herself.

Hugh, perceiving this, proceeded to put her at her ease.

'Why have we never met before?' he demanded, smashing through her discomfiture like a dog breaking through a flower-border. 'You never came to visit Cousin Everard.'

'It was my mother,' explained Dorothea seriously. She continued at some length about the late Mrs. Capper's moral outlook.

'I get you,' said Hugh. 'Your mother was a very clever woman. Now mine pushed Chris and me down Cousin Everard's throat for all she was worth, and she was a good woman, too, and like most well-meaning people she overdid it.'

Here the Grand Guignols arrived and Hugh handed one to Dorothea, saying, 'Here's luck,' and they both lifted their glasses and took a sip. Instantly for Dorothea the room swam round. For a minute she felt like someone under water; she seemed to stay there a long time, but it couldn't have been very long really, because when she came gasping to the surface Hugh was still talking about his mother. 'So all we got was good advice. And, to do the old boy justice, he may

119

have thought it worth more than a hundred thousand pounds.'

'I've noticed rich people often do,' agreed Dorothea, looking at the glass in her hand and wondering what would happen if she took another sip.

'Do they?' asked Hugh, who didn't seem to have noticed that he was drinking at all. 'I haven't had much opportunity of finding out that sort of thing. Most of the chaps I know are simply first-class at ear-biting. Making a touch, you know,' he added, seeing Dorothea's bewildered expression.

Dorothea took another cautious sip and felt more at ease. 'I remember Mrs. Merivale,' she confided. 'She's an Honourable in her own right, and she's one of the very special people of St. Sebastians. I mean, when she was nervous in an air raid she rang up the Vicar at once.'

She paused expectantly.

'Practically Royalty,' agreed Hugh, in respectful tones, perceiving that something was expected of him.

'Well,' Dorothea was smiling now and sipping away as to the manner born, 'when the Vicar wanted something done in the way of installing a new boiler, she sent him pamphlets by the dozen from some city firm, telling him how to renovate the old boiler, but . . .'

'Didn't include the cheque,' finished Hugh, seeing her face assume a slightly purple shade under the orange make-up.

'And she has a car and a chauffeur and still gets petrol from somewhere. But then her husband's in the Government.'

'That's bound to be the explanation,' Hugh said.

A waiter passed and he hailed him. 'Two Grand Guignols.'

'I really don't think...' said Dorothea doubtfully.

'Only the other half of what you've already had,' consoled Hugh. 'Do you think, then, that very few people are permitted by divine dispensation to have money because it has a deteriorating effect on the character?'

This question delighted Dorothea. It showed that this handsome young man (Hugh was 36 but to Dorothea he was young) took her seriously. She answered him in the same vein.

'Well, actually I shouldn't think so,' she said, swigging down the rest of her Grand Guignol with a fine flourish and becoming loquacious, 'because the unworthy ones go on having it, and if there's anything in your theory they ought to have a chance of being poor and pleasant. I mean, it isn't really fair to them.'

'I believe you're pulling my leg,' said Hugh. 'Ever been in Fleet Street?'

'I've often ridden through it in an omnibus,' said Dorothea carefully. 'But—strange though it sounds—I can't remember that I've ever actually walked through it.'

Hugh sent her a sharp glance. 'I'll buy it,' he said. 'What I meant was, you're not one of these people who write little improving verses, that look like prose till you read them aloud, for the picture papers. You know the kind of thing. Don't look where the bomb has fallen, but the sky from whence it fell, remember Heaven's up in the blue, and all will then be well.'

The waiter appeared with the next batch of Grand Guignols. This time Dorothea needed no encouragement. After the first sip she set herself to answer Hugh's question. 'I don't agree with you,' she said firmly. 'About all being well because—and anyway, it isn't—in the blue—Heaven, I mean.'

Hugh drained his drink at a gulp. 'You win, Cousin,' he said respectfully. 'All the same, it's a pity your Mrs. Merivale couldn't have met Cousin Everard. They'd have been birds of a kidney. On the various occasions when I tried to move the old boy's heart with a tale of my own lack of the ready, he only told me all the ways he'd discovered of keeping out of debt.'

'There's only one way to keep out of debt,' said Dorothea serenely. 'Have enough money for your needs. If you've got that'—she waved the glass in her hand at her horrified cousin—'all's well. If you haven't . . .'

Convinced that she was about to quote Mr. Micawber, Hugh broke in: 'That's always been my problem. How to have enough cash.'

'Or few enough needs,' added Dorothea. And then, before he could protest, she added in the most casual voice in the world: 'Is it true that Cousin Everard was murdered?'

'Is that the yarn Julia's spreading?'

'She was warning me,' Dorothea explained, in the absent Julia's defence.

'If you want to know, he fell down a flight of stairs in the dark, and you want to take care you don't do the same.'

'Out of the question,' said Dorothea tranquilly. 'I live in a flat.'

'Then don't fall off the roof. Remember this—Poverty's an orphan but an heir-apparent or whatever you actually are is everybody's friend. And people will do pretty desperate things for money. Even Chris and I—oh, I don't say we've monkeyed with murder yet—but we've even gone to work sometimes, though we don't say much about

123

it.'

Dorothea looked bland. She had finished her second drink and was looking about expectantly, as though a third might materialise out of the air. 'Tell me one more thing,' she said. 'Why are you and Miss Carbery so eager that nothing shall happen to me?'

Hugh looked uncomfortable. 'Oh well,' he said. 'I've never robbed a blind man or kicked a cripple to date.'

Unexpectedly the two Grand Guignols came into their own. 'Cousin Hugh,' cried Dorothea in ringing tones, 'kindly stop being patronising. I believe you think I'm incapable of looking after myself.'

'Come to that,' Hugh pointed out reasonably, 'you've let Julia into your house and she might have smothered you in your sleep. And you've come to lunch with me and I might have put something in your drink.'

'But you didn't,' said Dorothea simply. 'I watched you.' Hugh goggled.

'And Miss Carbery couldn't have smothered me in my sleep, because I locked my door and she's too big to come down the chimney. And since you're interested, Cousin Hugh, I may tell you I'm going to meet all my new relations. A danger that's in the dark is much more dangerous than a danger you've made come into the open. It's all very well for

Miss Carbery to tell me she knows all their little tricks. I want to know them too,' The two Grand Guignols were fast workers. Dorothea was collecting quite a nice little audience, and it is not so easy to do this at the Magnificent as you might think. 'Never have any truck with second-hand goods, my mother told me, and second-hand impressions are no more to be trusted than second-hand clothes,' wound up Miss Capper triumphantly, impervious to the fact that she had spent most of her life imbibing second-hand opinions.

Hugh looked round a little restively. The last thing he wanted to do was to attract attention. There were so many people lunching, it ought to be possible for one particular couple to pass unnoticed, but until to-day he hadn't realised there were people like Dorothea. Suddenly Dorothea began to giggle. Hugh went crimson to the tips of his ears. It was absurd that two drinks could do that to anyone.

'I was thinking,' explained Dorothea, 'that this is very like *She Vanished in the Dawn*, though, of course, it isn't dawn. There the heroine,' she giggled again, 'came suddenly into money and went out to lunch with a beautiful young man and afterwards he invited her back to his flat.'

125

'Did she go?' inquired Hugh respectfully, wondering if Dorothea had rather more enterprise than he had supposed.

'Well, she thought she would, because she argued that no beautiful young man had ever asked her to his flat before, and what was the good of having money if it didn't change things for you, but it was a mistake all the same.'

'Meaning it changed things for her beyond all hope?'

'When they got to Piccadilly Circus,' said Dorothea in sepulchral tones, 'the young man got out and said to the driver, "Take this lady to Maxwell Gardens." I think it was Maxwell Gardens. But when the driver arrived, no one got out of the cab, so at last he got down and opened the door and then he saw why no one had.'

'You've got a morbid taste in literature,' criticised Hugh mildly.

'Not books, films. I wouldn't read a detective story for anything. It would give me nightmare and keep me awake all night. But it's probably a very good thing, about the films, I mean. Forewarned is forearmed. Drivers never notice the faces of their fares, so you couldn't look for help there, and if I hadn't seen that film I might never have thought...' She paused dramatically.

'Thought what?' asked Hugh.

'That perhaps one day it would be me.' Her imagination overwhelmed her. Already she saw the shocked face of the driver, additionally shocked if her manner of dying had harmed his cab—the attentive police sergeant, above all, her own body, so modestly and unbecomingly shouded during life, made a public show.

She shivered with indignation.

'Cold?' asked Hugh.

Dorothea flung back her head. 'I'll not be murdered,' she cried in ringing tones. 'Seven to one—pah! I tell you, Cousin Hugh, it's no use. I will die like a lady in my own bed.'

II

When he invited his cousin to lunch Hugh Lacey certainly had not anticipated a display of fireworks on a scale unseen by him since his childhood days when he and his brother and their father regularly burnt off their eyebrows, terrified their mother, delighted the housemaid, and caused the cook of the moment to give notice.

Dorothea, however, was burning not just fireworks but her boats, and she meant to do it on a grand scale.

'Come and have lunch before someone grabs our table,' Hugh urged, putting out his hand.

Dorothea instantly drew back. Not the Vicar, not Georgie, not the late Mrs. Capper herself would have recognised her in this hour.

'The poisoned handshake,' she said clearly. Two or three people who hadn't noticed her before looked up with interest. Hugh didn't blame them. Women who are going to make spectacular observations in the Magnificent Bar shouldn't look like elderly girls up from the provinces for the day.

'And anyway,' continued Dorothea on the same piercing note, 'you can't tell me that Cousin Everard wasn't murdered.'

Hugh stood up in desperation and picked up his hat. 'We shall lose our table if we're not careful,' he said. 'I can't think where you get your information. If it's Miss Carbery, why not ask her why she didn't take it to the police.'

'Perhaps she thought there wouldn't be anything in it for her if she went to the police,' said Dorothea serenely.

Hugh looked nearly as staggered as he felt. What had happened to his little country buttercup? If the real woman was now coming to the surface Everard Hope, deceased, had clearly missed a treat. As they passed into the dining-room there was an atmosphere of applause so definite you were surprised not to hear the clapping of hands.

'The way I see it is this,' said Dorothea, talking all the way to their table. 'Someone, according to Miss Carbery, pushed old Mr. Hope down the stairs. If you have to commit murder it's quite an ingenious method, because it doesn't involve the use of a weapon. Did you see Humphrey Figgis in *The Foolish Virgin?*' Hugh shook his head. 'I saw it when it was released. I always wait because . . .' But her reasons were economic and uninteresting. 'Well, in that film the husband explains to his wife that when he kills someone it's going to look like an accident, and he suggests pushing someone downstairs. And he does actually push her downstairs.'

'The wife?' inquired Hugh, feeling a bit dazed and taking up the wine list. He wondered what would be safest to order.

'I shall leave the food to you,' said Dorothea comfortably. 'Doing my own housekeeping as I do, it's quite a treat to put the responsibility on to someone else.'

He chose what he hoped was a soothing wine and tried to calm his guest down.

'Now, as I see it,' continued Dorothea, 'it's to Miss Carbery's interest to see nothing happens to me. She's right, therefore, when she says she's my safeguard.'

'When you say nothing will have happened to you, don't forget Julia will be happening to you all the time. There are people who might think a sandbag less crushing.'

'But more permanent in its effects,' pointed out the new Dorothea born of two Grand Guignols and a glass of Liebfraumilch that, to Hugh's horror, she drank down as soon as it was poured out as though it were a glass of water. 'This is very nice wine,' she confided. 'Sweetish. I like my drinks to be sweet. Really, as I tell every one, Lord Woolton so far is the success of this war, but I do wish he could manage to give us a little more sugar. If you take extra sugar in your coffee as I do...' She snapped open the bag and showed him the little blue tin. It was no good, she was attracting as much attention here as she had done in the bar. It didn't occur to him that she might be doing it on purpose. He had an appalled feeling that she was going to put a lump of sugar into the wine.

Hurriedly he tried to change the subject. 'You don't imagine you'll ever be able to shake Julia off once you let her get a foothold?' he suggested. 'It's a question of begin as you mean to go on.'

'I have,' giggled Dorothea. 'I've left her at home and there aren't even any sardines.'

'Hell!' said Hugh,' I believe you're enjoying this.'

'It's a novel situation,' Miss Capper
agreed. 'Until to-day I don't believe I've ever
represented temptation to any one.'

Hugh thought this uncommonly probable.

'Of course, it has its disadvantages,' continued Dorothea, who, a quick mover in
some respects, had already reached the
slightly pompous stage. 'There is, as you
point out, an element of danger about the
position, but it does have a—a sort of bolster-
ing effect.' She looked at her modest curves
as though they swelled and flowered like
those scraps of coloured paper you buy at
street corners and put into a glass of water.

'Oh well,' said Hugh. 'When you're lying
in your coffin, don't blame me.'

'In any case I intend to have some fun for
my money,' continued Dorothea vigorously.
'And that's more than you can say for Cousin
Everard.'

'You're wrong there,' said Hugh. 'He
enjoyed being parsimonious. It was a hobby
with him.'

Dorothea was smiling inanely. She looked
at her glass and wondered who'd drunk all
the wine.

'Feeling all right?' Hugh murmured.

'I feel as though I'd been born this morn-

131

ing,' confided Dorothea. 'It's undeniably exciting to feel you matter to so many people.'

Hugh looked at her increduously. 'I begin to understand how it is that so many women sign their own death-warrants,' he ejaculated. 'I believe the average wife would rather be murdered by her husband than ignored by him.'

'It's more of a compliment,' said Dorothea seriously. 'Oh, what's happened?' For suddenly she saw that Hugh's attention had been riveted by a newcomer. Following the direction of his gaze she wasn't surprised. The woman who had just come into the dining-room must, thought Miss Capper, be rousing a perfect hell of jealousy in the heart of every other female present. This, she thought, must be how the Queen of Sheba felt when she entered Solomon's Court. The chic black and yellow model, the saucy hat with the audacious buttercup trimming, the narrow shoes, the fringed gloves, all these faded into insignificance by comparison with the modish appearance of the newcomer. She was probably a few years younger than Dorothea, but her face was ageless. It was difficult to believe it had ever been really young and it would probably look much the same ten years from now. She had a metallic perfection,

every gold hair trimly in place, polished, lac-
quered, perfect. Her hat—but there were no
words to describe that masterpiece. A minia-
ture top-hat of varnished black straw tilted
over one eye in a manner that would have
been absurdly reminiscent of a music-hall
artist of an earlier day but for the cloud of
white tulle and the white ribbon bow at the
back that gave it a mock feminine effect.

'Who is she?' breathed Dorothea. 'An
actress?'

'That was clever,' Hugh congratulated her.
'Yes, an actress all right, though she didn't
get far on the stage. That, my dear cousin, is
the second of your six mortal enemies, Mrs.
Garth Hope.'

'Well,' said Dorothea sensibly, 'I shall give
up the ghost now. I should never stand a
chance against a woman like that.' She looked
at the pearls, the furs, the sheer silk stockings, the high-heeled shoes with open toes.
Her handbag must have cost guineas.

'Do you notice,' asked Hugh unkindly,
'that she looks exactly like everybody else,
only a more expensive edition? If you want to
be noticeable, you have her beat to a frazzle.'

Dorothea looked round and admitted the
justice of his remark. 'All the same,' she said,
'I would prefer to look like her. Is that her
husband with her?'

Hugh laughed scornfully, but he felt a bit sick all the same. How Garth could allow his wife to go about with a posturing-waisted minny looking like a china reproduction of the Apollo Belvedere he couldn't imagine.

'Women like Lucille Hope don't waste time lunching with their husbands,' he told her dryly. 'Wonder how long this one will last.'

'He's younger than she is,' said Dorothea.

'Puss, puss! Oh, it's all right. He's got his living to make like any one else, and he only has a limited season. Listen to your Uncle Hugh and don't fall for a man with a perfect profile. It never goes with a bank balance. Well, why should it? There aren't enough talents to go round as it is, worked out at one apiece. Lots of chaps have to be satisfied with the rewards of virtue and nothing else.'

'Would you call good looks a talent?' asked Dorothea, doubtfully. She was sure the Vicar wouldn't agree.

'Whatever it is, it's a lot more paying than most,' her cousin assured her. 'I shouldn't think that chap ever has to buy himself a meal.'

'Does her husband mind her having lunch with him?' was Dorothea's next question.

Hugh laughed again. 'I don't suppose he's caught up with him yet. Lucille's boy-friends

134

are like Lucille's hats. The very latest thing while the fashion lasts and then off they go to the dress agencies. This chap'll be in circulation again pretty soon.' And because he didn't care for the subject he asked Dorothea if she'd have *crepes suzette*. But Dorothea, when she realised what she was being offered, said she'd rather have an ice, thank you. Hugh's last scruple died. A woman who preferred ices to *crepes suzette* deserved anything that might be coming to her.

'I must say,' said Dorothea, burying her face in the last glass of wine—not that she wanted it but she had been brought up to think that anything paid for must be consumed to the last drop or crumb— 'I'm enjoying myself very much. I'm sorry I never met any of you before. Families should hang together.'

She smiled tenderly at Hugh who couldn't help thinking it wasn't a particularly happy smile. Dorothea fumbled in her bag for a handkerchief and, feeling slightly overcome, what with one thing and another, pushed it off her lap, and immediately its great gaping mouth opened (Georgina had passed it on because the clasp wasn't too secure, though she hadn't given that reason, of course) and all the contents spewed over the floor. Hugh ducked his crimson face and recovered a

135

powderbox, lipstick, blue sugar-tin and some keys. To judge from the number of keys you might have thought Miss Capper was in charge of the Mint. Dorothea leaned languidly back in her chair while Hugh refilled her bag and fished for the errant handkerchief with the toe of the new black suede slipper. Hugh, thankful for a chance to conceal himself, wished a thunderbolt would annihilate her. Never, never, never he thought would he take this cousin out again.

But the final horror had yet to come.

Hugh ordered coffee for two, and was blandly contradicted by Dorothea who said not for her, thank you, the ice had left such a lovely taste in her mouth she wasn't going to spoil it with coffee.

'It's very stimulating,' urged Hugh, who knew also that it could be very sobering. 'You'd better change your mind.' He was really anxious that she should.

Dorothea giggled. 'I'm feeling very stimulated already,' she said, and he was almost sure she rolled an eye at the waiter as she spoke. Certainly she beamed across the room at Lucille, but Lucille didn't so much as notice her. She saw her all the same, as Hugh was instantly aware. Dorothea realised it, too, and bridled at the insult. After all, she didn't have to pay handsome young men to come out to lunch with her, and what a lunch. Grand Guignols, white wine, lobster, and an ice thrown in. She looked round for an opportunity to display her royal indifference to her cousin's tacit snub. Unfortunately—from Hugh's point of view at all events—an opportunity instantly presented itself. At the next table an elderly lady, being lunched by a much younger man, had been watching her neighbours with interest.

Her host was also offering her coffee and she was refusing it, but for a different reason.

'Now they've cut the sugar ration,' she said, 'I've had to cut my coffee. Of course, I ought to follow my neighbour's example and bring my sugar with me . . .'

Dorothea, intoxicated in more senses than one, leaned across Hugh and spoke in an urgent compelling tone.

'I'm not taking coffee,' she said. 'Do have my sugar.'

Hugh looked for an instant as though a bullet had struck him in a vital spot. Paralysed. There was no other word for it. By the time he had recovered Dorothea was leaning still further across, the little tin in her hand.

'It's perfectly all right,' she said. 'I've plenty more at home,' and broke into a confused explanation about some ridiculous friend called Georgie who didn't eat all her sugar ration and would pass it on. Naturally one wouldn't like Lord Woolton to know, but, between old friends . . .

'Dorothea,' said Hugh in a hoarse voice. 'You can't.'

'Of course I can,' said Dorothea scornfully. 'What's a war for if it's not going to make people feel more friendly?'

This explanation staggered him so much that by the time he'd recovered it was too late to do anything. Dorothea was babbling on. 'I do sympathise,' she was saying. 'Coffee without sugar is like marriage without love.'

One of her favourite stars—Arthur Bourbon—had said that in a recent film—*Not Wooed But Won*—presented at the Bush Gaumont the week before. The lady was smiling, her companion was one huge grin, every one at nearby tables was listening. Hugh looked round frantically for his own waiter. It wasn't worth it, not for a dozen fortunes. But who could have guessed his country cousin would turn out like this. He watched the elderly lady take the lid off the tin, and pop the sugar into her cup.

'Very kind of you,' she said, passing the tin back. In the circumstances, Hugh supposed she could do nothing else. He felt like a tame bear-leader when the bear won't dance but makes his master look a fool in front of everyone. How he'd flay that bear when he got it to himself. But he couldn't flay Dorothea, dearly as he'd love to. Of course, Lucille had noticed. He saw her turn her head and say something to her companion. Only Dorothea herself seemed unmoved. She was beaming with pleasure at her simple act of Christian courtesy.

She had no notion that what she had just done was to mark a milestone in her life.

CHAPTER SEVEN

I

LUCILLE HOPE was an angler of considerable skill. She could play and land a fish as neatly as any woman living, and she never, so to speak, allowed the fish to go stale on her. Eric Bennett, the young man of the moment, knew that it was doing him a power of good to be seen everywhere with her. He knew, too, that both recognised the rules of the game. There would be no talk of divorce, nothing embarrassing, no scandal. He and she provided an enchanting interlude for one another, and for him the whole affair had an economic rather than a romantic basis. One must eat to live and to eat one must work. Unto each man his destiny, unto each his crown, etc. As Hugh had observed, Mr. Bennett was exploiting his talent to the utmost. One of these days he would find it was no longer powerful to bring in dividends. Then he would have to settle down to work in earnest. Work to people like Eric meant marriage, and marriage, naturally, meant money. He was still in a position to pick and choose, young men having a value in England that they have in no other country in the world, and good looks being regarded as quite absurdly important. Mr. Bennett might have been in the films, but for his voice, that betrayed him at every turn, being consciously old-school-tie; he might have been an actor where his voice would have mattered less but for the fact that he couldn't act. And even that would not have been so important, with his looks, if only he had been prepared to work Equity hours. As it was, he simply had to be a dancing-partner and Lucille was the sort of woman it did a man credit to be seen with.

What he hadn't realised was that Lucille, who should have known better, was quite ridiculously in love with him, and meant to keep him at all costs. All reasonable costs, that is. Since neither of them had sixpence the circumstances weren't reasonable.

It was part of Mr. Bennett's duties to keep abreast of contemporary social history, and the paragraph about Everard Hope's eccentric will had not missed him. Already he was laying plans for the future. As befitted a business man he kept a card index and a spiritual ledger in which were entered the names of other possible employers. He wasn't a nice young man but he knew his job and knew, too, that if you mean to get a living it's no use being mealy-mouthed about details. Arthur

Crook, who he was the indirect means of introducing into the Hope affair, would have supported him there. All or nothing, said both, like the famous poet who would have approved of neither. And with both of them it was all.

To-day Lucille was at her liveliest and jauntiest. She recognised her cousin before he had seen her, and she regarded his companion with the keenest curiosity.

'What on earth has Hugh picked up?' she murmured, drawing her companion's attention to the odd-looking couple. 'Surely he's not going to the good before he's forty?'

Mr. Bennett glanced across the crowded room. 'Second cousin once removed up from the country,' he suggested.

'Buys in the ready-made department,' added the critical Lucille. 'What on earth persuaded a woman with her complexion to wear yellow?'

'Perhaps she's just come into money,' Eric suggested.

And stopped.

The same thought struck them both simultaneously.

It was Lucille who spoke first. 'It's ridiculous,' she said firmly. But her tone lacked conviction.

'The heiress!' exclaimed Eric. 'How enterprising of your cousin.'

'Much too enterprising to be true,' retorted Lucille. 'Why, Hugh's never out of bed before lunch. If it were any one it would be Chris.'

'It's not his wife surely,' murmured Mr. Bennett.

'So far as I know he hasn't got one.'

'Well, she isn't the little blonde in the side-street. Perhaps he's just blazing the trail on his brother's behalf. You must hand it to him that he hasn't lost much time.'

'He's wasting it now,' said Lucille, carelessly. 'For, of course, that fantastic will won't be allowed to stand. Everard's money will go to Everard's nearest relative.'

'Isn't this Miss Capper a relative?'

'So far off that none of us had ever heard of her.' Lucille took a cigarette from a narrow gold case and tapped it on the cloth. 'Match?'

Eric produced the lighter she had recently given him. 'Your cousin looks as though he were prepared to make her a bit nearer.'

'That's nonsense. By the way, I've got a box for the first night of Hurlingham's new play. It ought to be pretty good. Benson's backing it. He's got a new girl—a refugee or something.'

'Let's hope it's something,' said Mr. Bennett coolly. 'This refugee stunt has really

143

been overdone.'

'We shall be able to judge for ourselves on Friday,' said Lucille more crisply than ever.

Eric was glancing at a little green leather diary he had taken from his pocket. 'It's too bad,' he exclaimed. 'Did you say Friday? I'm on fire-fighting duty then. What a shame!'

'They must have changed the rota since last week,' said Lucille dryly.

'One of the chaps has gone sick,' said Eric glibly. 'I'd change, if I could, Lucille, but I hardly like, during a war, to upset the whole round just because I want to go to a first night.'

'You'll be free by nine,' Lucille reminded him.

He shook his head. 'Too late, I'm afraid. You do understand?'

'I understand perfectly,' said Lucille.

He saw that she did. He was ruthlessly ending one chapter and preparing to open another. 'As a matter of fact,' he went on smoothly, 'I meant to tell you, I believe I'm getting a new job. Very hush-hush at the moment...'

'Dear me!' said Lucille tight-lipped and smiling. 'What can that be? Modelling for the American export market?'

Eric looked at her slyly. If Nature had intended him to earn honest bread she shouldn't have given him those lashes that curled so absurdly or that capacity to shake the heart of even a hard-boiled married woman by a single sidelong glance.

'You don't think much of my capacities, do you? I shall have to grow a moustache for this new job.'

'So you're not going into the Navy.'

He looked across the room and caught Dorothea's eye and smiled. It was quite ravishing, that smile. Dorothea felt her heart twist in her breast. It made him look so young, and youth in the other sex appeals to women as no virtue or mental qualification can do. Eric had the wit to realise that. Though actually it didn't require much wit to see it. Women offered you the truth on a dish with parsley round the edge. He'd practised that smile as a ballet dancer practises his steps with heart-breaking earnestness. After all, it was his gift and you can only spend the money you have in your purse.

Lucille flashed him another glance. He was still looking across at Dorothea. She knew then she'd lost him. You'd never catch him supporting a losing cause.

'Funny how nature camouflages, isn't it?' Eric said coolly. 'Who'd guess that dowdy little creature had a hundred thousand pounds coming to her?'

'If she lives long enough,' said Lucille mechanically.

He sent her a sharp look. He'd always known she was ruthless, but he hadn't guessed she'd stop at nothing to get what she wanted. He couldn't have told you how to spell pity, but even he felt a pang for that helpless, charmless, insignificant creature on the further side of the room. He knew she didn't stand a chance.

II

The most nerve-racking lunch of his career over, Hugh offered to call his companion a taxi, regretting aloud his inability to accompany her owing to a feeling at the War Office that their personnel should put in a limited number of appearances in the week. Dorothea said thank you very much, she wouldn't have a taxi, she'd really like a little fresh air and walking cleared the head, didn't it? It had been a lovely lunch, but it had been warm. And anyway she had some shopping to do. On their way out she passed quite close to Lucille and her Adonis, but though the young man smiled again you might have thought Lucille and Hugh were strangers. Dorothea beamed back, stumbled over a chair, recovered herself with a slight effort and another beaming smile and went out.

'Sure you won't have a taxi?' inquired Hugh, tensely, thinking that in this state she was quite capable of kissing a policeman.

'I've only a few steps to go,' Dorothea assured him. 'Thank you for my nice lunch. I shall look forward to meeting my other cousins quite soon.'

'I'm sure that's mutual,' said Hugh, and, realising she was serious about not taking a taxi, called one for himself and wished he could tell the driver to crush Dorothea under the wheels. She, poor creature, with no notion of this, stood swaying slightly, looking up and down as if she wasn't quite sure the pavement was where she hoped it was. But after an instant, even as she had declared, the fresh air restored her and she turned with a firm and steady step in the direction of Piccadilly Circus. It had occurred to her that women who looked like Lucille Hope never bought their corsets, as Dorothea invariably did, at the summer sales in Kensington High Street. In fact, they didn't wear corsets at all but foundation garments costing guineas and guineas and fitted on the person, instead of being picked out of a great tossed pile on a bargain counter and thrust shamefacedly into an attache-case now that the Government wouldn't allow them to be wrapped. Therefore, thought Dorothea, she would take the

147

bull by the horns and copy their example. At the thought of the fitting-room she quivered with dismay, but what other women had done she could do. And assistants regarded you as that anonymity, a customer, not a person. Like doctors, thought Dorothea, wishing she had accepted Hugh's offer of a taxi even as far as Swan and Edgars, because the new shoes were still smart and narrow and hurt her feet abominably. By the time they had spread and accommodated themselves, they would have lost their Bond Street air. The Vicar was right, thought Miss Capper, no rose without a thorn.

There was a dark-blue taxi creeping up behind her and she thought of hailing it, but desisted, because Hugh was driving this way and might notice her and he'd think it so peculiar. Like a good many people who have lived secluded lives, Dorothea supposed that her actions were bound to occasion notice if they were in the least out of the ordinary.

The blue taxi drew abreast, passed on. Then it was halted by the lights. The door swung open, a young man stepped out. Dorothea gasped. It was Lucille's beautiful young man and he was unmistakably making in her direction.

'Miss Capper?' said the young man. 'You'll think this awful cheek but just listen to what

I have to say and perhaps you'll understand why I'm butting in. In fact, I'm sure you'll understand.' And he smiled yet again.

Dorothea felt it didn't matter whether she understood or not. Her heart was shaking at his youth and nearness and the impression he contrived to convey of being defenceless and a secret Galahad, he whose middle name was Granite and whose favourite proverb was the one about self-preservation. She wished she could give him half the hundred thousand pounds and so free him from Lucille's clutches.

'I saw you at the Magnificent,' Mr. Bennett went on. 'That was your cousin you were with, wasn't it?'

'Yes,' agreed the ravished Dorothea. 'That was Hugh. He very kindly asked me to lunch. It was really very good of him as of course he'd expected to get something out of Mr. Hope's will.'

'Instead of which it all comes to you?'

'I don't feel I've the right to keep it all,' said Dorothea solemnly. 'We could divide it perhaps, after I've got it.'

'I knew you'd say something of the kind,' exclaimed Mr. Bennett eagerly. 'I have intuitions.'

'Perhaps you're a novelist,' suggested Dorothea eagerly. She had always wanted to meet one, not realising that you wouldn't recognise them from any one else if they sat in rows in the tube.

'Oh, perhaps we'd better not talk about my work,' he warned her lightly. 'You know what they say—walls have ears.'

'Secret Service?' breathed Dorothea, feeling this was one up even on the novelists.

He let her believe that. His real career would have been quite as unintelligible to her.

'I feel I ought to warn you, though you'll think it's foul of me coming straight from lunching with Mrs. Hope, that they're going to try and do you out of that money.'

'That's what Julia says,' murmured Dorothea reflectively. 'And Hugh. Do you think if everybody's combined to tell you something, it's necessarily true? I know, of course, on the surface it ought to be, but so much truth at the same time seems to me against nature.'

'Well, I can't say anything about the motives of the others, of course,' said Mr. Bennett, contriving to look quite adorably shy, and concealing the fact that behind his heart-fluttering lashes his eyes were about as soft as a railway sandwich, 'but I obviously have nothing to gain by telling you, and I do think you ought to know that they're planning to upset the will.'

'You mean, Mr. Hope is planning . . .?'

'They're all in it together,' said Mr. Bennett reluctantly, 'including the one you call Julia. They're saying the old man was mad.'

'I should think he must have been to leave the money to me,' agreed Dorothea simply. 'But I dare say they won't be able to prove it.'

'Don't you see, that'll make things more dangerous for you than ever? You see, I'm pretty sure they know they can't upset the will, in spite of all their talk, but they mean to have the money whatever happens. That's why they're all approaching you in their separate ways, trying to win your confidence by warning you against the others.'

'What,' inquired Dorothea, feeling deliciously fluttered by this encounter and hardly taking in the bit about her own peril, 'do you think I should do?'

Hook, line and sinker, thought young Mr. Bennett, metaphorically rubbing his hands. 'What you want to do is go straight to your lawyer and lay all the facts before him,' said he firmly.

'As a matter of fact,' confessed Dorothea, 'I have none. My mother used to say they were luxuries only for the rich.'

'You're one of the potentially rich, aren't you? You'll be able to afford luxuries pretty soon, only not unless you have this chap to

151

uphold you. A kind of speculation, see?'

She didn't see anything but his charm and his smiling lips and his air of vitality and something she herself had never had. She foamed inwardly at the thought of all that being exploited by Lucille.

'I suppose you couldn't recommend me to anyone?' she murmured. 'It's so difficult getting the right man.'

'That's true.' He looked sober. 'I could put you on to a chap,' he admitted. 'Only how do you know I'm not in the racket too?'

Dorothea said one of those things for which women of her age are notorious.

'I think I'm quite a good judge of character,' she said.

'Are you really?' He looked at her admiringly. 'Now I'm always being led up the garden. Still, this man would be all right. Fellow called Dick. He's not one of these hoary old blighters who want an Act of Parliament before they'll sign a letter. And he doesn't mind taking a few risks.'

'Risks?' Dorothea turned the word over in her mind. She didn't want a lawyer who was prepared to turn the tables and put all the other claimants out of the way, just someone clever enough to uphold her rights without making her feel a godless, selfish woman for wanting to keep what was, after all, hers by will and testament.

'Well, if you should lose you'd be in a spot, you see,' explained Mr. Bennett with engaging frankness. 'And lawyers have to live like anyone else. That's what I meant.'

Dorothea looked a little surprised. 'I shouldn't dream of employing a lawyer if I couldn't meet his account,' she said gently.

'You'd be surprised how many people do,' Mr. Bennett assured her. 'Look here, shall I get in touch with this fellow and just explain?'

'If you would,' said Dorothea gratefully.

'I'll ring him up now,' said Mr. Bennett, 'and if you take my tip you'll go right along and see him. These legal affairs are like modern battles. The chap who's on the spot first with the heaviest ammunition carries the day. And you know,' his experienced glance united them in a common bond, 'people like you and me have to be up early in the morning if we're to get any worms at all. These other chaps know all the ropes, and they aren't going to stand aside to let you pass. You go and see Harry Dick and tell him I sent you. Bennett's my name—Eric Bennett.'

'Oughtn't I to make an appointment or something?' murmured the fascinated Miss Capper.

'Tell you what,' said Mr. Bennett. 'I'll just

pop into that telephone booth and find out if he's got a spare quarter of an hour this afternoon.'

He walked with incomparable grace into the telephone box that always, to the imaginative Dorothea, looked like an upended scarlet coffin, and picked up the receiver. Dorothea watched him talking, smiling confidentially as though the invisible Mr. Dick could see him. He seemed to be explaining things very fully. How kind, how more than kind, thought the grateful Dorothea, feeling her spirit brim over with emotion, partially induced by the liquid part of her lunch, to take so much trouble over a faded spinster he'd never seen before.

The scarlet door swung open and he rejoined her. 'Have I kept you waiting ages? I thought I'd better just tell him about the others, to make things easier for you. Look here, he says he can see you right away. You'd better take a taxi...'

But Miss Capper said quickly that the tube from Green Park or Piccadilly would get her to Russell Square in no time, and if he lived in Bloomsbury Street that wasn't far—and the Government asked you not to travel for pleasure—and petrol cost men's lives...

He let her run on, smiling down at her very nicely. Oh, she was a peach, he thought.

With her there would be no need to fan the flame of passion. Eternal youth and the woman whom love passed by was the card to play here. No one living could play it with greater appeal.

CHAPTER EIGHT

I

HER HEART fluttering like a butterfly on a pin, Miss Capper descended to the bowels of the earth. Her intention of buying a foundation garment she thankfully thrust into a niche in her mind, doubtful whether the bliss of its possessing would compensate for the embarrassment of its acquiring. At Russell Square she got out and blinked doubtfully at her surroundings. She knew nothing of London east of Cambridge Circus, and she stood on the pavement staring at the names on the streets. When at length she found Bloomsbury Street she realised she had forgotten the number Mr. Bennett had given her. Still, there were a good many lawyers here, and she only had to look on the brass plates in the doorways to locate her man. She was going conscientiously from entry to entry when she became aware that she was being watched. A stout rather common looking man wearing bright brown clothes was standing at the street corner watching her with open amusement. She felt herself flush under his regard, told herself she didn't care what he thought, then stiffened with horror as he began to cross the street and come towards her. She went quickly inside a doorway and was very busy reading through the names on the wall when she realised that he had followed her in and was standing beside her.

'Lost your bearings?' he inquired in a loud common voice.

'I'm—er—I have an appointment with a Mr. Dick,' said Miss Capper primly.

'Dick, eh?' He looked at her thoughtfully.

'Yes,' repeated Miss Capper, rapidly losing her composure under that sustained gaze. 'I—I don't know this part of London very well. I was given Mr. Dick's name by a friend, and as I very unexpectedly have to consult a lawyer—about a legacy, that is . . .' Go away, go away, go away, screamed her mind. This is nothing to do with you. I expect I do look a fool, but why should you care?

'If you're so keen to get rid of your legacy, why not give it to the Salvation Army?' inquired this extraordinary person. 'Save you a lot of trouble.'

'He is a lunatic,' thought Miss Capper. 'Probably of the most unpleasant kind. The kind that annoys women.'

Sane men who annoy women won't pick spinsters nearing the forties, she thought. Then she remembered she was wearing a very

157

dashing ensemble and that younger women were scarce these days. She trembled till the buttercups in her hat shook with her. 'I have no wish to give away my legacy,' she said, turning back to the wall.

'Then why go to see Mr. Dick?' inquired her companion. 'Believe in reincarnation, Miss—er...'

'My name is Capper,' said Dorothea nervously, giving the whole game away. 'And I do not believe in reincarnation.'

'Well, if you did,' said Mr. Crook, in no wise disturbed by her agitation and obvious disapproval of his entire existence, 'you might think Dick was once a boa-constrictor. Just thought I'd warn you, that's all.'

His commonplace words, his jaunty, disinterested air, did something to poor, slightly bottled Miss Capper. Suddenly she saw herself as she must appear to other people, a foolish, gullible spinster, being taken up on account of her money, to be dropped as soon as it was dissipated. A great wave of distrust of Mr. Dick, Bennett, indeed of the whole world, swept over the demoralised creature. Suddenly she realised her utter defencelessness. As Hugh had pointed out she had, perhaps, one enemy in her home and the others were stalking her from the four corners of the earth. This description was more picturesque than accurate, but it did express Dorothea's feelings. What, after all, did she know of Mr. Bennett but that he made his living by being pleasant to not-so-young women? And if he were prepared to prey on Lucille, why suppose he wasn't equally prepared to prey on her? She gave vent to a sort of moan.

'Already,' she said, 'I am beginning to wish I hadn't inherited Cousin Everard's fortune.'

'Well, you haven't yet,' pointed out Mr. Crook, who had placed her at once. 'And if you go and see Mr. Dick you never will.'

'But what am I to do?' demanded Dorothea.

'Come with me,' said Crook. 'I know a lot about your Mr. Dick, and I probably know a lot about the chap who recommended him, too. Nearly as much as you'd know after you'd been in their clutches a fortnight.'

Miss Capper prayed desperately. She prayed for a sign. After all, miracles had happened once so why not now? And they seemed to happen to quite insignificant people, so why not to her? What on earth was she to do?

'Nervous of me?' asked Mr. Crook, as if he couldn't believe it. 'Why, ask any bobby what they know about me. They'll tell you.'

As though his words had conjured up the man out of empty air, a policeman suddenly

159

appeared beside them. Crook nodded to him. The policeman replied with a friendly grin.

'Afternoon, Mr. Crook.'

'Like to assure this lady she's safe with me?' Crook inquired.

The policeman grinned more broadly. Dorothea felt hopelessly at sea. Still, she'd asked for a sign and got it. For faith's sake, she couldn't refuse to abide by it now.

'When a lawyer's on speaking terms with the police,' Crook was explaining, 'you can hope to see Heaven opened and the angels of God descending on the sons of men.'

'Perhaps I should be wise to get some professional advice,' agreed Dorothea, trembling more than ever, partly with nervousness and partly with disappointment, because she'd always thought lawyers were tall, handsome men with eyeglasses on watered silk ribbons and white slips to their waistcoats.

'Payment by result only,' Mr. Crook reassured her, leading the way to the top of the building—the very top, Dorothea discovered. 'If you don't get your legacy, I shan't charge you a penny. Put it down to Profit and Loss account.'

'How kind!' murmured Dorothea, saying firmly to herself, as she always did at the dentist, 'I shall feel better when it's all over, much, much better.'

Certainly she could not complain of any lack of professional zeal on Mr. Crook's part. He took her very carefully through her story, even stopping her to try and recall the precise expressions used by Miss Carbery in her telling of the tale.

'So she thinks there was some funny business, too?' he observed. 'Well, it could be, Miss Capper, it could be. What you've got to watch out for, Miss Capper, is that there's no funny business where you're concerned.'

'I intend to be exceedingly careful,' Dorothea assured him.

'You've taken one step in the right direction,' Crook told her encouragingly. 'You've put the matter in my hands. You couldn't have a better man. You know, I can't help hoping that old boy can watch developments from his side of the screen. It 'ud be too bad if he was to miss all the fun.'

'Fun!' cried Miss Capper indignantly. 'I find it anything but amusing myself.'

'Fun for him, I meant,' explained Crook. 'After all, you must expect to pay something for coming into £100,000.'

'I always understood the possession of money to be enjoyable,' said poor Dorothea.

'But not the acquirin' of it,' Crook pointed out. 'That's generally an affair of blood and sweat, and in your case it looks like bein' more blood than sweat.'

Dorothea shuddered.

'And anyway,' continued Mr. Crook, complacently, 'if you ain't enjoying this, I am. And there's one more thing.' He leaned forward impressively. 'Suppose this chap, whoever he is, does stop your coming into the inheritance, I can promise you I'll run him to earth, if it's the last thing I do.'

Miss Capper gaped, horrified. 'You mean, if I don't—if he—you mean, if they—but,' her voice was shrill with indignant horror, 'it wouldn't help me, if I'd been murdered.'

'It would be a victory for justice,' said Crook in reverent tones. 'But that's just by the way. I wouldn't like you to think I'd leave a stone unturned, and you mightn't be able to get a message through to me, wherever you were.'

'It's quite new to me to have enemies,' said Miss Capper, pathetically.

'It's new to you to have prospects,' Crook pointed out. 'By the way, watch your step with Midleton.'

'But he's a lawyer,' protested Dorothea.

'That don't make him the Archangel Gabriel. I mean, he has to eat like the rest of us.'

'It seems to me it's better to be without money,' burst forth the unhappy spinster.

162

'Better,' agreed Crook, 'but not so interestin'. For the other chap, I mean.'

It was only too obvious what he meant.

'But what are you going to do?' Dorothea demanded.

Mr. Crook looked a little hurt. 'Give me a chance, lady. What can I do until the other side have made the first move? Unless you're suggestin' goin' out and knockin' them off their perches before they can knock you, but I ought to warn you that even I couldn't promise you'd get a verdict of Justifiable Homicide if you did. No, no, you wait till one of them shows his hand and as soon as you provide me with a neck, I'll fit the rope necktie all right. You can count on me for that.'

Somehow or other that seemed to be the end of the interview. Miss Capper found herself back on the stairs with tears literally pouring down her face. She couldn't have told you what she anticipated, but she felt she must be the loneliest woman in the world. Which was absurd when you reflected that she was the envied of thousands. But she was realising that the people are right who say that lawyers aren't really interested, except in the rich, and then only so long as they remain so, which, once they've been introduced to the legal profession, is usually a remarkably short time.

As soon as she had gone, Crook clapped his hands like a pasha and Bill Parsons appeared like a genie. 'Beer,' carolled Mr. Crook. 'Bill, d'you remember my telling you about a fishy sort of funeral down in Hornshire not long ago?'

'Yes,' said Bill, who knew that if he didn't he soon would.

'Well, it was fishy,' said Mr. Crook, like a prophet making an announcement.

'No body?' asked Bill, pouring beer.

'There was a body all right, and what our Miss Capper's afraid of is there's goin' to be another, and I wouldn't be surprised if she was right.'

'Surely not,' said Bill politely. 'Not now you're in the picture.'

'I didn't say whose body,' pointed out Crook. He explained the situation. 'Now, what does logic suggest, Bill?'

'To you?' asked his A.D.C. 'I wouldn't know.'

'What does it suggest to you?' inquired Crook.

'That whoever was responsible for bumping off the old man may take a potshot at the not-so-young young lady.'

'Sound enough for Euclid,' approved Mr. Crook. 'Though, between you and me, I thought that chap pulled a few fast ones in his time. Only nobody wanted to look a silly ass and pretend he didn't understand. As you know, Bill, it isn't often you catch me backing Bishops, but the one who said that ignorance is the greatest ally of evil was right. Which one was it?'

'All of them,' said Bill, 'from Augustine onwards. And a few lady novelists as well.'

'I remember those two old girls in the pub,' Crook continued enthusiastically. 'Now, they knew there was something queer but they didn't do anything about it. Well, naturally. There wasn't anything in it for them. How does one get to Fox Norton, Bill?'

'You've been there,' Bill reminded him.

'Come back from there,' Crook corrected. 'That's different. In these days of Home Guard autocracy they're only too thankful to see you coming back from a place. Getting there's a very different matter.'

Bill, who, differing from Crook on many points, was at one with him in the belief that it's ridiculous to do anything you can get any one else to do for you, picked up the receiver and called the head office of the G.W.R. Then he looked at the watch on his wrist. It was a very handsome watch. It had once belonged to a very handsome gentleman. But Bill, an expert in those days, had removed the inscription that had once ornamented it. Since his last encounter with the police, that had left him with a bullet in his heel, Bill had worked for righteousness as exemplified by Arthur Crook.

'You can't do it to-day,' he said, putting the receiver down. 'But you could catch the 8.17 in the morning, change at Hamerton (20 minutes wait and it's too early for the pubs to open), get the connection at 10.8, change at Riverhead, another 20 minutes wait, catch the connection to Wolf Norton, and you can get a local train from there.'

'I will say one thing for the Churchill Government,' declared Crook handsomely. 'They know we're fighting for freedom and they don't want to rob us of more than they can help, so we're free to go to a place like Fox Norton, but they make it as damned difficult as they know how to get there. How about the next train?'

'If you wait till 12, you can get there at 2.30, with a drink at every change,' said Bill. 'Going to unearth the truth about the old man's death?' He refilled their glasses.

'Private circulation only. Well, no one's paying us to find out what happened to him. But the odds are the two affairs will link up. The old woman's right. Rich old men shouldn't die when their relations are on the premises. It don't look right.'

Since he could not travel that afternoon, Crook characteristically began his work from the London end. Miss Capper had supplied a list of the relatives, and, though he hadn't told her as much, none of the names was strange to him. For all his unconventional standards he was a sincere believer in the pattern theory of existence. If Arthur Crook stumbled on a mystery, the Power interested in crime clearly intended him to play some part in that mystery's solution. During his earlier visit to Fox Norton he had, as he expressed it, snouted round for information about the household at The Brakes, and on his return to town he had followed up some of the hints then received. He put a man on to discover any further developments and turned his attention to the case of a forgery. It was going to take him all he knew to prove that his client had not signed another man's name when, on his own admission, he had. But Crook was being paid to prove it and, able, like the devil, to cite scripture for his own purpose, he believed the labourer was worthy of his hire only so long as he earned that hire. Similarly, had Miss Capper asked him to prove that she hadn't bumped off her relatives one after the other, he would have accepted the commission and gone to all lengths to win the case. Not that he thought she had. All his professional life, he would mourn, he had been looking for Lucrezia Borgia in modern dress, and it was his grief that, even if he did meet her, some other fellow would step in front of him and mess matters up.

'Fact is women have too much conscience,' he would say. 'It's one of the diseases of the modern world. If Lucrezia came back now I don't say she wouldn't do her bit of poisoning, but she'd write out a full confession and die penitent on the scaffold, and what's the good of a first-class crime if you're going to disown it afterwards?'

'There's one thing it's safe to bank on,' he told Bill. 'They all needed money, most of them had tried to touch the old man, he'd turned 'em all down flat, half of 'em at least had had a hell-and-glory row with him, none of them can tell a coherent story about his death, they none of them have alibis, and there's about as much proof against any of 'em as 'ud go under a sixpence. Apart from that, the affair's just child's play.'

He settled down cosily for a night's work.

II

When she turned the corner into Blakesley Avenue, Dorothea thought at first there must

168

have been an accident. A number of men of various ages but of curiously similar appearance was lounging near her gate, or where her gate had been before the local borough collected it for salvage. As she stopped instinctively, all the men turned towards her like a herd of feeding cattle. And as cattle Miss Capper treated them. That is to say, she followed the tactics she always observed when circumstances compelled her to cross a field of cows. Staring straight ahead, she walked with quick resolute steps, trying to believe that what she refused to see would also refuse to see her. However, as she drew nearer they closed in and she realised they were journalists. She looked at them helplessly. They were asking for a story, like children at bedtime. What had she felt like when she heard the news? Had she met any of the cousins?

Desperately, Dorothea stood still. 'I've nothing to say,' she told them. 'Absolutely nothing. You see, I haven't got the money yet.'

One man, an ill-mannered fellow with a ragged black moustache, said: 'You must give the law a little time. The old man's not been dead a week.'

'And, of course, I may never inherit,' added Dorothea, more flustered than ever.

'In your place I'd see to it I did,' said some-one else.

'Naturally I shall do my best,' retorted Dorothea, 'and my lawyer will help me. But he says, and I am sure he is right, it's much easier to have fatal accidents when you're rich or expecting to be rich, than when you're poor. He says that even Providence is more interested in the rich.'

What further indiscretions she might have committed it is difficult to say, but at that moment the front door was flung open and Miss Carbery appeared.

'I told you you couldn't see Miss Capper,' she stormed. 'Come in at once.' This was to Dorothea. 'Don't you know it's dangerous to talk to the press?

'Life is very provoking,' murmured poor Dorothea. 'When one has nothing and is therefore safe no one takes any interest, but when you are on the highway to a fortune and people want to talk to you, you have to remain aloof.'

'It's only for a month,' snapped Miss Carb-ery. 'Once you've got the money you can make a will leaving it to a Cats' Home, and after that your cousins will take no interest in you.'

'But the secretary of the Cats' Home will,' said Dorothea sadly.

Miss Carbery stumped up the stairs 'That friend of yours, Miss Trent, rang you up again,' she announced. 'And Mr. Midleton's written—know his scrawl anywhere—and there's a letter from that wife of Cecil's. Came in the afternoon post. You seem to have had a very long lunch, though I must say I'm surprised to see you back at all.'

'I don't think they can be so dangerous as you suppose,' said Dorothea, reminding herself that this one was only an elderly spinster, too, without even the hope of a hundred thousand pounds. 'After all, I've had lunch with one of them and it hasn't killed me'

'I should think you did the killing,' retorted Miss Carbery, swift as lightning. 'Oh well, I suppose if you want to be conspicuous, getting yourself up like a queen wasp is as good a way as any.'

'I hadn't had anything new for ages,' Dorothea defended herself. It seemed a shame she should be made to feel guilty when it was her money and her coupons that she'd squandered. Under Miss Carbery's derisive eye she pulled off the black hat, that instantly ceased to look fashionable. Even the buttercups drooped as though they were about to shed their petals.

'I know where you picked that up,' said Julia, eyeing it with disfavour. 'It's got Shaftesbury Avenue stamped all over it. Oh well, it's probably all right so long as you only wear it in the daytime.'

In silence Dorothea slit open the first letter that came to hand. It was signed Lilias Tempest and contained an invitation to tea.

'It's very kind of her,' murmured Dorothea, buoying herself up with the thought that she had at least a lawyer to guard her interests, and anyway there's more than one kind of death.

'Are you going?' demanded Miss Carbery.

'I expect so,' said Dorothea.

'Where's my invitation?' asked her companion.

Dorothea shook the envelope. 'It doesn't seem to be there.'

'That doesn't strike you as suspicious? No, dare say it wouldn't. After all, you haven't met Cecil.'

'I never shall if I refuse their invitations. Anyhow, tea at their own house . . .'

'There are four steps up from the street,' said Miss Carbery. 'Take care you don't fall down them. It's very easy, especially with a little assistance.'

'I must go,' said Dorothea. 'I don't want to look proud because one day I may be rich.'

'Not if your relations have any say in the matter,' snorted Miss Carbery.

The telephone hiccoughed and shrilled and Miss Carbery leapt to the fray.

'Probably that woman again,' she hissed. 'Don't you trust her, either.'

'I must trust someone,' complained Dorothea.

'Much better not. Hallo' she bellowed into the mouthpiece. The next moment she turned to Dorothea, wearing a puzzled expression.

'I can't make it out,' she said, imperfectly covering the microphone with her hand. 'I don't know the voice at all. It isn't any of those men . . .'

'Perhaps it's my lawyer,' said Miss Capper.

But actually it was Mr. Bennett.

'I do hope you didn't have any difficulty in finding Dick,' said a charming voice in her ear.

Dorothea blushed guiltily. 'I—as a matter of fact, I didn't get there, after all.'

'But—we had made the appointment.' The young man sounded a little shocked. Well he knew Dorothea hadn't got there, having telephoned Mr. Dick for particulars of the interview.

'I thought perhaps I'd wait a little—till I'd seen the other lawyer,' temporised the cowardly Dorothea.

'Well, you know these lawyer wallahs,

173

they're pretty busy. They don't like having their appointments cut.'

'You must explain,' said Miss Capper. 'Really, I'm very sorry'

'If you haven't already seen Midleton I'm sure you'd be wise to consult a solicitor on your own account first,' continued Mr. Bennett inexorably. 'I'm sure Dick would stretch a point . . .'

Miss Capper was sure he would. She looked so distressed that she allowed Miss Carbery to snatch the receiver from her.

'Who's that? Who? Well, Miss Capper isn't able to talk to anyone to-night. She's sickening for influenza. She's going to bed right away. No, of course she can't see a lawyer. When she does she's going to see Mr. Tatham.' She hung up with a slam you could hear on the ground floor. 'That wasn't a lie,' she announced to the astonished Dorothea. 'He's a very good man, if he did marry one of my relations. I made an appointment for you this afternoon. You're to see him at ten tomorrow.'

Dorothea pulled herself together sufficiently to gasp: 'But I have my own lawyer. I've seen him already and left everything in his hands. Really, Miss Carbery, I'm sure you mean to be kind, but there's no need to treat me like an idiot. I am perfectly capable

174

of managing my own affairs.'

As Miss Carbery said to a friend the next day, it was enough to make you abandon your philanthropic instincts and start thinking about yourself.

CHAPTER NINE

HUGH'S RETURN to his rooms coincided with his brother's arrival from the M.O.I.

'How's the Far East?' asked Christopher politely, it being understood by both that this was Hugh's special pigeon.

'Stands Libya where it did?' murmured Hugh. 'By the way, our new cousin's hot stuff.'

'Well, well, well,' said Christopher. 'You've not wasted much time.'

'Thought someone ought to break the ice,' explaind Hugh. 'And whoops, there I was over my head before I'd got my bearings. You wait till she makes tracks for you. She's already seduced Lucille's latest, and if Lucille finds out there'll be another family funeral.'

'She's a brave woman,' murmured Christopher. 'Poisoned chocolates would be just Lucille's cup of tea.'

'And she'll make Garth provide the poison.'

'Oh, as to that, it's not so hard, as you and I know. I could guarantee to get enough to poison the whole family between here and

176

Cambridge Circus. What's she really like?'

'Lucrezia Borgia with the sex appeal left out. Leave her alone with a bottle of brandy and she'd probably finish us all. Gosh, is that the time? I'm taking the only girl on earth out to dinner. Lend me a fiver, will you? Our dear little cousin's cleaned me out.'

II

In the flat in Blakesley Avenue the modern version of Lucrezia Borgia was vehemently defending her rights.

'No, Julia,' she said for about the hundredth time (it having been agreed that Christian names might be used since we shall all employ them in Heaven and may as well get accustomed to them in good time), 'I am not going to see Mr. Tatham to-morrow. I have my own lawyer and it would be most improper for me to consult another.'

'At least you can tell me his name,' urged Miss Carbery, but Dorothea said it wasn't in the least essential.

'Suppose anything happens to you?' inquired Julia. 'We may need to get in touch with him.'

'If anything should happen you can count on his getting in touch with you. But I'm convinced nothing will. You see, he has explained to me that he works solely on the

177

payments by results principle.'

'That's very unusual,' snapped Miss Carbery. 'Half the lawyers I know would be in the Bankruptcy Courts if they practised that.'

'That's why I am convinced I am safe,' said Dorothea simply. 'I am certain that he has never done nothing for nothing in his life. He will therefore ensure that no harm overtakes me until he has been paid. And since he cannot be paid unless and until I receive my inheritance, it follows as the night the day,' wound up Miss Capper lyrically, whose mother had been a Tennyson fan, 'that I shall actually inherit.'

'You ought to take a course of logic,' snapped Miss Carbery. 'I don't know what your cousin gave you to drink . . .'

Instantly Dorothea became dreamy. 'Two Grand Guignols and some delicious white wine. I don't quite know how much wine, because every time I looked at my glass someone had filled it up, but I don't feel I'll ever quite forgive my mother for bringing me up a teetotaller.'

'You've plenty of time,' Miss Carbery reminded her. 'At least, one hopes you have.'

'But so little drink obtainable,' mourned Dorothea. 'Do you know,' she chuckled reminiscently, 'I'm not sure I wasn't just a little bit overcome. It was so very hot at the

Magnificent. I even think I rather shocked Cousin Hugh.'

'Your cousin Hugh is an excellent amateur actor,' said Carbery in crisp tones.

'It was when I offered the sugar to the old lady.'

'You did what?' Miss Carbery stared.

'It seemed so unkind,' babbled Dorothea. 'I mean, she wanted coffee and she hadn't any extra sugar, and I had extra sugar but didn't want coffee. So I gave her mine—my sugar, I mean.'

Miss Carbery looked disapprovingly. 'You won't get many invitations to the Magnificent if you do that kind of thing.'

'Hugh tried to stop me, but I felt I had to. Why, on the Feast of the Annunciation the Vicar told us that true courtesy is always perfectly natural.'

Julia looked at her as though she had come out of the Zoo. But she let the point go.

'I shall certainly accompany you to Mr. Midleton's office,' she announced firmly. 'You will need a supporter.'

Dorothea looked at her with loathing. She had, she thought, done pretty well for a first attempt. She had bought a new suit, lunched at the Magnificent, seen through the machinations of a gold-digger, and found herself a lawyer, all without Miss Carbery's assistance, in fact in the teeth of her opposition.

'She exaggerates,' Dorothea told herself, deciding for once to forgo her usual conscientious hair-brushing. A hundred strokes morning and night, brushing the hair upwards, was her rule, but she couldn't endure the thought of disturbing all those little curls, and she knew she would never be able to re-set them herself. So she made a number of little ineffectual dabs with brush and comb alternately as a sop to conscience, tied on the lemon-coloured veil she had been coerced into buying at the beauty shop, and opened the pot of face-restorative she had somehow found marked up on her bill. Hormone cream it said. Miss Capper had no notion what hormones were, but they must be something pretty good, she thought, considering the price. In delirious ignorance, she smeared the stuff on her cheeks and settled down for the night, feeling pretty pleased with herself.

Next morning she wasn't so sure. She had no intention of handing over the reins of management to Miss Carbery, so she was up bright and early, throwing back the bed-clothes with abandon and wondering what new adventure this day would hold. When she came into the living-room Miss Carbery, black with disapproval, was looking at the paper. It was one of those popular journals that, to judge by their advertised sales, delight the hearts of hundreds of thousands of readers. That is to say, when the news is good, they underline it, telling the public that in some mysterious way they are responsible for the success involved. But when news comes of reverses, then the paper tells its readers that it's because of this or that weak link in the Government, that they themselves had pointed out long ago, the leaders foam like beakers of beer, the editor demands an inquiry, and the reader feels that even if battles are being lost something is being done about it.

'Look at that,' invited Miss Carbery pushing the paper, open at the middle sheet, under Dorothea's nose.

Dothea saw a really impressive advertisement issued by the National Savings Campaign depicting Mr. and Mrs. John Citizen standing on the shore, looking across the narrow sea at a shop labelled 'Things You Don't Need.' In the sea between ramped a shark with a Nazi trade-mark on his near fin.

Underneath was the superscription— 'Would you buy it if you had to swim for it?'

Dorothea's conscience smote her. Her comment was characteristic.

'What a good thing I didn't see that yester-

181

day morning,' she said. 'I wouldn't have dared . . .' Buy my suit, she meant, but her voice died away before the blast of Miss Carbery's scorn.

'Let it be a lesson to you then from now on,' she said.

'It shall be,' promised Dorothea meekly. 'I had meant to go out again this morning, but now I shan't.'

'And you'll refuse Mrs. Tempest's invitation?'

Dorothea looked surprised. 'That won't help the war effort. And it would seem so rude. No, I don't mind going without the foundation garment I meant to buy, because honestly I can do without it. . . .' After all, she had done without it for thirty-eight years, but . . .

'Foundation garment? Have you taken leave of your senses? Did you see what I showed you?'

'The—the War Savings advertisement,' faltered Dorothea. 'War Savings!' Miss Carbery used the same tone as if she derived Fifth Column activities. 'No, the paragraph next door. The one with the photograph inset.'

Dorothea hurriedly bent her head. The paragraph was entitled:

RICH WOMAN'S DEATH MYSTERY

POST-MORTEM ORDERED

Lady R. Olgason of Portman Square was taken suddenly ill after lunching out at a London restaurant yesterday. She died in considerable pain last night. A post-mortem has been ordered. Mrs. Olgason is the mother-in-law of Mr. L. Lewis-Lewis, the racehorse owner. Mr. Lewis recently filed his petition for bankruptcy.

'How terrible!' said Dorothea mechanically.

'If a woman like that couldn't look after herself,' began Miss Carbery... 'With that chin!'

Dorothea looked at the photograph. Then she started. She felt the room begin to revolve slowly round her, and held on to the table to make sure that that at least remained firm. For the picture, fuzzy and blurred like all newspaper reproductions, was nevertheless unmistakably that of the lady who had sat at the next table yesterday at the Magnificent and to whom she had passed the two pieces of sugar.

She wrestled with mounting panic. Sheer coincidence, she told herself. The sort of thing that happens once in a hundred times, and this time it had happened to her. But even while she thus strove to reassure herself, she was remembering Hugh's horror-stricken face as he tried to prevent her passing over the little tin box. Perhaps Julia was right. Perhaps she was in greater danger than she dreamed.

'You see?' said Miss Carbery's hateful voice in her ear. 'It doesn't tell you who she was lunching with, but most likely it was the son-in-law.'

'Perhaps it was,' whispered Julia. 'Anyhow, he was much younger.'

Julia stared at her. 'What are you talking about? You didn't know her, did you?'

'She was at the Magnificent yesterday. I gave her my sugar,' whispered the stricken Dorothea. 'No, don't ask me any more questions. It's all too horrible. I didn't know people did things like that, even for money.'

'You'll learn a lot more before you're through,' Julia assured her grimly with possibly more truth than either of them realised at the time.

Dorothea found she couldn't face any more breakfast. She had to ring up Mr. Crook, but she couldn't do it while Miss Carbery was in the flat. And it didn't look as though Miss Carbery ever intended to leave the flat, even for half an hour. Or anyway not alone. She announced with great firmness her intention of accompanying Dorothea to Mr. Midleton's office, on the ground that he wasn't a beautiful young man and there could be no question of three being one too many. Dorothea realised she had about as much choice as a man with a revolver nuzzling his ribs.

The appointment had been made for 10.30, and no ingenuity on her part made it possible for her to get in touch with Mr.Crook before they left the flat, so, rather despairingly, Dorothea made up her mind she'd have to exercise her wits after they left Mr. Midleton and somehow shake off her difficult companion.

Mr. Midleton kept them waiting the regulation five minutes, and then interviewed them in a room as different from Mr. Crook's as proverbial chalk from cheese. Crook said his clients liked a man's office to look as though he were busy, and he kept papers on all the desks and chairs and part of the floor as well with the same regularity as he kept beer in the cupboards. Mr. Midleton's office reminded Dorothea of a maiden lady's bedroom. There was the same pitiless chastity, the lack of mystery, the feeling that here a spade was a spade and everything was aboveboard and sanitary. It chilled Miss Capper to

185

the marrow.

Mr. Midleton's stiff little grey brows rose when he saw his timid new client come in followed by Julia Carbery, like a ship in full sail, as determined as a British destroyer in charge of a convoy and about as scrupulous as a U-boat.

'Miss Capper asked me to come with her,' said Julia, without blinking an eyelid. 'Not knowing Mr. Hope, you see. . .'

'I take it Miss Capper was not expecting to see Mr. Hope,' said Mr. Midleton in his unsympathetic way.

'Of course not,' said Dorothea. 'But—you will understand how strange it all seems to me. I've lived so very quietly until now, and suddenly to be told I've inherited a hundred thousand pounds . . .'

'The opportunity of inheriting a hundred thousand pounds,' corrected the lawyer frigidly. 'It is not precisely the same thing.'

'That it isn't,' put in Miss Carbery cheerfully. 'You want to watch your step with lawyers, Miss Capper. I've told you that before.'

Mr. Midleton looked at her as though he perceived a noxious insect issuing from a law report.

'I never saw Mr. Hope,' contributed Dorothea nervously. 'His—his death was so very unexpected.'

'Particularly by himself,' agreed Mr. Midleton. 'I was to have visited him on the Friday, as no doubt Miss Carbery has told you. Naturally, I cannot tell what was in his mind. . . .'

'I could make a good guess,' said Julia, but the man of law had no intention of being over-ridden in his own office, so he said, 'Guessing is not regarded as evidence in law,' and turned back to Miss Capper.

Miss Carbery was not so easily silenced. 'I was his housekeeper and confidential secretary for fifteen years,' she announced.

Mr. Midleton disregarding this, Dorothea felt it incumbent upon her to say: 'I think it was wonderful of you,' though she had herself looked after sick relatives for quite as long a period and never expected any praise at all. Still, as there are different laws for rich and poor, so, she knew, there are different standards for the Julias and Dorotheas of this world.

'Life's what you make it,' said Miss Carbery.

Mr. Midleton surprised them both by saying: 'And so is death.'

Dorothea gaped, but Julia was equal to the occasion. 'I see your suspicion approximates with my own, Mr. Midleton.'

'I did not use the word suspicion,' said Mr.

Midleton, at his most glacial. His manner implied that it was far less rare for rich old gentlemen to fall downstairs in the middle of a house-party than the layman would suppose.

Dorothea wondered why he had sent for her. He didn't seem to mind in the least that his late client might have been the victim of foul play, any more than it mattered to him if the prospective heiress pitched suddenly in front of a tube train. That's one satisfactory thing about money, provided there's enough of it. There's always someone to inherit, and inheritors always need a lawyer, just as a lawyer needs a legatee to keep the family pot boiling. Naturally an unsuspicious client is preferable to a nosey one. Mr. Midleton was sedately pleased Mr. Hope hadn't left his money to Julia.

As soon as the two ladies found themselves alone on the stairs Julia voiced her perplexity.

'Don't be soft,' said Miss Carbery in a scornful voice. 'He can charge as much for one visit as for half a dozen letters.'

It required some enterprise on Dorothea's part to separate herself from her companion when at length they reached the street. She did it by putting into practice a scheme she had evolved while Mr. Midleton painstakingly explained the situation.

'Oh dear,' she said, as they reached the pavement, 'I believe I left my umbrella in Mr. Midleton's room.'

Julia saw that she had, but she had no intention of letting Dorothea go back for it. She suspected the wily spinster of wanting a private audience with the lawyer, and so she said that she would go up herself. This was what Dorothea had anticipated. While Miss Carbery stormed the staircase, Miss Capper attracted the attention of a passing taxi and asked the driver to wait a moment for a lady. As soon as Julia reappeared, she leaned out of the cab window, snatched the umbrella and said: 'Thank you so much. I shan't be late home. I have an appointment,' and drove off before the astounded Miss Carbery could collect her senses.

Crook, who was taking the midday train, beamed when he saw Miss Capper.

'Well?' he cried expectantly. 'Got it with you?'

Poor Dorothea yammered at him. 'It? But I don't understand?'

'The poisoned sandwich or whatever it was. Mean to tell me no one's made an attempt on your life yet? That's the worst of these blue-blooded families—no enterprise. In their place I'd have had three or four shots by now—always supposin' the first hadn't

189

come off.'

'There has been an attempt,' said Dorothea huskily and told him about the lumps of sugar. She noticed that after this Mr. Crook treated her with more respect. 'Of course,' she added, 'I haven't any proof.'

'That's all right,' said Crook. 'What are lawyers for?' He looked thoughtful. 'Miss Carbery didn't come with you?'

'Well, she did, but I shook her off.'

'Take care you don't shake her off altogether. I mean, she's in a hot spot too. When you're looking out for attempts to put you six feet deep in the earth, remember she has enemies as well.'

'You think there may be an attempt on *her* life?'

'I only say watch for it,' said Crook, 'and, if there is, mind you tell me at once.'

'Oh dear!' said the sadly-teased Miss Capper. 'I thought she was supposed to be looking after me.'

But Mr. Crook only asked her if she'd never read *Alice Through the Looking-Glass* and didn't wait to hear her reply.

CHAPTER TEN

I

MR. CROOK reached Fox Norton half an hour before the local closed. It wasn't long, but it was long enough for him. He went to the Dog and Lizard in the sublime faith that they would remember him, and it turned out that they did.

'Nice part of the country this,' suggested Crook, ordering a pint and saying, 'How about you?' as he swigged it down.

'Suits me,' said the barman. 'Say, you've got a thirst, haven't you?'

'Murder's thirsty work,' returned Crook, saying, 'Same again.'

The barman refilled the tankard. 'Whose murder? Yours?'

'Not yet, we'll hope.'

'Down here last week, weren't you?' asked Sam.

'You ought to be in the Home Guard,' Crook told him.

The barman said he was, of course.

'What's it like?' asked Crook.

'With our lot,' said the barman grimly, 'we'll probably get a good chance to die for our country whether we get the invasion or not.'

Crook asked casually if Sam had known the old boy at the Brakes.

'I know who you mean,' said the barman.

'Not much use to you,' suggested Crook.

'No use at all,' said the barman. 'Why, he was so mean he'd have wanted the refund on empties before he took 'em away.'

'Died in a bit of a hurry, didn't he?' offered Crook.

'Took about eighty years to make up his mind,' said Sam.

'Live here all the time?' asked Crook.

'Only the last fifteen years. Mr. William had it before that. Now he was a gentleman you could be proud of. Nothing stand-offish about him. He'd be down here most nights and bring his friends with him.'

'Brother Everard being among the friends?'

'Oh him! He wouldn't have drunk water if it hadn't been free?'

'And he didn't stay here?'

'He stayed whenever his brother would have him. Mind you, I've often thought Mr. William went a bit further than he would have done just to see what Mr. Everard would say. My brother don't like me, he'd tell the world. He knows he comes into anything I leave, and he's afraid I won't leave

192

enough for him to put into money-bags.'

'Not married?' asked Crook experimentally.

'Well, not to say married, not so far as we know,' agreed the barman. 'But he didn't live a dull life.'

'I get you,' said Crook. 'How about the others? Did they come down in Mr. William's time?'

'Mr. Christopher, he'd come sometimes, and Mr. Hugh now and again. Mr. William wouldn't have the others. Spoilsports, he called 'em. Of course, he couldn't keep Mr. Everard out, and he came and lived free when he got the chance. It 'ud got so he was practically living there that last year or two. And of course Miss Carbery was there as secretary—well, no one was jealous of her, of course—and she stayed on, helping Mr. Everard to sort things after they found Mr. William, and he kept her after that. Well, if he hadn't there'd never have been a woman about the place. She was the only one could coax them to stay.'

'None of the old lot stayed then?'

'They said they preferred to eat, even if Mr. Hope was an ostrich and could get along on pebbles and bits of glass and what not. It was along of Miss Carbery that Maggie Martin stayed.'

'Had she been a bit of Brother William's fun and games too?'

'He said she was worth her weight in gold.'

'Valuable party to have about the place,' suggested Crook.

'Still, she couldn't stop Mr. William enjoying himself his own way. It was queer really. I mean, him keeping her when you remember his ladies. But she didn't mind. We thought she'd come into a bit one of these days, and perhaps she would if Mr. William hadn't gone it a bit strong even for him, and fallen out of that window. It was a nasty fall,' he added.

'The Hopes seem to run to falls,' suggested Crook.

'Bitter March weather it was, and he was leaning out of the window, to clear his head, it's supposed, and out he fell plonk into the snow. He was a big man. Made quite a crater as you might say. But I'll tell you one thing. There wasn't a soul roundabouts that didn't mourn for him.' He looked at the clock. 'Sorry, sir,' he said.

'So am I,' said Crook, rising reluctantly from his stool. 'Still, we might meet again. Anyone living at the house now?'

'Maggie Martin's still there, sort of caretaking. The place is full of furniture and pictures, and they can't do anything about it yet, see.'

'Rum will,' observed Crook, coming into the little square in front of the inn.

'Lot of feeling about that,' agreed the barman. 'Lady quite a stranger, you know.'

'There wouldn't be much mourning if she stopped a stranger to that fortune to the end of her days,' offered Crook.

'If you ask me,' said the barman, with the wisdom of the married man, 'women don't know how to get real fun out of money. All geegaws and curls to put in their hair and new clothes. Now if Mr. Christopher or Mr. Hugh had got it . . .'

'Perhaps they will yet,' said Crook.

'No air-raids on London are there these days?' asked Sam.

'Hitler's not the only chap with gumption,' Crook assured him. 'That's the house, isn't it?'

The barman nodded. 'And a mortal ugly place it is. Won't sell that in a hurry.'

Crook said good-bye and moved off in the direction of The Brakes. As Sam had observed, it was a great barn of a place with an air of suspicious discomfort. He rang the front door bell, and when no one came he moved round through the dripping shrubberies to the back of the house. Enormous kitchen premises stretched to an unkempt

195

kitchen garden. He rapped on the window and a face appeared behind the glass. When it saw Crook it brightened and a hand indicated the back door.

'I always keep the front door on the chain,' Mrs. Martin told him. 'I don't like this house and that's a fact.'

Crook tilted his brown bowler to the back of his head. 'Has a suggestion of corruption and decay,' he agreed. They came together into the front hall. It was, as she had told him, a dour place with damp streaming down the walls, the pale afternoon light illuming the cracks in the ceilings, the blackened mouldings, the fine carved bannisters that were clammy to the touch. All the rooms were immensely high. Light seemed lost before it reached the ceilings, leaving pockets of shadow in the corners. Crook admired the woman for remaining there alone. It wouldn't be difficult to hear the sound of an old man tapping along with a stick, or the anguished cry of another ghost who had plunged to his death on a bitter March afternoon sixteen years ago.

Mrs. Martin was full of the house's tragedies. Crook was shown the great landing window, occupying the whole of one wall, from which William Hope had fallen. Heavy curtains covered it, darkening the landing.

'That's because of draughts,' said Mrs. Martin. 'They're always like that. When Mr. William fell he must have caught at the curtains. We found them all dragged.'

'Nasty thing to happen,' suggested Crook.

Mrs. Martin sighed. 'He was always fond of his glass,' she said. 'That's how it was. It was Mr. Everard found him, coming back from a walk.'

Leaving the window he was conducted to the head of the staircase whence Everard had stumbled to his hideous death. Crook looked down into the darkness below. His imagination, that could be acute enough when occasion demanded, pictured the little shrivelled figure staggering on the edge of eternity, throwing up his arms perhaps, dropping down, down... If witnesses were to be believed, he must have been panic-stricken. Yet at the inquest no one, he realised, had remembered hearing the old man speak. Of course, the babel must have been intense at the time, so many feet moving to and fro, torches flashing, candlelight dancing and throwing great shadows on ceiling and wall—yet no one had heard Everard Hope speak, and the fact troubled him. It was almost as though—as though...

He felt his brain buzzing like a hive of bees.

Stooping down he examined the rent in the carpet that had theoretically caused the old man's death. It was a great gash in a carpet already worn threadbare by years of the coming and going of feet. Since the tragedy it had been roughly sewed together with thread that didn't quite match the carpet. Under Mrs. Martin's slightly disapproving eye he proceeded to cut the stiches.

'Are you the police?' she demanded suddenly.

'You ask them and see what they say,' Crook told her. 'H'm. I wondered. That wasn't an ordinary hole. That was a deliberate cut.'

'You mean, he was meant to fall down those stairs that night?'

'I mean, someone knew there was going to be a fire alarm and that Everard Hope would be on this staircase instead of the little one by his door. What d'you make of that?'

What he made of it himself threw an entirely new light on the situation.

II

In London Miss Capper had returned to the Bush, brooding darkly on Crook's warning.

'Of course,' said she to herself, for, like many solitary and shy people, she was frequently her own sole audience, 'Miss Carbery is right when she says she's a danger to whoever did murder Mr. Hope, always assuming it was murder. It's even possible she knows who did it—(but if so, asked Miss Capper's common sense, why didn't she tell the police?) Well then, perhaps she knows but has no proof. Or perhaps whoever is responsible has some hold over her so that she daren't go to the police.' This situation was so common in the films to which Miss Capper was addicted that its extreme improbability, presented no difficulties to her at all. 'If that is the case,' Dorothea continued her ruminations, 'then he or she will probably try to get rid of Julia before she can put me on my guard, knowing that I shall be quite helpless.' She hoped that the guilty party wouldn't realise that Mr. Crook was now included in the cast, and might, therefore, play very prettily into his hands.

All the same, the situation was hardly a cheerful one. Even Mr. Crook could not be in two places at once, and while he was protecting Miss Capper the villain might work his will on Miss Carbery. The only way to prevent this appeared to be for the two ladies never to be separated, and Dorothea honestly thought death might be preferable. Still, if anything did happen to Julia she, Dorothea, would be practically helpless. It was sheer good fortune that she wasn't dead already, and even as it was some unfortunate old lady had paid the bill.

'Defenceless!' repeated Dorothea and shivered. Like someone sent out into an air-raid minus gasmask and tin hat. She reached Russell Square and got into the tube. On the platform she noticed a queer individual leaning against the wall watching her. When she pressed forward into a non-smoker she saw that he followed her into the same carriage, though she was convinced that an instant earlier he had been smoking. At South Kensington she left the train to get a bus to the Bush and, as she meekly joined the small queue, she perceived that her shadow was at her heels. In a moment of frenzy she waved at a passing taxi and was driven away. Peering out of the window at the back she saw that the mysterious, rather seedy-looking personage had taken a little notebook out of his pocket and was writing something down.

'The number of the taxi, of course,' thought Miss Capper. 'Oh dear, I wonder what will happen next.'

(But actually he was only making a note of his betting losses and hadn't noticed Dorothea at all.)

Still fearful of being traced, Miss Capper

stopped the taxi in front of one of the Panda teashops and joined a queue for a cup of soup, a plateful of spaghetti, and a wholemeal roll. By the time she had struggled out of the restaurant it was getting on for two o'clock, she was amazed to see. She simply couldn't have spent all that time there, could she, just reading a noon edition, short story, betting notes and all. When she reached the flat she hurried up the stairs and pushed her key into the lock, calling out apologetically: 'Any one at home?' It was absurd that she should have to feel like this about an uninvited guest, but she felt as though she had returned to childhood and must placate an outraged adult.

Miss Carbery, however, made no reply. Dorothea hurried into her room, removed her hat and coat, pulled on a flowered cretonne overall, and went into the living-room. Still there was no sign of the visitor, but on the table lay a box alongside its paper wrapping, a box marked 'Chocolate Peppermint Creams.' Dorothea looked at them with delight. She picked up the wrapping-paper and saw, a little disappointedly, that the chocolates had been sent to Miss Carbery.

'But she's left them out to show we're meant to share them,' she thought. 'My very favourite sweet.'

She went out into the corridor, as though

201

Miss Carbery might be hiding under the carpet, but there was no sign of her, and Dorothea decided she must have gone out to lunch.

'Naturally, she thinks I'm out to lunch,' she argued, and unless you liked tinned beans there wasn't much to eat in the house. 'But she certainly wouldn't mind me having one of her peppermints.'

They looked so glossy, so brown, so pre-war. Their smell was so appetizing. The Vicar had once said that gluttony was a breaking of the seventh commandment, but one peppermint surely wouldn't be gluttony. And as Miss Carbery was having breakfast, lunch, tea and dinner (or supper) with her hostess, and as so far she hadn't offered to put her hand in her pocket, one peppermint cream could hardly be an unfair exchange. She took one of the tempting lollipops and put it into her mouth. The next instant she heard a groan and the faint creak of the bathroom door. Extraordinary, she reflected, that it hadn't occurred to her that Miss Carbery might be there, but more extraordinary still that she hadn't answered when she, Dorothea, called out. She wasn't a person who suffered from excessive modesty in the ordinary way. With a sense of guilt Dorothea took the unbitten chocolate out of her mouth and dropped it into the pocket of her overall.

Julia tottered into view. But what a Julia! Gone was all the exuberance, all the cocksureness, all the impression she normally gave of not thinking much of the world, and knowing that, if the job had been left in her hands, it would have been much more capably done. This Julia had damp hair, a damp pale face, hands that shook.

'Oh dear!' exclaimed Miss Capper. 'I'm afraid you're ill.'

Miss Carbery leaned against the wall. 'Heard you come in,' she mumbled. 'Tried to call out. Couldn't make you hear. But you haven't, have you?'

Dorothea looked at her, bewildered. 'Haven't what?'

'My fault,' groaned Miss Carbery. 'Ought to have guessed. But it was diabolically subtle. Every one who knows me knows what I'm like about chocolate peppermint creams.'

A great wave of comprehension swept over Dorothea, leaving her for the moment almost as dizzy and sick as her companion.

'The peppermint creams!' she repeated.

Miss Carbery lolled her sick head against the wall in imitation of a nod.

'And when I saw they were from Dubois...' She crept forward, Dorothea falling back as she advanced till they were both in the sitting-room. Dorothea picked up the lid of the box. It was gold and red in candy stripes with Dubois stamped right across it.

'My very special kind,' continued the ravaged Julia. Sickness didn't improve her, Dorothea had to admit. Her hair had fallen out of curl and her clothes looked as though she and a tramp had slept in them. Dorothea's hand, holding the cardboard lid, began to shake. I ought to have suspected, she thought. Mr. Crook warned me. But oh what luck, what luck—that she hadn't eaten the chocolate, she meant.

Miss Carbery's eyes fell on those trembling hands. 'You hadn't taken one, I suppose.'

Dorothea felt like a little girl caught pilfering jam. In just such a voice had the righteous Mrs. Capper spoken to a small daughter about to be slapped.

'I—I didn't think you'd mind,' she faltered.

'You fool!' hissed Miss Carbery. 'You'd better take an emetic. Quick! I tell you, they're poisoned. I know. I've every reason to know.'

Dorothea's hand went guiltily to her apron pocket. She drew out a sweet with the tooth-marks still on the shining chocolate.

'I was just going to bite it,' she whispered

204

shamefacedly.

'You're lucky,' said Julia. 'Damn' lucky! D'you know what I did? I took two. Two! Both together, one in each cheek. I always say you get more than twice the pleasure by having two at the same time. It wasn't till after I'd swallowed them that I thought there was something queer. To begin with, they didn't taste quite right, but then in a war you can't complain if your chocolates are a bit below par, like everything else. And then I thought it was queer there wasn't a card with them, and who was likely to send me chocolates from my own special shop? Then I realised it was a trick. It was done to get me out of the way. No one but Mr. Hope's precious cousins knew about me and the chocolate creams, and none of them loved me so much he was going to take all that trouble just to give me pleasure. You can't buy them from the shops, you have to get them from the makers. Then the sickness began and I knew if I didn't act quickly I was a goner. So I took salt and water.' She retched slightly. 'It did the trick, of course. Not even a pin's head of poison or of anything else can be inside me now.'

Dorothea said, 'Oughtn't you to see a doctor?' but Miss Carbery said, 'No.' She would be all right and everyone knew what doctors were. All the same, she added, she was going to get to the bottom of this. She'd send the chocolates to Mr Hollins, the chemist at Fox Norton who knew her and had his own views on Mr. Hope's death. If he confirmed her belief that the chocolates had been doctored, then they could take them to the police.

'But whoever worked this is pretty clever,' she added soberly. 'You see, they're so big— the sweets, I mean—and it's only a half-pound box—that they can't get more than three in a row. Well, the sender knew I'd take two at once and probably guessed I'd offer you one at the same time. That would dispose of the top row, and it was meant to dispose of us as well. Then probably you'd find the rest of the chocolates were quite O.K. Give me that one in your pocket. That's the test one, though actually I'll send the entire box to Mr. Hollins.'

'Won't the writing on the outside wrapping tell you anything?' murmured Dorothea, wanting to be helpful.

She picked up the sheet of brown paper, but the address had been carefully printed. As for the postmark, it was too blurred to afford any clue.

'I blame myself,' said Miss Carbery, shakily. 'I ought to have thought. But when I

206

came upstairs and found this little box on the step outside your door it never occurred to me . . . But so few people know where I am I should have realised at once it came from one of the cousins. Well, we'll keep everything—box, paper, string. They may feature as exhibits 1, 2, and 3 in a murder trial yet.'

CHAPTER ELEVEN

I

CECIL TEMPEST was horribly troubled. The firm of bookmakers was becoming increasingly unpleasant. His lofty remark about anticipated royalties they treated with the scorn it deserved, since they had met writers before and they knew that it is quite unusual for them to receive cheques of four figures and, where they are married, to be able to conceal this fact from their wives or be permitted to retain the amount. Mr. Beresford, the senior partner of Bens, wrote a sharp note saying that unless he received payment within seven days he would place the matter in the hands of his solicitors. Cecil was frantic. It was no use trying to find anything in the house that would sell for a tithe of the sum. If there had been anything it would have been sold long ago. Lilias was not one of those useful wives who get unexpected legacies or manage to save large sums out of the housekeeping or earn a private living in addition to running the house without servants, making and mending the clothes, cooking, cleaning, washing, ironing, making jam on inadequate sugar supplies, bottling fruit, drying vegetables, collecting for a local Savings Group, and nursing the family when it was sick. On the whole, Cecil thought he'd had rather a scurvy deal. Meanwhile, there was Mr. Beresford.

To crown everything, Dorothea Capper, on whom he had relied for assistance (Cecil belonged to the old-fashioned school that still believes in miracles), had refused his wife's invitation, *tout court*.

'Why on earth should she do that?' demanded Cecil, feverishly.

'Perhaps she doesn't trust our tea,' suggested Lilias.

'Did you only ask her to tea? Good heavens, that's worthy of Cousin Everard himself. You should have asked her to dinner and got a fowl.'

'You can't get fowls,' pointed out Lilias mildly, 'and even if you can I don't see why we should buy fowls for someone who's going to inherit a hundred thousand pounds. Why, she'll be able to buy peacocks on that.'

'I particularly wanted her to come,' said Cecil desperately. To make things worse, he had made a sickening blunder at the office only yesterday morning, and Mr. Whaley had murmured something about his nephew who was coming out of the army, after all. Something about his heart not being right. A lot of chaps are like that in a war, Cecil had muttered to himself. A more logical man might have reflected that, since he was probably going to lose his job in any case, he might have stopped worrying about Mr. Whaley's reactions, but Cecil wasn't made like that. There was always, he hoped, the chance that the nephew's heart might stop altogether, and then, if he could settle this betting debt, he was pretty safe. But not once Mr. Whaley found anything out, for Mr. Whaley knew that men who bet also drink and ill-use their wives and are the prey of every degrading lust known to reformers. These things go together like flotsam and jetsam, oil and vinegar, Pig and Whistle. When he realised that Dorothea wasn't, in Miss Carbery's phrase, going to play ball, he began to think of some fresh bait to put on his trap, though that is not how he would have phrased it. Somehow, somewhere, he and Dorothea must meet. Searching the rather dusty recesses of his mind, he remembered that when he had been courting Lilias he had pleased her by gifts of flowers. All women liked flowers, particularly the middle-aged who have not been sought in marriage. Cecil hurried along to the Metropolitan Line Station, wondering who could be trusted to deliver flowers at this stage of the war. Probably, he reflected gloomily, only a place that charged a good deal. Much was said and written about risking a sprat to catch a whale, but his sprats didn't seem to come of a successful stock. He sighed, remembering a story of his grandfather who had been three times married and who had, on the occasion of each wife's funeral, for all three pre-deceased him, hired a wreath of laurel and everlastings, subsequently returning this to the funeral upholder, on payment of a small fee. Progress still had a lot to learn from the past, thought Cecil.

He hesitated in front of a shop window. How about a pot of daffodils—three-and-sixpence seemed a lot with so little to show, and she might think daffodils mean. Besides, they are the flower of youth, and though Cecil was exactly the same age as the heiress and still thought of himself as a man just on the threshold of his prime, everyone knows it's different for women. So reluctantly he abandoned the idea of daffodils and settled instead on a potted hydrangea at five shillings. With congratulations from Cecil and Lilias he wrote on the little card they gave him. There was a really magnificent plant if he could have run to half a guinea, but he decided it wasn't necessary and after all it's the thought that counts. Under the first line he wrote in his incredibly neat impersonal hand:

> Can you come to a concert of sacred music
> at the Alexandra Hall on Sunday? I have
> tickets. If all right, please meet me Box
> Office 2.20.

He wanted to add a tea invitation, but there
wasn't room, and he didn't like to ask for a
second card in war-time. Besides, she'd
already shied at one invitation to tea. He put
his office telephone number, because he
wasn't including Lilias in the invitation. He
felt matters might go better without her. She
had a way of blurting out the things better
left unsaid. Like most wives, she didn't in the
least appreciate the romantic creature she had
married.

Leaving the shop Cecil hurried to his
office. He hadn't, of course, got the tickets,
and he didn't mean to buy them yet. He
didn't want to be stuck with them, and she
might have another engagement, a meeting at
the Y.M.C.A. or something, and in a war you
have to remember that money fights, like
bullets, and neither should be wasted.

It was on Friday morning that the
hydrangea arrived, and when she ran down
the stairs and opened the street door Dorothea couldn't at first believe it was really

meant for her. It seemed incredible that last Friday she had practically never heard of Everard Hope, and here she was with his secretary-housekeeper-companion under her roof, and his cousins sending her poisoned sweets and pot-plants and only heaven knew what was to come. She carried it proudly upstairs, so delighted that at first she didn't even read the rest of the message. Miss Carbery was washing stockings rather messily in the bathroom. When she saw what Dorothea was carrying she fixed her with an eye like a nail in a coffin.

'Well?' she called, as her companion made no attempt to take her into her confidence. 'Who's it from? Father Christmas? or the Vicar?'

'It's from Cecil and Lilias,' said Dorothea slowly, trying to remember a distant day when her life belonged to herself and she had—God forgive her!—dared to think it dull. 'They want me to go to a concert of religious music on Sunday.' (For it didn't occur to her that Lilias wasn't to be of the party.)

Miss Carbery sniffed awfully. 'The things that are done in the name of religion can scarcely be credited,' she announced.

'At the Alexandra Hall', continued Dorothea.

'A very good place for falling downstairs,'

213

countered Julia. 'You be warned in time. There's been too much falling downstairs as it is. I suppose Cecil doesn't suggest my accompanying you.'

'He—well, no.' agreed poor Dorothea.

'Of course not. Not to be expected. Oh well, if you are murdered don't say I didn't warn you. And take care how you handle that plant. Drench it in the bath before you go sticking your nose into it. It might have one of those infected darts you get in Africa hidden in it somewhere.'

'It's come direct from the shop,' offered Dorothea.

'Cecil chose it, I suppose,' returned Miss Carbery tartly. 'What was there to prevent him putting something lethal into it when the assistant's back was turned? He knows all about that sort of thing too. He writes boys' stories for that idiotic Press sometimes, and they think nothing of blowing darts or rolling canoes over prostrate bodies.'

'I don't think...' began Dorothea, but Julia swept over her like a tidal wave.

'Not that I imagine he's done anything of the sort on this occasion. Otherwise, he wouldn't be wasting money on tickets for the Alexandra Hall. Does he say whereabouts they are?'

Not on the card. Well, there isn't much

room,' Dorothea apologised.

'If I had to guess,' said Julia with awful joy, 'I'd say the front row of the balcony. Ever been in the balcony of the Alexandra Hall?'

'I don't think so,' said Dorothea, beginning to understand how it is that apparently devoted men murder their wives. They can't stand those flat triumphant voices yap-yapping at them.

'Long way to fall,' said Miss Carbery succinctly.

'I shall go, though,' said Dorothea, who by this time would have walked into a tiger's cage just to assert herself over her companion. 'I can't spend the rest of my life hiding in corners like a mouse and saying No.'

'If you accept all these invitations you won't have much time to bother about,' Julia warned her darkly.

But Dorothea paid no heed to that.

She rang up Cecil at his office as he had directed. Cecil said in a quick high voice: 'You can? That's delightful. I'll look out for you at 2.20. I—we're looking forward to meeting you.'

Dorothea thought: 'They might have suggested lunch, but I suppose they have their meat ration over the week-end.'

Friday and Saturday were quiet days. On Saturday afternoon the two ladies went to the local Gaumont and saw a splendid film about a companion who murdered her employer and hid the body in an oven. Thoroughly exhilarated they came back to toast and margarine and a cake described as Plain Lunch.

Sunday morning was wet. Dorothea went to church as usual, and, not as usual, observed quite a shiver of interest pass over several faces as she walked to her pew. She had buried her face reverently in her hands and was wishing that milliners would design hats suitable for devout women, when someone jabbed her in the ribs, and there was Julia.

'Move up!' said she, looking round with a lively eye. 'What's all this about? Haven't been in a church for years—unless you count Mr. Hope's funeral.'

Her voice, that she barely troubled to subdue, was painfully audible. Her personality was almost impossible to overlook. A sort of shock of pleasure ran through the congregation. As the service progressed Miss Carbery sniffed her disapproval from time to time and once she said: 'Well, why not go to the circus and have done with it?' But she didn't go out as Dorothea passionately wished she would before the sermon.

The Vicar this morning chose simplicity as his subject. 'My little children, keep yourselves from idols,' he said, looking straight at Dorothea. Sometime, he was reflecting, as he elaborated his points, he must call. But not too soon. He mustn't give the impression that the money really made any difference, and in a way it didn't. Money as money didn't excite him, but he was the shepherd of his flock, and their burdens were his burdens. A hundred thousand pounds was a quite considerable burden, and it was his duty to try and lighten it if he could.

Julia, who drank in the sermon and never took her glittering eyes off the preacher, grabbed Dorothea by the arm the moment the service was over and marched her into the street.

'I'm glad I came,' she announced. 'That's something I hadn't thought of before.'

'What hadn't you thought of?' asked poor Dorothea, prepared to be told that Miss Carbery had noticed the devil hiding behind a pillar, waiting to spurt living flame at his victim.

'The Vicar,' said Julia. 'You take care or he'll lift your money for you, and make you feel he's done you a favour by the way.' She frowned. 'When you get it,' she said, 'you'll have to make a will.'

217

'I suppose so,' agreed Dorothea faintly.

'Don't leave it to the Church whatever you do.'

'I haven't any other family,' Dorothea explained.

'I've never met such a woman,' flared Julia. 'I thought your Church forbade suicide.'

'So it does, of course,' said Dorothea, staring. 'Like every other church and every moral society.'

'Well, you seem set on committing it. First of all, you inherit a family you've never heard of, and you seem bent on giving them every conceivable opportunity to put you out of the way—and then if I do succeed in heading 'em off till the month's over, you want to put temptation in the way of those who're supposed to be experts on the subject by leaving it to a society that's one of the champion beggars of the world.'

'Monomania,' thought Dorothea. 'That's the word. She's a monomaniac. Perhaps she's seeing danger where it doesn't exist. Perhaps those chocolates weren't poisoned, after all.' She hadn't had an answer yet from Mr. Hollins. Miss Carbery watched the post like a hawk, and said dourly that silence probably meant the worst. Perhaps, after all, Cecil did just want to be friendly. If so, it was a shame not to give him a chance. And if he was dangerous—well, what about her vow to be a wild bird of heaven and risk the snare of the fowler? She positvely thrilled at the thought of the afternoon's encounter.

II

Dorothea arrived a little early for her appointment. There was a large crowd pouring through the big entrance at the Alexandra Hall. Dorothea took up her position at the head of the steps, because she couldn't get any closer to the Booking Office. From what she could hear, most of the people were inquiring for the lower-priced seats. She wondered where Cecil's places were. If the tickets had been given him, as seemed probable, because no one buys tickets for concerts like this in order to make a good impression, they go to the theatre instead, they might be stalls. She knew that in the amphitheatre of the hall the echo ruins the music for those who are capable of appreciating it in the first place, but she wasn't musical, not really, and she did like the thought of a comfortable seat. She had been watching the crowd, twisting her head round at the most painful angles, for some time before it occurred to her that she wouldn't know her relatives when they did appear, and they wouldn't know her. They ought to have arranged some sign. If she'd said, 'I'll be wearing buttercups in my hat,' then they would have known her at once. Or Cecil might have put a daffodil in his button-hole.

There were other solitary females haunting the steps, but sooner or later these were joined by their friends, mostly of the same sex, and melted away through various entrances. Dorothea glanced at the watch on her wrist. It was almost the half-hour. She began to feel panic-stricken. Supposing she didn't recognise him and he didn't find her, would she spend the afternoon here? She felt desperately conspicuous. Then she saw a man eyeing her a little uncertainly. Perhaps that was Cecil. She moved forward a step or two, smiling doubtfully in his direction. She thought he moved towards her; her smile widened. Her lips began to form phrases. Then the man walked past and greeted a girl in a grey suit who was running up the steps. Blushing with mortification, Dorothea turned hastily to a notice on the wall and pre-tended to be absorbed in that. 'How awful!' she thought. 'He probably thought I was trying to pick him up.'

She felt furious with Cecil for making such a situation possible. Probably the man, who had looked rather attractive, was telling the girl how a female like a camel had tried to accost him. Actually, of course, the man hadn't even noticed her existence. By this time they would be striking up the overture. That meant that, even if Cecil did come, they would be late and would have to fall over a lot of strangers' feet on their way to their places. Dorothea was angry for two reasons. One, that she went out so seldom at someone else's expense that she couldn't bear to miss a minute of her free entertainment, and two, she hated to be stared and muttered at as people always did stare and mutter if you had to disturb them once they were seated. She felt a hot flush run all through her body and a pulse began to beat furiously.

A voice spoke in her ear. 'Miss Capper?'

She turned sharply, and saw a thinnish, shabby-ish man with a nervous manner, wearing a black bowler hat, that he raised experimentally.

'Yes,' she acknowledged, feeling disappointed at the sight of her escort. This was a tremendous come-down from the Magnificent with its Grand Guignols and its dashing companion. And how worn he looked. Dorothea knew, because Miss Carbery had told her, that Cecil was thirty-eight, Dorothea's own age. She thought, 'Do I look like that? So shabby? So worn?' But decided that she didn't, because naturally one never does.

'Sorry to keep you waiting,' said Cecil, who had had some difficulty in getting away from Lilias, whom he wasn't taking into his confidence. 'Look, we're upstairs. I always think one hears better upstairs.'

He evidently cherished this belief to the utmost degree, for he had taken seats at a height that made Dorothea feel dizzy. He chattered eagerly about the performers as they climbed into what the muddle-headed Dorothea thought of as the bowels of the sky. Of course, he said, she'd realise that during the week he hadn't much time for this sort of relaxation.

Dorothea, dizzily catching the conversational ball, said she understood that they didn't hold Sunday concerts on week-days. Cecil laughed breathlessly. His laugh sounded like a stirrup-pump that doesn't function quite right. They hurried into their places, disturbing an artistic-looking woman with hair like an empty bird's nest. Cecil began to say something, but she glared at him so fiercely he subsided.

The concert began.

As Dorothea had suspected, it was a very long programme. The atmosphere had that quality of solemnity proper to the occasion. Sacred music creates a feeling all its own.

Cecil leaned forward, apparently absorbed. Dorothea glanced surreptitiously round her, her ears open for possible comment when (as she put it) the piece was over. She wanted to seem intelligent and it was clear that Cecil 'knew all about music,' which is disconcerting to those who do not but lack the honesty to admit their philistinism. After a long piano recital by someone Dorothea had never heard of, Cecil flung himself back and asked: 'Have you ever heard Solomon play that?'

'No,' said Dorothea eagerly. 'Actually, I never have.'

The artistic woman on her other side said audibly: 'And nor has anyone else.'

Cecil, who couldn't help but hear, changed the subject. 'I do hope you liked my few flowers,' he said.

'They were lovely,' returned Dorothea. 'Blue's such a nice colour.'

'It's my favourite colour,' said Cecil. 'In flowers, that is.' He added the last words hurriedly in case she thought he was criticising her rather staggering bright yellow get-up.

'And it's the colour of health,' contributed Dorothea. She felt extraordinarily tired. Perhaps that was emotion induced by the music. Perhaps one could be subconsciously musical. Only, more likely, she admitted honestly, it was the effect of Cecil. Cecil was like a wet flannel. She glanced at the watch on her wrist. An outspoken woman like Julia Carbery would announce that she had a headache or even that she'd had enough music for one afternoon, but Dorothea wasn't made of such stern stuff. She sighed when she saw his absorption in the next item. When that was over he turned to her with a smile and said: 'I often think the Saturdays and Sundays of our lives are like arriving at an inn in the mountains up the long trudge of the working-days of the week.' (The manner of literature he produced made this sort of thing quite easy for him, and he didn't say what he meant simply and directly because his readers would have felt there was a catch somewhere if he had, or else that they weren't getting their money's worth.)

'Yes,' agreed Dorothea, not knowing what else to say. 'I expect you get awfully tired at your work.'

Cecil smiled—the author's experienced beam. 'The curse of Adam,' he told her. 'In the sweat of thy brow ... you know.' Though actually he didn't sweat much.

'Miss Carbery tells me you've written heaps of stories,' Dorothea continued, wishing she could remember the title of just one. 'I've often thought I'd like to write. And then I feel: "Well, who's likely to want to read my silly common-place thoughts.'''

Cecil, who was as exhausted by this musical treat as Dorothea herself, missed his cue there. He said in profound tones, 'Ah, who indeed?' and before Dorothea had conquered her shock, someone bounced on to the stage and began to sing an Italian aria.

Dorothea looked horrified. 'Do you think they ought to sing Italian songs in war-time?' she inquired.

The artistic lady, who kept her head on her chest during the performance, here lifted it to hiss: 'Vandal.' Then she dropped her arrogant chin back on her magnificent bosom.

'Art knows no barriers,' said Cecil, soberly, and his face took on a rapt air. Dorothea suppressed a yawn. Hugh might have tried to murder her, but at least he had entertained her expensively first. And her guardian-angel had been there to foil his purpose. You couldn't blame any guardian-angel from slipping away from the Alexandra Hall. When the aria was finished she didn't venture any comment, but sat there listening to the driving of the rain on the roof. Luckily she had brought an umbrella, but not her mackintosh, because she'd wanted to look smart for Cecil. It wouldn't have mattered if she'd worn the bath-mat so far as he was concerned, she told herself savagely. And her first glance at him had warned her he wouldn't be good for a taxi.

All round her people began getting up, and she thought, with a stab of incredulous joy: 'Why, it's over. It's over.' She could almost join in the applause, so great was her relief. She fumbled for her umbrella and got up too.

'Like to stretch your legs?' asked Cecil. 'Right you are. It is a bit cramping up here.'

Then he realised his mistake and hurried to add all the advantages of a seat 'among the gods,' though he failed to stress the chief of them, which was that it was very, very cheap.

'It's been marvellous,' said Dorothea, trying to sound enthusiastic, and on the whole succeeding pretty well.

'The best,' quoted Cecil, as became one of his profession, 'is yet to be.'

Dorothea contrived to conceal a start of dismay. Cecil took her arm and guided her into the corridor. A number of other people were standing here in little groups, or strolling casually to and fro. Cecil moved across to one of the open windows, and they stared over the dripping city. The rain seemed to have set in for the duration. The gutters were rivers; the black streets deserted.

'Not a very jolly day, is it?' suggested Cecil, leaning out of the window and surveying the dripping gardens. This is your chance, old man, he was saying to himself. Take it before it's too late. It may not come again.

'Not very,' said Dorothea.

'See where a Jerry got that statue to Music,' continued Cecil.

'I remember seeing the broken arm lying at her feet the next morning,' contributed Dorothea.

'Did you really? I say, it is a downpour, isn't it?'

'They say rain's very healthy,' ventured Dorothea.

'Nature's sanitation, I call it,' returned Cecil. He shot a sly glance at her. He hadn't expected anything wonderful, but it did seem unfair that such a dowdy creature with nothing to say for herself should have the prospect of a hundred thousand pounds.

'She won't know what to do with it,' he told himself angrily.

Dorothea, racking her brains for something to say, murmured desperately, 'I'm so sorry your wife couldn't come with you this afternoon.'

He thought grimly that might have been better phrased, but it gave him an opening on which he pounced gratefully enough. 'She's very disappointed, as a matter of fact, but she hopes you're coming to see us soon. I believe

227

she did invite you, but you couldn't quite make it.'

'I'd like to come,' said Dorothea. 'It's different now I've met you.'

You couldn't imagine a worm of a man like Cecil Tempest becoming involved in anything desperate. Which only shows you shouldn't judge by appearances.

'One of the children,' continued Cecil doggedly, 'has a bit of a throat.'

'I hope,' said Dorothea politely, 'it's nothing serious.'

'That's just the trouble,' returned Cecil. 'You never can be sure. And you don't want to take any risks where children are concerned.'

'My mother,' said Dorothea, tossing diplomacy to the winds, 'used to say it was a mistake to fuss too much over children.'

Cecil bridled. 'Perhaps your mother had no children,' he observed sharply. Then perceived the folly of his retort. 'Ours are extremely sensitive,' he said hurriedly. 'And one does feel so responsible. My boy, now, Douglas, he's doing extremely well at his school. I only hope we shall be able to keep him there. He's fourteen and—well, times are hard.'

'What school is that?' asked Dorothea, stifling another cavernous yawn and thinking that if Douglas were as dull as his father it wouldn't matter whether he stayed at school or not.

'St. Benedicts. It's an excellent school, but the fees . . .'

'Couldn't he have got a scholarship?' asked Dorothea tactlessly.

Cecil looked at her with loathing. He proceeded to explain how highly-strung his boy was, that he inherited it from his father who (said Cecil with a little deprecating laugh) made absurdly heavy weather over trifles. Now his little daughter, aged 12, was like her mother. Cecil often envied Lilias her placid outlook on life, but, of course, he added, with a sigh, it must help to know that the responsibility of keeping up the home lies on other shoulders. All this bread-winning. . . . He looked at Dorothea. 'I think you don't work,' he suggested.

'I'm not paid,' said Dorothea, remembering the years of nursing and household drudgery that lay not so far behind her.

'Well, life's paying you your wages now with interest.' commented Cecil smartly. It was a phrase he'd used more than once in his serials. He rather liked it.

'I hope so,' smiled Dorothea. 'Is that meant for a warning?'

Cecil gaped. The poor thing, he thought,

must be a natural. Probably that would explain her extraordinary reaction to the concert.

He leaned over the sill of the window. How minute the people down below seemed. He'd heard that if you surveyed the world from a height it dwarfed your own anxieties. It didn't, unfortunately, dwarf his, but perhaps he wasn't high enough. The taxi-cabs dwindled past like shiny black insects. He spoke without turning his head.

'Come and look at these!' Dorothea moved a step or two, mistrustful of his mood. 'Being up here,' said Cecil, 'has given me a new idea. I wanted a plot for my serial and here it is. Look there.'

Impelled by his tone she looked down. Instantly she felt giddy. The street seemed to rush up towards her—its blackness invaded the corridor in which they stood. She felt as though a hand squeezed her throat. Another hand, she was certain of it, caught her in a death-grip by the wrist.

'No,' whispered Dorothea in a ghastly voice. 'No.'

Cecil glanced stealthily over his shoulder. The second half of the concert had begun. The corridor, save for themselves, was deserted. He hoped that no one inside the hall could hear any sounds from without. Dorothea was struggling like a demon. It was enough to make a man want to throw her from a window. She broke into a froth of words.

'Cousin William died from falling out of a window. History repeats itself, they say. Someone came into a lot of money when he died.'

'It's no use,' said Cecil contemptuously. 'No one's listening. It's no use at all.'

He came closer. Dorothea felt something prick her wrist. Looking down she saw a sharp glistening point. She almost fainted with horror.

'He is drugging me,' she thought. 'When I am unconscious he can do what he pleases with me. Then I shall be lost indeed.'

With a last wild effort she dragged herself from his grasp. Two or three drops of blood fell from her wrist to the yellow frock. Cecil swung round. She saw his arm come towards her. By some miracle she evaded it, and the next moment she was at the head of the stairs, pouring herself down them like water going down a chute. Down, down, down, spiralling madly, feeling at any moment she might lose her footing and plunge, as Everard Hope had plunged, to a sickening death in the hall below. Her ears were astrain for the sound of following feet. If she heard them, she thought, if they came too close, she would hurl herself over the well of the stairs. Death in any form would be preferable to being in that fiend's power.

Down, down, down, another flight, and when she reached the foot of that yet another. Oh, the duplicity of Cecil luring her here. The meanness of Cecil in buying such cheap tickets that they had to go to the very top of the house. She reached the hall at last, and a startled attendant ran forward, but she brushed him wildly aside and pelted, without even putting up her umbrella, into the fury of the storm.

CHAPTER TWELVE

I

CECIL had not left the window. When Dorothea flung away from him so madly he was for an instant like a man paralysed. Then fear held him. He feared her, her ferocity, the strength she had displayed; and with fear came terror and despair. It was no good, his best effort was no good, and he'd never have the courage to make it again. And how had he aroused panic in her mind? He had meant to be so careful, so discreet, so that almost before she realised what was happening his object would be achieved. He stared down at the black, glistening pavements. The taxis rolled slowly past. It had occurred to him a few minutes ago that he might get a book out of that—a procession of taxis going along the road, each holding a single passenger—or perhaps one might have a married couple—or a couple who weren't married, at least not to one another. The possibilities were endless. And then he could link up the five stories— five taxis would be enough. It would be built, of course, on the pattern of The Bridge of San Luis Rey. Of course, lots of other people had had that idea, but he didn't think any of them had done it with taxis. But he could put it out of his mind, because for him there wasn't going to be any future. He hadn't been able to summon up courage just when courage was most needed. She was only a weak woman with no one at her back, so to speak, weak and bewildered. He'd seen that at once. It shouldn't have been so hard to put his plan into action. But he'd failed. Leaning out, he saw a wild black creature, like a little beetle, come diving into the rain; a crawling taxi slowed down altogether; he saw the rain in the gutter pour itself over the kerb. The black creature jumped inside and the taxi drove away.

Feeling more tired and dispirited than he had ever done in his life, Cecil went back to the hall. He couldn't go home yet, it was too wet to walk, he'd paid for his ticket. So, on all counts, he might as well occupy his seat. The second part of the concert had begun some time ago. The woman who had sung the Italian aria was now singing something in French. Cecil found he had to pass the artistic woman once again in order to reach his own place. She looked at him as though he were an insect, a cockroach or something, she couldn't quite bring herself to crush. He waited till the song was over so as not to disturb her.

234

She looked at him impatiently 'Is your wife coming back?'

'My wife?' Cecil looked distraught. 'Oh no. No. She had to go. One of the children has a bit of a throat.'

'Don't know what she came for at all,' said the woman bluntly. 'She doesn't know one note from another.'

Cecil muttered something incoherent and edged humbly into his place. As he passed the terrifying female she suddenly uttered an exclamation and caught him by the sleeve.

'Look out!' she said. 'You're a public danger. Keep that to prick your wife with, if she talks too much, I suppose.'

Cecil looked down. From the cuff of his coat the stranger had plucked a long wicked-looking needle.

Cecil felt the perspiration break out afresh. He muttered more busily than ever. Then the piano-player returned, and he sank down with a sense of relief. But for all he heard of the remainder of the programme, it might have consisted exclusively of 'Pop Goes the Wesel.' All he could think of was his recent disastrous encounter with Dorothea. Again and again he told himself he'd made an absolute mess of it. He'd never get another chance. Lilias could write and invite her to the house, but she wouldn't come. He knew it. No, the

235

truth would be revealed, he'd lose his job, Lilias would leave him, the children would have to go to Council Schools—his ignorance was so dire that he didn't realise Douglas was already past school-leaving age—he'd be so discredited no one would take his serials—it might be as well to pitch himself from a window, even if he had made no provision for Lilias.

He was so sunk in these melancholy reflections that it took a loud clear voice behind his seat to rouse him.

'I don't see any sense coming to a concert,' said a fluent feminine voice, 'if you know so little about tunes you can't recognise "God Save the King."'

He looked round with horror and saw that every one else was erect. Hurriedly he pulled himself to his feet. It was still pouring when he left the hall, but men who make a mess of their lives and are defeated in a crisis by an hysterical spinster have no right to taxis. Without even turning up the collar of his coat, Cecil walked miserably into the rain.

II

Had it not been four-thirty on a Sunday afternoon the driver of Miss Capper's taxi would unquestionably have thought his fare was drunk. Her hand, as she opened the door, trembled like a leaf, her voice giving him her address ran up and down the scale in an original but scarcely a reassuring fashion; when she had fallen into the seat of the cab she bounced and muttered and peered in a way that gave the driver gooseflesh. More, she kept looking over her shoulder.

'I take off my 'at to 'er,' he told a mate later in the evening. ''Ow she managed to get in that state by arf-past four of a perishing Sunday afternoon, I don't know.'

The other driver said perhaps it was drugs.

The first one said she'd come out of the Alexandra Hall.

The second said funny things happened in these halls, if you asked him.

Still, Dorothea had been so shaken that she'd confused half-crowns and pennies and had enormously overpaid her driver, so that was one thing to the good. Miss Carbery was sitting comfortably in Dorothea's best chair, pouring out her fourth cup of tea, when the flat's owner tottered into the room.

'Didn't he even stand you tea?' she demanded.

'No,' said Dorothea flatly, coming in and leaning against the table. 'He tried to throw me out of a window, and then he tried to drug me with a hypodermic syringe. I thought I'd never get away from him.'

'I told you not to go,' said Julia unsympathetically. 'Was Lilias there?'

'No,' said Dorothea. 'The little girl has a sore throat. Look at that.' She extended her wrist, on which could be seen the faintest of scratches. 'Of course, he meant to make me unconscious and then when I couldn't stop him . . .' she gasped.

'Tip you into the street and, if questions were asked, say you'd gone to Ladies and had fallen out of the window on your way. Well, you can't say you weren't warned. One of these days, when it's too late and you're lying on your death-bed, on a pavement or down a lift-shaft or whatever it may be, perhaps you'll remember what I've said.'

But this was undue optimism even for Miss Carbery.

When she had recovered from her shock and had a cup of tea and when her trembling hand could once more hold a pen, Dorothea sat down to write to Mr. Crook. Keep in touch, he'd said, and she desperately wanted something or someone solid to cling to. Mr. Crook was as solid as the Rock of Gibraltar.

She wrote tirelessly, page after crowded page in her small spinsterish writing. At last she drew a long breath and pushed the pad away.

'Finished?' asked Miss Carbery kindly.

238

She was engaged in knitting a petunia woollen helmet for a mine-sweeper. The wool had once formed part of a jumper of her own, but she believed that in a war we should make the supreme sacifice, and a petunia helmet could never confused with any one else's.

'Not quite,' said Dorothea, pushing her hair off her forehead. 'Writing to lawyers is very close work.'

'Why not go and see them?' inquired Miss Carbery, sensibly.

'I thought you said that cost more.'

'It won't make any difference in the end,' Julia assured her. 'Take it from me, they've already made up their minds how much they're going to have. And they'll see they get it.'

'Besides, they confuse me when I see them,' added Dorothea, feeling confused at the mere thought.

'That's the idea,' said Miss Carbery brightly. 'If you're confused enough you won't notice how big their account is.'

Dorothea bent over the page once more. It was long past post-time, and anyway it was far too wet a night to traipse to the pillar-box, but she had been brought up with a verse over her bed:

Leave not till to-morrow's sun

What to-day you might have done.
Brief must be the human span,
Do the utmost that you can.
Sinner, heed this timely warning,
For you may be dead by morning!

and all her life she had been meeting people who exemplified that advice.

'Much better wait till I've heard from Hollins,' added Miss Carbery. 'Then you will have something definite to offer. After all, you can't prove that Cecil tried to throw you out of the window and you might have scratched your arm yourself.'

'Do you think Mr. Hollins will be long before he answers?' asked Dorothea irresolutely.

'These things take time, or so I should imagine. I can't pretend to be much up in murder attempts. In books, I know, the detective, generally an amateur, takes one glance at the cup of coffee and tells you how many grains were dropped in, but it isn't usually as easy as that in real life. Especially if Mr. Hollins has had to pass the sweets on to a higher authority, as he might have done, since he's very conscientious.'

'I might wait till after the first post,' agreed Dorothea.

'You needn't make it sound like a favour,'

said Julia. 'Don't forget you're very lucky it's only chocolates that are being analysed and not the contents of your stomach.'

When the first post came in, however, there was nothing from the chemist, and Dorothea wouldn't listen to her companion's suggestion to wait till the afternoon, because a letter posted on Sunday from Fox Norton couldn't possibly get to London first thing next day. She felt she'd be happier once the letter was in the box and so, in fact, she was. It was strange, she thought, that, though Crook didn't look like a gentleman and didn't even pretend to be one, he did convey a sense of security. You felt that once he'd taken on a job he'd see it through, and what was more, see it through successfully.

III

It could not be denied that Dorothea was having an exciting time. She never had had so much excitement in her life before, and there was still quite a lot ahead. Actually, she owed more to Miss Carbery's presence in the flat than she realised, though, later on, when Crook and she had their promised meeting, he made her see this and she felt rather humble about her own attitude. Still, that was later.

The next development came in a letter

from Garth. He wrote in his rather stiff manner to say that he felt he should inform Miss Capper that he had taken legal advice and was contesting the late Everard Hope's will. He said frankly that the matter might prove both long and costly, and it would, perhaps, be advantageous to both sides to effect some compromise. He proposed Miss Capper and he should meet in private for preliminary discussion. He emphasized that any decisions they might make at such a meeting would have no value in law until formally enacted in the presence of their respective representatives, and indeed the letter was headed in capitals—WITHOUT PREJUDICE.

Naturally, wrote Garth, adopting the role of the candid Englishman, if I were convinced of the ultimate success of my proposed action, I should not be making this suggestion to you now. On your side, there is a grave doubt whether a court of law would uphold the will as it stands. In any case, nothing is lost to either of us by a frank discussion of the situation.

He made it quite clear that this was not a social occasion, and suggested a meeting at his office in Balmoral Row. Dorothea considered this proposal carefully, even telephoning Mr. Crook for his advice. But Mr. Crook was out of town, and she didn't care to discuss the position with a subordinate. And it did seem, to her optimistic feminine nature, that here was a suggestion that might ease the tension before the end of the fatal thirty days. For, she acknowledged, there would be little use in inheriting a fortune if she had gone out of her mind before payment fell due. One might surely gibber behind bars on nothing a year with as much satisfaction as on the income of a hundred thousand pounds.

She read the letter again. Garth was a lawyer, Garth knew what he was talking about. She committed herself to nothing by meeting him and, if she were cunning enough, she might draw him out, get him to lay his cards on the table; she could then prance round to Mr. Crook and put those same cards before him. She decided that Garth was more likely to be frank with her than with another member of his own pro-fession. When those two met it would be all fencing, all legal phraseology. She began to feel positively uplifted. She had never meant, she told herself, to retain the whole amount for herself. No, she had strong views on these matters. She was unmarried, without descen-dants. Obviously she should share with her kindred. The difficulty about the kindred was that, hitherto, they had appeared to be ready to share with anyone except herself.

But if she could come to some amicable arrangement with Garth, she could retain part of the fortune for her own use, find a more convenient flat and, above all, get rid of Miss Carbery, who surely wouldn't want to stay once she realised there were no pickings for her.

Deciding that the yellow and black suit was too flighty for the occasion, Dorothea put on her brown æolian dress, her brown matching coat, her varnished brown straw hat, her lace-up brown shoes, her plain brown gloves, took her sturdy crook-handled umbrella and her stout brown bag and travelled by tube to Chancery Lane. Her experiences of the past week or so had bred in her an exaggerated caution. On the platform she took care to stand well back from the edge; in the street she would hesitate so long before negotiating a crossing—for the number of street accidents was alarming and what was she among so many—that frequently the green lights would snap back to red before she had done more than dab an experimental foot in the gutter. A man, well-known for his humorous illustrations, watching her, observed to a companion: 'See history repeating itself. My Aunt Maria looked exactly like that, except that she wore ballooners instead of skirts, when she went bathing at Brighton.' And, indeed, the analogy was not without point. Sooner or later old Aunt Maria found sufficient courage to take her dip, and sooner or later Miss Capper got herself across the road.

When ascending or descending stairs she clung tight to the bannister rail; she regarded escalators as the invention of a criminal mind, and she had ceased altogether to attend the cinema. Every deed that is done in the dark shall be revealed in the light, proclaimed the Reverend Clifton Bryce from his pulpit, but it wouldn't help a victim much once the deed had been accomplished. Like most of her sex, Miss Capper had very little feeling for abstract justice.

Reaching the pavement outside Chancery Lane, Miss Capper nearly twisted her head off her neck trying to see street names. She wasn't sure where Balmoral Row was and she didn't like to ask any passer-by, in case he were one of her relations in disguise. But presently she saw a postman and, knowing the King's uniform (as she supposed) was safe, she inquired directions from him. Never at home in the city, she took several wrong turnings and reached Balmoral Row fifteen minutes late for her appointment. This annoyed Garth, who was the soul of punctuality. She increased her enormity by spending a further five minutes explaining how it was

245

she was late.

'I allowed myself an ample margin,' she repeated several times.

Garth looked at her and groaned inwardly. It was inconceivable that this little creature should be able to ruin them all.

Miss Capper thought him terrifying at first, but she kept reminding herself that his fate was largely in her hands. If she chose to force him to the ropes, she might well defeat him. Garth, who knew this far better than she did, knew also that he stood no chance of getting the will upset, except by guile, concealed his impatience and approached the matter with caution.

'I'm very glad to meet you,' he said gravely, 'and only sorry that we have to meet in such inauspicious circumstances.'

'I do feel it's wrong to let money make so much difference,' agreed Dorothea in earnest tones. 'After all, it's people that matter, not things.'

Garth wasn't as startled as might be supposed. Like many of his profession he was used to rather peculiar maiden ladies. It was going to be easier than he expected.

'Of course, I was simply staggered when I heard the news,' continued Dorothea, who believed that the way to show you were at ease was to talk fluently and without a break.

'I couldn't imagine why Mr. Hope should have left the money to me.'

'It was a little surprising to us all,' agreed Garth smoothly.

'I do think the Vicar's right,' said Dorothea. 'Money does make more trouble than anything else in the world.'

'Lack of money makes trouble too,' Garth pointed out.

'Of course it does,' agreed Dorothea warmly 'You mustn't think I'm unsympathetic. And, of course, when you've given hostages to fortune, naturally you have more responsibilities.'

Not all Garth's temporary good nature could supply an answer to that.

'When I first heard the news,' continued the guileless spinster, 'I thought at once—We all ought to share this. After all, a hundred thousand pounds is a lot of money. I wouldn't know what to do with it. I live very quietly, and I think I have a retiring sort of temperament. I don't mean, of course, I couldn't do with more money. There are so many people one would like to help. But, naturally, one's own family should come first. And that's why,' continued Dorothea, rushing on her fate, 'I'm so very glad you asked me to meet you in this friendly fashion Then we can exchange views. You shall tell me what you think and I'll tell you what I think about what you think, and then I can consult my lawyer with your suggestions, and he'll tell us both what he thinks of what I think of what you think.'

Garth pricked invisible ears. 'Lawyer?' he said. 'You mean Mr. Midleton, I suppose.'

'Oh no.' Dorothea tried to sound nonchalant. 'I have my own lawyer. Mr. Crook of Bloomsbury Street. I don't know if you've heard of him.'

Garth clasped his big hands quietly on the desk before him. 'Oh yes,' he acknowledged. 'I've heard of him.' Of course he had. The point was how had Dorothea stumbled on this one man when there must have been a huge choice. And how unfortunate for—well, everyone. Garth believed he had considered the situation from all its angles, but he had never dreamed of being involved with Crook. He had about as much chance against such a man as a sparrow against a king vulture. Crook had no conventions, no scruples, and he hadn't, in the best sense of the word, any reputation to lose either. Moreover, he had a nose for cash like a bear for honey. He'd never agree to Miss Capper handing over four-fifths of her fortune to her relations. In fact, he'd see to it that she didn't. And he would know that there was no validity in any

248

private agreement Miss Capper might make with her cousin. Not with Mr. Crook handling affairs.

So now, thinking fast, he sat looking like something carved in bronze—a head by Epstein or someone, thought Dorothea vaguely.

'He's quite good, isn't he?' asked Dorothea rather nervously. She was like one of those ambitious women who, having for years had their hair set locally, take their courage in both hands and march into a Mayfair beauty parlour.

'Who has been doing your hair, madam?' asked the supercilious attendant, and the unhappy woman mutters that she's been living out of London for a long time—not an easy journey—eventually is compelled to admit that she lives in the suburbs, and listens in silent shame to this same creature who probably lives in the suburbs himself, say it's worth taking a little trouble over one's hair, at least that's what ladies seem to think, and cheap treatments are generally more expensive in the long run. So now Dorothea, feeling that Mr. Crook must be suburban from his mere appearance—besides, his private address was Earls Court, she'd looked up in the telephone directory—began to excuse herself for employing any one who looked so entirely unlike one's idea of what a lwayer should be.

'I wonder,' said Garth thoughtfully, 'how you came to know him. But perhaps your mother . . .'

But Dorothea denied that at once. 'Oh no. We didn't actually have a lawyer. There was old Mr. Merridew, but he died and mother didn't care for the new concern, for the remaining partner amalgamated with another firm, and really we didn't need a lawyer. The Bank looked after our little affairs, never anything very considerable, you understand, and they've gone on looking after mine. But when I heard about this money it did seem to me I ought to have someone to—to guard my interests—and, anyway, I don't understand about money at all, I'm not a bit a progressive woman—and that's how I met Mr. Crook.'

'He was introduced to you by a friend perhaps?' suggested Garth inexorably.

'Well, not exactly. I—it was quite a chance my meeting him. I was looking for someone else and I got into the wrong office, and he said he could look after things for me just as well.'

'I see,' said Garth. 'Sailing a bit near the wind, wasn't it? Lawyers aren't allowed to advertise any more than doctors.'

'Aunt Amy,' began Dorothea, as though

she were invoking the oracle, 'used to say there are very few rules that doctors and solicitors can't get round. And she was a woman of the world.'

Garth said nothing to that. Dorothea was afraid she had offended him. She thought he looked rather like Napoleon, though it is improbable anyone else would have traced the resemblance.

'And does Mr. Crook know your circumstances?' inquired Garth.

'Oh yes,' said Dorothea. 'I've told him all about the will and the poisoned chocolates. . . .' She brought that in very naturally, so that if he had had a hand in sending them he would betray himself before he could stop. What they called shock tactics. But Garth was staring at her with knotted brows.

'You mean someone has sent you poisoned chocolates?'

'Actually they were sent to Miss Carbery, but whoever sent them knew she'd offer them to me. Killing two birds with one stone,' she added innocently.

'Have you reported this to the police?' asked Garth.

'Miss Carbery's taken steps,' Dorothea told him. 'I expect there'll be another development quite soon.'

'Have you no suspicions?'

'I couldn't have any, because I don't really know any of the people who might have sent them, and Miss Carbery won't talk. I think she knows a lot.'

Garth was regarding her steadily. 'Be careful of Miss Carbery, Miss Capper. After all, it must be obvious to you that she's in this for what she can get.'

'Isn't everyone?' asked Dorothea with an innocent generalisation that sent his brain spinning.

Garth let that pass. 'Actually, that wasn't quite what I meant when I asked if you'd told Mr. Crook all the circumstances. I meant— about yourself.'

It was Dorothea's turn to look bewildered. 'I don't understand.'

Garth leaned forward. 'Miss Capper, don't you realise why my cousin left his money to you?'

'I've thought and thought, but I can only suppose that he did it to spite the rest of you.'

'You didn't even know he was a relation, did you?'

'My mother never wanted to talk about him. She wouldn't speak of him to me.'

'And that didn't rouse any suspicions?'

'Suspicions?' Dorothea looked uneasy. 'What should I have thought?'

'Miss Capper, did your mother ever speak

252

to you about your father?'

Dorothea's startled face came up with a jerk. Her companion's manner had changed. It was now definitely menacing. She thought it might be like the film, 'She Knew Too Much,' in which the lawyer had whipped out a revolver and taken a pot shot at the hapless heroine, only missing because the hero had known he was going to do this and had emptied the chambers of the revolver the night before. Miss Capper was not a realist and it did not occur to her that it is highly improbable a lawyer of repute will risk his reputation and his life by shooting a lady across the office desk in broad daylight. It should be said for lawyers that, when they plan murder, they usually employ more subtlety than other men. Anyway, you need a licence for a revolver, and Garth, as a lawyer, knew this. Besides, he didn't stand to gain anything by swinging for murder.

'Your mother,' he repeated in tones that reminded her of Edward H. Robinson in one of his famous gangster pictures. 'Precisely.'

'Why do you say precisely?'

Garth leaned back. He felt like a fisherman who has at last persuaded a salmon to take notice of him.

'Miss Capper, do you remember your father?'

253

'He died when I was a child,' said Dorothea quickly.

'Not quite a child,' murmured Garth.

'My mother always told me he had.'

'No doubt she meant he was dead to her.'

'I know he treated her very badly.'

'I believe that's true. But did she never tell you anything about him?'

'She just didn't want to talk about him. Mr. Hope, what are you trying to say?'

'I meant to break it to you gently. That is, if you didn't know already.'

'Know what?' said Dorothea, who wasn't very quick in the uptake.

'After we heard my cousin's will,' said Garth, 'I thought it would be interesting and probably instructive to find out why he should have left that money to you, so I made some inquiries. And I found out that, in a way ...' he paused. It wasn't going to be quite so simple as he had supposed, even for a lawyer who was not unused to embarrassing situations. Dorothea was regarding him steadily, and though she would have been the first to laugh at any suggestion that she resembled a lioness guarding her cubs or anything fantastic of that kind, she did wear the look of one prepared to go to outrageous lengths. So before she could dive in so deeply she saturated them both he said quickly:

254

'You mustn't think I'm saying anything that could be construed as casting any sort of slur on your mother's name, Miss Capper.'

'I shouldn't think even you could do that,' said Dorothea quickly, who had the advantage of remembering the late Mrs. Capper. If a sculptor wanted to put up a memorial to Female Virtue he could have done a lot worse than get Mrs. Capper to sit to him.

'And, of course, as soon as she found out the sort of man your father was, she didn't stay with him another day. All the evidence goes to prove that.'

That took the wind effectually out of Dorothea's sails. 'You mean, he didn't desert us but we deserted him?'

'That isn't quite the way your lawyer would put it, but it's the fact, just the same.'

'He must have been even worse than I thought. And anyway,' she added, 'I don't see why we have to discuss my father. I came here to talk about the money.'

'Well, in a sense,' said Garth in a deprecating voice, 'it's his money—or was.'

'His money? Oh, but that doesn't make sense. It was Cousin Everard...'

'Uncle Everard to you,' said Garth gently.

'You mean—William Hope was my father?'

Garth inclined his head. Incline was the

255

only word.

'And—I'm really Dorothea Hope?'

M 'Not in law,' said Garth.

'You mean, my mother took her maiden name by deed-poll after she left my father?'

'I mean, she never had a legal right to any other.'

'But—she was married to him!'

'She thought she was, but, in fact—no.'

'But they were,' clamoured Dorothea furiously, feeling the words bursting out of her brain as if they were a flock of pigeons she couldn't control. 'Why, I know the church . . .'

'I told you your mother thought she was married to him, though not for long. I mean, she didn't think it for long. William Hope neglected to inform her at the time that he had a wife living (though she died a couple of years later, without issue). As soon as she found out, she left him.'

'Of course she did,' said Dorothea warmly. 'My mother had a very strong character.'

Garth agreed. 'Only a woman with a very strong character could have got Cousin William to the altar.'

'I'm beginning to understand,' said Dorothea. 'In a way, I am entitled to that money. That makes a difference.'

Garth looked up sharply. He hadn't anticipated this reaction. 'Not more than any of the others,' he said.

'Of course I am,' contradicted Dorothea. 'None of the others are William Hope's children.'

'I meant—his other children. There are others, you know.'

'But they're not legitimate,' burst out Miss Capper, and then turned crimson, because, of course, from Garth's pedantic and materialistic viewpoint, she wasn't either. She felt she'd gladly have forfeited the hundred thousand pounds rather than learn that. Various remarks of her mother came back to her now wearing new faces. When the young Dorothea had played Home and Husband in her isolated nursery Mrs. Capper would say: 'You mustn't suppose marriage is everything. Sometimes it's the hardest cross any woman can be called upon to bear.' She remembered once how she had said, 'Isn't it worse not to be married?' and hadn't understood why her mother caught her hand and slapped it hard, telling her not to be impertinent. She'd thought it—not unfair, because mother was always right, but incomprehensible. And there had been other occasions when Mrs. Capper's manner and response had puzzled her, but everything was clear now. Poor Mother, oh poor, poor Mother. And—as an afterthought—poor Dorothea. If Garth's story was true—and it must be or he wouldn't have asked her to come and see him—she was a—a by-blow, a come-by-chance. And it was worse to be a female than a male by-blow. In fact, there was hardly anything worse you could be, except a daughter of shame. Here she caught her breath sharply, because that was just what she was. A daughter of shame. There was a book she had read once called, *Splendid Sons of Sin*, but no one had ever written a book called, *Splendid Daughters of Sin*. She lifted her scarlet shocked face to her companion.

'Does any one know this besides you?' she whispered.

Garth shook his head. 'I wanted to see you first.'

'Is there any reason why the others should know?'

'None,' said Garth frankly. 'Not if we can come to some arrangement.'

'Arrangement?'

'Well, of course, if it gets as far as the courts the facts are bound to come out.'

She thought of all the people who would learn the truth—the Vicar, Georgie, the other worshippers at St. Sebastian with whom she sometimes went to tea. It was appalling. But it did settle one thing, once and for all. Her

258

mother had refused to take any of William Hope's money, even after his death. That, of course, was the explanation of Everard's letter offering an allowance, after he came into the money. She'd regarded her whole connection with the family as tainted and, in loyalty to her mother, Dorothea wouldn't touch it either. She had just enough to live on, and her brief experience of being a prospective heiress had brought her no happiness.

Garth was watching her anxiously. It was a very ticklish situation. Crook would be sure to throw a monkey-wrench into the works if he could. Crook wouldn't let a client of his part with a hundred thousand pounds if he could stop it, and there weren't many ways of stopping Crook once he was on the warpath. He leaned forward.

'We could come to some agreement,' he said, 'by which all Everard Hope's relations would share his fortune in equal quantities. A fifth share...'

'No,' said Dorothea sharply. 'I wouldn't touch a penny of it.'

'That is taking a rather exaggerated view of the situation, if I may say so,' suggested Garth.

'I must do as I think right,' said Dorothea, who could be loyal to more than just her own comfort. 'My mother wouldn't touch the money and nor can I. But I can't shirk a responsibility that has been laid upon me without any—any co-operation on my part,' she added desperately, not sure that co-operation was the word she meant. 'And you tell me yourself that my father had other—other responsibilities. I think his money should go to *them*.' She fumbled with facts. She couldn't thrust them forward naked as truth under Garth's nose. But she intended to make herself clear just the same. 'Naturally, I can't find *them* and I couldn't intrude into their lives if I did, but—there's a society that's always in need of funds, that looks after people whose lives have been ruined by men like my father.'

Garth was looking at her like a man demented. She couldn't mean what her words seemed to suggest. But her next speech made it obvious that she did.

'It's called The Society of the Lost Sheep,' she continued steadfastly. 'As soon as I get this money I shall hand it over to them. That's all I can do to expiate the wrong my father did me and my mother and, according to you, a great many other people. I feel I owe that to his memory, because, after all, he was my father, even if I would rather not have known it.'

Garth felt something boiling up inside him. He thought he'd seen every possibility, but this one had never occurred to him. 'You do realise,' he said, 'that such action on your part would involve the whole story being dragged into the light of day.'

'I dare say there would be a little talk just at first,' Dorothea agreed. 'A nine days' wonder, perhaps, but probably not so much as that. We are in the heart of a war, and we—the country—are spending money at such a colossal rate that a hundred thousand pounds is only a flea-bite really. People would soon forget, and even if they didn't— well, it's a chance I must take. You see, if I agreed to your proposal and kept everything covered up, I'd never feel right with myself, and so, of course, I wouldn't be happy at all.'

Garth felt that if he'd had a hammer at hand he'd have hit her on the head with it, whatever the consequences, just to relieve his feelings.

'If you're prepared for the publicity,' he muttered, 'I suppose no one can stop you from going ahead. Though I should be inclined to discuss the matter with Mr. Crook before you take any steps. I fancy he won't see eye to eye with you.'

'I don't think he'll mind what I do with the money so long as I get it, and pay his bill,' said Dorothea, with deplorable candour.

'My intention to contest the will stands, of course.'

'I don't think you've a chance of winning,' Dorothea told him. She had got her second wind by this time; she even felt a sort of peace descend upon her. She couldn't shilly-shally any more. Her path lay before her, direct and unmistakable as the path of the righteous towards the Eternal Day. 'Everyone will think it most natural that Mr. Hope should try to recompense the person his brother wronged so desperately. And since my mother is no longer alive to benefit—though, like me, I know she would have refused to take a penny—then that he should will it to me. In fact, I've a much stronger case now than I had when I came into the room.'

Garth thought: 'Damn it, yes, you're right.' He sought desperately for some way to save the situation.

'Since you're resolved, we must just go through with it,' he said. 'I'd have saved you this exposure, if I could.'

'That,' said Dorothea clearly, 'is just a lie. If you'd wanted to save me you'd never have told me the truth. There's another truth, though, that you haven't stressed, and that is that you want the money or part of it, and you think you can force my hand. Well, you have, but not in the way you expected. Nothing will move me now, not you or Mr. Crook or Miss Carbery or a time-bomb.'

He saw that she meant what she said. He also saw that she meant to take this story piecemeal to Mr. Crook, and knowing Crook's reputation, realised that this meant the ruin of his own. Crook wasn't a fellow to mince his words, and though it wasn't really fair to call this attempted transaction blackmail, that's precisely what Crook would call it. And Crook's labels were apt to stick. Shakespeare had observed somewhere that there is nothing bad or good but thinking makes it so, and it didn't take much acumen to know what Crook would think. Dorothea meanwhile had stood up. She hadn't anything further to say. Garth was desperate. He knew she was all set to go on to Crook at once.

But she didn't get there.

CHAPTER THIRTEEN

I

SEEING HER READY for departure, and realising that nothing he could say would alter the position, Garth came round the side of his table, admonishing her: 'It might be worth while thinking this over before you go to see your lawyer. You came up by lift?'

'No, I walked.' Her decision taken, Dorothea was horrified to find herself shaking from head to foot. 'There didn't seem to be a liftman.'

'You can work it yourself,' said Garth. 'I'll show you.' He opened the door and went in front of her, down the mosaiced passage. The lift was slow and old-fashioned. Garth pulled open the floor gate and, leaning into the void, hauled on a steel rope until the lift came into view.

'It's quite simple,' he said. 'You just pull on the rope till you get to your floor, and then you pull on it the other way to stop it.'

'I think really I'd rather walk down,' said Dorothea nervously.

'It's a long way,' said Garth. 'I'll take you.' He put out his hand. 'Hallo! Light seems to be off. It frequently is, but it doesn't matter.

Sometimes it comes on when you get into the lift. Something to do with the weight of your body on the floor.'

He stood back, and at that moment a telephone shrilled. Garth started. 'Get in and wait for me,' he said. 'Shan't be a moment, but I'm expecting a call. . . .'

He hurried back to his room. Dorothea stood by the lift, feeling childishly indecisive. 'I'd much rather go down by myself,' she thought. 'It would be much simpler and much less embarrassing. But I suppose it would look rude as he asked me to wait. Besides, he may want to say something else and I ought to listen.'

At that moment she heard feet on the stairs and a man came into sight. When he saw Dorothea he called out something sharply about the lift, and her heart beat with instant trepidation.

'Of course, he has been trying to get it and we had it at this floor, so he's had to walk. He sounds very cross.'

She thought she might just dodge inside and, if he were discourteous enough to stop and complain, she could tell him about Garth. Or perhaps Garth would appear just in time. Or, best of all, the man would go down and pay no attention to her.

The outer gate stood wide. She turned and

stepped through the entrance. But instead of the floor of the lift, she was conscious of only a sickening jolt as her foot found only the blackness of unfathomable space.

II

As she lost her balance she thought: 'They've beaten me at last. It's taken a lawyer to do it, but they've beaten me.' It was astonishing how many thoughts could fly through your mind in the course of a second. She knew that Garth wasn't really answering that telephone. It had been part of a plan to call him away at the crucial moment when her attention was distracted. For he had known the lift wasn't there any more; by a skilful move he had sent it higher, conscious that she would step to her death and intending that it should be so.

Some people, however, have remarkably efficient guardian angels. The man coming down from the floor above, seeing the little spinster waiting by the open gate of the lift, had shouted a warning that it wasn't working properly, that she must use the stairs. (Dorothea had thought he was complaining he'd been forced to use the stairs.) When he saw her turn and step into the chasm he hurled himself down the remaining steps, though he knew he couldn't hope to save her. But there was a second's grace. The crook of the umbrella she carried caught in the lift gate, and, being made of some kind of fancy metal (it had belonged to the late Mrs. Capper) supported her for an instant, and during that instant the stranger, a wiry enterprising kind of man, had caught her by one arm, worked his other round her shoulders and dragged and yanked and hauled her back from what was literally the gate of death. She was a bedraggled-looking object, her face all smears, her hat tilted over her nose, hair loosened, mouth fallen open in terror. For a moment she was like a creature without reason. She clawed, she wept, she babbled. The stranger held her fiercely by the arm and told her to pull herself together, she wasn't dead yet.

'I'm not,' panted Miss Capper, 'but that's no thanks to him.'

It didn't seem to occur to her that it was entirely thanks to the stranger that she wasn't lying crushed and defaced at the foot of the shaft.

'No thanks to whom?' asked the stranger, looking puzzled.

'Mr. Hope. Oh, I ought to have foreseen this. I was warned. But how could I guess he would do anything so horrible?'

'Now, look here,' said the stranger firmly.

'No one pushed you into that hole, and don't let your imagination persuade you that he did. I was coming down the stairs and I saw you step in quite deliberately, and there wasn't any one standing with you, either.'

'Of course not,' gasped Dorothea. 'He'd just gone to answer a telephone. But—he knew the lift wasn't there. He meant me to fall.'

'Sounds a bit unusual,' said the phlegmatic stranger. 'I mean, why . . . ?'

'Because of the money. Don't you see? I'd just told him I wouldn't let him have the money, so his one chance was to get rid of me before the end of the month.' She stared frantically into her companion's steady face. You really couldn't blame him for not believing a word of it. In his experience lawyers of reputation do not try to throw their visitors down lift-shafts. If they want money there are plenty of other ways of jockeying it out of the pockets of the amateurs, and Mr. Grey thought it probable that Garth knew them all. He began to feel sorry for the absent man. This panic-stricken little old maid was obviously one of those rattle-pated creatures, of whom there are many, whose very insignificance has unbalanced them. Just as, after a notorious murder, numbers of exhibitionists come forward confessing to a crime that, as

268

the police proceed to prove, they cannot possibly have committed, so she, realising how unlikely it was that she would ever attract attention, had to take this desperate step. Most probably, thought the stranger, he ought to hand her over for medical examination.

'You mustn't make these wild accusations,' he told her, severely. 'The fact is, I've assured the landlords more than once that sooner or later there would be a fatal accident and they'd be responsible. It's these old-fashioned lifts. Of course, they make the excuse now that there's a war, but I was telling them about these lifts before the war. The only safe kind of lifts are the sort that can't operate unless the outer gates are locked. In this instance, the outer gate can be pulled back and the lift can be manipulated by a rope.'

'He pulled it up,' said Dorothea, her voice still shaking. 'And then, when I wasn't looking, he—he sent it down again or up—I don't know.'

The stranger was looking at her very severely indeed. 'That's just it,' he said. 'You don't know, and you make statements that might bring you into court. As a matter of fact, the lift is out of order to-day, has been since ten o'clock. Some loss of pressure or

269

something of the kind—I'm not an engineer, but what happens is that unless you step in immediately the lift starts to sink. That's obviously what's happened here. Your friend pulled up the lift, you stood there talking, he went to answer a telephone, and by the time you turned back to the lift it had sunk out of sight.'

'How clever!' whispered Dorothea. 'Oh, how diabolically clever. Don't you see, that's what he meant to happen? He kept me talking on purpose, knowing I didn't know about the lift being out of order. He asked me if I'd come up in it, and I said: 'No, I walked.' Of course he couldn't allow for you coming down the stairs at that exact minute. . . .'

As he spoke, a door behind her opened and Garth reappeared. When he saw her talking to a stranger he looked surprised.

'Have you been waiting for me all this time?' he said. 'I'm sorry. It was rather a ticklish conversation.' His quick gaze took in the metamorphosis that had overtaken Miss Capper. The brown hat was dented and tilted over one eye, her clothes looked as thought they'd been thrown on to her at a Fair Competition, she was trembling and stammering and her bag hung open. His inquiring gaze went from one to the other.

'This lady tried to step into the lift,' said

the stranger crisply. 'She didn't know it was out of order.'

'Nor did I,' said Garth promptly. 'It was all right when I came up in it this morning.'

The stranger explained; Garth looked staggered. 'Do you mean that you very nearly... But how appalling. And how criminal of the authorities not to post notices that it was out of order, on every landing. I've protested several times about the use of this type of lift.'

'A fat lot of good that is,' said the stranger. 'Your tongue could fall out and your hand fall off before they'd listen to you. As it happened, this lady very nearly lost her life, thanks to their carelessness.' He looked at Dorothea. 'I think you should leave your name and address, madam, in case any action is taken.'

'Mr. Hope knows what that is,' said Dorothea, and turning she scurried down the stairs, away from those unsympathetic voices, those gimletty eyes. Down and down—she seemed to spend so much time these days on stairs.

'Is she all right?' asked the stranger of Garth. 'I mean, it was a close shave and it was enough to distress any one, but she told me quite seriously it was a deliberate attempt at murder.'

'Another?' ejaculated Garth.

'You mean, she's got a bee in her bonnet?'

'She's been telling me that she's getting anonymous boxes of poisoned choclates, you know the sort of thing.'

'And no motive at all, of course,' said the stranger. 'For their own sakes, people like that ought to be shut up. One of these days she'll fall over a tube platform through sheer hysteria and then accuse some absolute stranger of shoving her.'

Garth drew a deep breath. 'These border-line cases are so hard to deal with,' he acknowledged. 'They seem more or less normal most of the time, and doctors naturally are nervous of signing 'em up without quantities of evidence.'

'You want to watch your step,' said the stranger, but Garth said she wouldn't be calling on him again. He'd seen to that. As he went back to his office his mind was tangled with his own troubles. It was the worst luck conceivable that that interfering fellow should have turned up just when it looked as though all their troubles were at an end. With Dorothea dead in the lift-shaft they could all have drawn a breath of relief. As it was—the telephone rang again and he lifted the receiver mechanically—he must think of something else.

III

'You do like putting your head in the noose, don't you?' was Miss Carbery's candid comment on the situation. 'Still, there's one thing. Now they've all had a shot you can probably rest on your laurels. I mean, there won't be any more of these attempts on your hundred thousand pound life.'

But she was wrong. The worst was yet to be.

IV

A little to Dorothea's surprise nothing happened that night. No one parted the curtains and came stealing into her room after dark, no invisible hand fastened a string at the head of the stairs to trip her, no taxi tried to run her down when she went out to do the housekeeping—a loaf of bread and a small hake. Dorothea had 'discovered' hake since the war, and was as conceited as if she had invented it. When she came in Miss Carbery said: 'Hold your horses. Man named Crook telephoned you. Wants to see you this afternoon. Said I thought you were engaged.'

'Oh no,' said Dorothea, wide-eyed. 'Why should you think that?'

'So far as I'm concerned,' said Julia emphatically, 'you're always engaged when a stranger telephones.'

'But he's not a stranger,' said Dorothea, and went over to the instrument.

'That you, sugar?' Mr. Crook's hearty voice hailed her. 'Just got your letter. Been out of town, see. Not ordered your coffin yet, I hope?'

'No,' said Dorothea, not quite sure how to take this.

'That's right. With all this timber shortage *and* Arthur Crook on the trail—damned unpatriotic. Coming round at three o'clock this afternoon?'

'Yes,' agreed Miss Capper carefully. 'Yes. I could manage that.'

There were several more things she wanted to say, but Julia was listening. Mr. Crook knew she wanted to say them, but he was a busy man and, though she might have found this difficult to believe, he had innumerable other clients all of whose affairs were at least as important as her own. Besides, whatever she told him now she'd tell him all over again this afternoon. He wasn't a lawyer for nothing. So he rang her off, saying cheerfully, 'Bye. Be seeing you'; and Dorothea hung up the receiver and wondered if she'd cut the hake into cutlets and fry them in egg substitute, bread-crumbs and cooking fat, or boil it whole. While she was debating this household problem the front door bell rang, and she jumped up at once. The woman who occasionally 'did' for her didn't come this morning, so she must answer her own doors.

'Better leave it to me,' said Miss Carbery grimly. 'Don't want a jab in the bread-basket with a bayonet, do you? That's one of the thing they haven't thought of yet.'

But Dorothea felt it wouldn't be sporting to allow her guest to face the bayonet, and went down to the front door herself. A short sturdy man in a familiar blue uniform stood on the threshold.

'A.R.P.,' he said. 'Miss Capper? Come to inspect roofs and attics. You've got a trap-door, I suppose?'

'Yes,' said Dorothea, approaching the stairs in a crab-like walk. 'And a ladder.'

The A.R.P. man came on like the hosts of Midian. Poor Dorothea was quite breathless by the time she reached her own flat.

'Got a loft up there?' He squinted at the ceiling.

'There's a space between the ceiling and the slates, I think,' said Dorothea doubtfully. 'I've never actually been up there myself. . . .'

'Better take a look,' said the man. 'Where d'you say the ladder's kept?'

'In the kitchen,' said Dorothea, leading the

275

way. Behind them Miss Carbery panted like a significant grampus.

The A.R.P. man brought out the ladder, knocking some of the plaster off the kitchen wall, and planted it clumsily under the trap-door. He mounted carefully, looking rather like a Walt Disney elephant from below. Miss Carbery clutched Dorothea's arm.

'Have you ever seen him before?' she hissed.

'I—I don't think so,' returned Miss Capper, catching the inflection and hissing in her turn.

'Then how can you be sure he is who he says he is?' hissed Miss Carbery.

'He has the uniform,' hissed Dorothea more faintly.

It sounded like a snake's nest at feeding-time.

'How many women do you suppose have been ruined by a uniform?' demanded Julia. 'You remember *Pickwick Papers*? We know, Mr. Weller, we who are men of the world, that a good uniform must have its way with the women sooner or later.'

The A.R.P. man, hearing this quotation delivered in the voice reserved for quotations, stuck his head out of the trap-door and asked rudely: 'Speakin' to me?'

'I was not,' said Miss Carbery coldly.

The head disappeared.

Dorothea tried to defend herself. 'I don't know all the A.R.P. men on this section,' she pointed out.

'That's Hitler's strongest weapon,' said Miss Carbery at once. 'Lack of observation. That's how he's managed to turn Europe into Greater Germany. If people were to get to know the faces of local policemen, clergymen, civil defence workers, they wouldn't be so easily taken in.'

The A.R.P. man reappeared, saying that seemed to be all right. He removed the ladder and knocked a treasured china cat off a little bookcase that Miss Capper kept in the hall. Dorothea rescued the cat, minus its tail.

'Look what you've done,' said Miss Carbery in ringing tones.

The A.R.P., who had a muzzle like a pug, leaned towards her.

'Lady,' he said, 'p'raps you hadn't heard there was a war on.' He charged into the kitchen and replaced the ladder. 'Got all your 'quipment in order?' he wanted to know, knocking over a chair as he came out again.

'On a shelf in the linen cupboard,' said Dorothea, opening the door quickly, before he could wrench it off its hinges. 'All ready for emergencies.'

The A.R.P. representative overhauled

everything with quick clumsy hands. 'Didn't they give you a cardboard box with your mask at the Town Hall?' he demanded, looking derisively at the neat leather case in which Dorothea's mask was slowly rotting.

'Yes. But this is so much more convenient for carrying when you're shopping,' explained Dorothea, guiltily aware that she hadn't carried a mask for months.

'Rots the rubber, deteriorates the eyepiece,' said the A.R.P. man, breaking the strap of the case as he tore at the mask. 'Just as I thought. Cracked. Have to take that back to the Town Hall, though you'll be lucky if you get another. There's a rubber shortage you may have heard. Japs have got ninety per cent of the world's rubber. It was in the papers,' he added.

'I'll take it back,' promised Dorothea, literally shaking in her shoes, and reflecting that in all the important aspects of daily life the prospect of a hundred thousand pounds seems to make no difference whatsoever.

'H'm. What's this? Torch? Don't you know you've got to cover a bulb with not less than three thickenesses of tissue-paper? Axe?' For the first time he sounded slightly respectful. 'That's a nice specimen. D'you think you could break down a door with that?'

Miss Capper, eager for approval because the visitor was a man and must therefore be placated, said: 'Well, I don't know about that because I've never tried, but when I bought it the man said that it would be very useful for hitting any one over the head.'

Her visitor laughed shortly. 'Have you tried that?'

'Well, no.' She looked abashed. 'But after that woman was murdered in West Brompton I used to put the hatchet by my bed every night for—oh, quite a month afterwards.'

'See it doesn't get rusty,' said the A.R.P. man dropping it on the floor. 'All right, don't worry, it missed my feet. Got a stirrup-pump?'

'The people on the ground floor have that. I'm afraid they aren't in during the day. If you could come after six in the evening . . .'

'I'm off duty then. Do you mean they're never in during the day?'

'I think they do war-work. Anyway they go off in taxis as often as not quite early and don't come back till quite late.'

'Sounds exactly like war-work,' said the A.R.P. man dryly. 'One thing, they won't be able to go on doing that much longer. Got any pails?'

'The first floor have those. I'm afraid they're out, too.'

279

'And they don't come back till six either, I suppose?'

'Sometimes it's later. They work in Government offices, even on Sundays sometimes.'

'Nice quiet house,' said the A.R.P. man. 'There are going to be some fire practices at the Convent starting next week. You'll get a notice.'

'I'll try to come,' promised Dorothea, wondering how her cousins could turn such events to good account.

'You've got to come,' said the man uncompromisingly. 'The Government's shilly-shallied long enough about women being conscripted for fire-fighting. Why shouldn't women defend their own homes? If you were in Russia,' he eyed Dorothea's skinny form with contempt, 'you'd be in the army.'

'Pity we're not in Russia,' broke in Miss Carbery vigorously. 'Nothing I'd like better than being in the army. Stop all this nonsense about the superiority of men. Why, half these chaps in civil defence are better off than they've been for years. You needn't tell me. I've studied statistics.'

Metaphorically Dorothea wrung her hands. There wasn't any need, was there, to arouse antagonism? Her experience was that there was plenty knocking about without going on to your doorstep and inviting it in.

But the A.R.P. man was a match even for Julia. 'Nice thought, isn't it, that you have to have a war to get a chap a job?' he demanded belligerently. Seeing that she had no reply ready, he thudded down the passage and went out, slamming the door violently. When Dorothea went to straighten the mats and replace the curtain over the bathroom door (it had fallen down in the draught), she realised that he'd broken the front-door lock. 'Oh dear!' she said. 'Now I must ring up Powells, but they won't send anyone to-day. They never do. They'll only tell me there's a war on. It may be the end of the week before they can attend to this.'

'You've got a bolt on the door,' said Miss Carbery approvingly. 'You can shoot that, and if you take my advice, you will.'

'It's all right really,' faltered Dorothea. 'Only it's a nuisance, my having to see Mr. Crook this afternoon.'

Miss Carbery said in cheerful tones that she'd stay, it was her job being watch-dog, wasn't it? Then her face changed. She looked troubled.

'What is it?' whispered Dorothea, susceptible to every rise and fall of the temperature.

'I don't know,' said Julia, frowning.

281

'Only—I believe I've seen that man some-where before.'

CHAPTER FOURTEEN

I

PUNCTUALLY at two-thirty Dorothea set out. It was raining, a steady bleak downpour that looked as though it might go on for the duration. Dorothea put on her black mackintosh, her black goloshes, and took the famous crook-handled umbrella to protect the buttercups in the black straw hat. She felt quite pleasantly excited at the thought of retailing to Mr. Crook all that had happened during the past few days. Of course, he had had her letter, but letters weren't the same thing.

Mr. Crook, however, speedily stripped her of her self-conceit.

'You know,' he said, 'it beats me how you women ever stay out of jail. Haven't you got a dictionary?'

Dorothea, looking considerably startled, said of course she had.

'Never looked up the meaning of libel, I suppose?'

'Libel?'

Crook nodded. 'Practically every statement in your letter could be regarded as libellous. First of all, you say your cousin Hugh tried to poison you in the sugar you put in your

283

coffee. How much evidence have you got to support that? Why, you don't even know for certain that the sugar was tampered with. What if the old lady did die? You don't know it was because of the sugar. That disposes of your case against Cousin Hugh. Then you say that Cousin Cecil tried to throw you out of a window. Try taking that to court and see what happens. Cousin Cecil takes the stand, swears you went hysterical on him and dashed out into the rain. Any witnesses that he made any attempt on your life?'

'He was far too careful,' said Dorothy indignantly. 'Besides, what about the needle?' She held out her wrist on which a sharp eye might still discern the remains of a scratch.

'And you take that to the police surgeon and ask him to swear on oath it was made with a hypodermic needle. Why, the man ain't living that 'ud do it, and if he was living the right place for him would be the bat-house. You might have scratched it on your own brooch or the pin in your collar. You might be one of those dames with persecution mania. I've known them do some damned odd things. Why, they'll cut 'emselves— quite badly—so that it hurts, I mean—and swear they've been assaulted. It's a common joke to say a chap's guilty till he's proved

284

innocent, but take it from me, it ain't so. If you and Cousin Cecil go to court, Cousin Cecil's not only goin' to get the verdict, he's goin' to get the commiseration of everyone who hears about it. Why, you can't even prove motive.'

'The money, if I die . . .' began Dorothea, but once again Crook cut her short.

'Who says it's goin' to him? And even if it does, who says he's goin' to risk murder to get it? For it would be a risk. You mightn't break your neck in the obligin' way Cousin Hope did. You might stay alive long enough to whisper your secret into a policeman's ear. And I know those windows at the Alexandra Hall. You might chuck yourself out or be heaved out. It couldn't be an accident. Well, Cousin Cecil would have to prove you'd chucked yourself out or anyway suggest it. You couldn't fall out by accident. As for the prick, you'd have to show he's got a hypodermic needle and drugs and knows how to use them. You couldn't do it, sugar. Take it from me, you couldn't do it. From a professional point of view, that rules Cousin Cecil out.'

'And I suppose you're going to tell me that Cousin Garth didn't know the lift was out of order?'

'Don't see how you can prove he knew. It *was* in order when he used it in the mornin',

285

so unless you can find someone who saw him come out of his room and try to get the lift later in the day but before your arrival, you're stymied. What you have to realise, sugar,' and here Mr. Crook leaned closer, pushing his amiable pig's face into hers, 'is you're either nuts or else you're up against a real tough bunch of crooks.'

Dorothea supposed that if you were drowning you'd feel as she felt now. Crook's calm assembling of the facts was as pitiless as a wave closing over her defenceless head.

'There were the chocolates,' she whispered.

'Any proof that they were poisoned?'

'Not yet,' agreed Dorothea, 'but Miss Carbery has sent them to Mr. Hollins, the chemist at Fox Norton, to have them analysed. We're waiting for his reply. She says he may have had to send them to a doctor.'

'Anyway, they weren't even sent to you. And how were your cousins to know you liked sweets?'

'I'd told my cousin Hugh. He may quite well have told his brother.'

'What the soldier said ain't evidence. I'm always tellin' women that.'

Dorothea prepared to depart, looking shaken and crushed. 'I can see you think me very foolish,' she said. 'But my life is valuable to me, if to no one else.'

'Don't ride your high horse with me,' Crook warned her. 'I don't want to spend my time with a telescope looking for you. Of course your life's valuable to you, though no one but me might guess it.'

'I don't understand,' said poor bewildered Dorothea. 'I can see you think I'm imagining danger where no danger exists.'

Crook stared. 'Be your age,' he said. 'Who told you that? I think you're in a pretty hot spot if you want to know. Point is now—who's goin' to win the round—X. or me? X. bein' the chap who wants to see your little light go out like that.' He snapped his fingers.

'So I am in peril?'

'Hadn't you guessed it?' asked Crook kindly. 'You might expect to do something for a hundred thousand pounds. No rose without a thorn—and you're a pretty hefty thorn yourself, come to that. To the rest of the family, I mean. Oh yes, you're like St. Paul, standin' in jeopardy every hour. Now look here. You prepared to take a risk?'

'I don't seem to have any choice,' said Dorothea sadly.

'Well, you know what the strategists tell you. Attack not defence is the secret of victory. All the amateurs of the country have been tellin' Mr. Churchill that for months. Now you've been on the defensive ever since you heard about this money. What you want now is a little enterprise.'

Dorothea, who felt she had employed a good deal of enterprise in avoiding the various forms of death that had come crashing her way of late, looked and felt disgusted by this observation.

'Well, see it straight,' urged Crook. 'Who are your natural enemies? All the people who want you out of the way. Who are the people who want you out of the way? Anyone who might benefit by your death. And, if you're right, most of 'em have had a pot-shot already at puttin' you where poor Jamie lies. Whereas you, with just the same opportunities, haven't grasped one of 'em.'

Dorothea gaped like a bilious chicken. 'The same opportunities?'

Crook felt some sympathy with Miss Carbery, who said Dorothea must have been a parrot in a previous existence.

'Why d'you let them ride you?' he demanded with some exasperation. 'If you'd been whole-hearted about this fortune of yours you wouldn't have hesitated. The fact is, you're like most women, particularly unmarried women. You prefer your conscience to your cash. Well, if that's the case, say good-bye to the cash, only I'm afraid it means sayin' good-bye to life, too.'

'I don't want the money,' cried poor Dorothea. 'I've already told Mr. Hope that.'

And, crimson with shame, she explained the circumstances.

'You are a card,' said Crook admiringly. 'Always done what mother thought best, haven't you?'

'Yes,' gulped Dorothea.

'Then why not do something different for a change?' inquired Crook simply. 'After all, what's progress for if it isn't to put new ideas into circulation? Besides, all this nobility—it ain't so hot. Half the time it's just shirkin' issues. Now, how about doin' a bit of attack? It's about time.'

He looked at her earnestly. A great light broke over Miss Capper.

'Do you mean, I might take the initiative and—and murder them?' But he couldn't mean that, of course.

'You're getting there, sugar,' said Mr. Crook approvingly. 'Mind you, I wouldn't put it that way myself. When you've been a lawyer as long as I have you'll know that two-thirds of your success depends on the right way of puttin' things. Words, that's what we juggle with. Novelists tell you the same.' He shook his formidable head. 'All punk, sugar. What a novelist can do with words is nothing to what we can do. No, your job is to suppress your enemies. F'r instance, why not have sent the chocolates on to one of the cousins? How were you to know they were poisoned? When Cousin Cecil tried to push you out of the window, couldn't you have turned the tables and sent him crashing? He's only a little whipper-snapper, you say. You started at plus, too. No one suspected you. There are times,' continued Mr. Crook, sadly, paying no heed to his companion's goggling eyes and stammering tongue, 'when I'm sorry I stand for law and order. 'Course, I know all about professional integrity and all that, but there are times when I envy the free-lance. Take it from me, a married man's not the only chap who's given hostages to fortune.' And he sighed for opportunities lost for honour's sake.

'Then what would your advice to me be?' asked Dorothea, catching the infection of his mood.

'What the Prime Minister, whom I'm damn sure you adore, has been tellin' the country for longer than they've bothered to listen to him. See what the other chap's goin' to do, and then *do it first*. Of course, if he's no more ambitious than you, you can sit back and take it easy. But—you may not have noticed this, so you can take my word for it—there's always a few ambitious fellows roaming about, and they're the ones you've got to watch.'

'Perhaps,' said Dorothea, achieving a fine irony, 'you can tell me what I should do now to—er—get square with my more ambitious relations.'

Mr. Crook beamed and cuddled into his deep chair.

'That's the girl,' he said. 'Now you and me'll go into conference.'

II

Leaving Mr. Crook's office, elated, desperate, feeling like a falling star that can't do anything but fall, and therefore takes no thought for the future, Dorothea was surprised to find that it was still raining. The fireworks had flashed so brightly upstairs that the contrast of the murky streets was as dazzling as sunlight. Dorothea didn't feel she could go home yet; it seemed such a deplorable anti-climax. She remembered a notice in last Sunday's *Recorder* about a film entitled 'Lady Mind Your Step,' a real hell-for-leather smash-hit, said the reviewer. Dorothea was feeling rather that way herself. Reluctantly she decided to let Julia Carbery know where she was, as otherwise that lady would start telephoning police stations, and at the present delicate stage of operations the police were the last people Dorothea wanted disturbed on her account. So she stepped into a telephone booth and announced her change of plan.

As she had anticipated, Miss Carbery was obstructive. 'Thought I warned you not to go to cinemas alone,' she said. 'This Crook person isn't coming with you, is he?'

'Oh no,' said Dorothea, sounding shocked. 'He's a very busy man.'

'Where is this picture?' Julia wanted to know.

Dorothea named a cinema in Leicester Square.

'I'll meet you there. What time does it start? 4.25? That gives me heaps of time. Your man isn't likely to come about the lock now. Of course, I shall probably catch my death of cold in this rain, but what's that to you?'

Dorothea forlornly hung up the receiver. It had been too good to be true to suppose she'd be allowed to go by herself. She looked at the rain and shivered. She would be horribly wet by the time she got to Leicester Square, in spite of the goloshes, the mackintosh, and the umbrella. A taxi came slowly past, and on the spur of the moment Dorothea hailed it. No sooner was she inside than she remembered *The Clue to the Cruising Cab*, in which the villain, disguised as a taxi-driver, followed his prey from pillar to post, and eventually crushed her to death on the Embankment. His own escape was due to the fact that he was, in private life, a contortionist, which enabled him to swing himself clear just before the crash. However, this time Miss Capper seemed fortunate. She reached the cinema without mishap and, having twenty minutes and more to wait, went into the café for a welcome cup of tea before Miss Carbery arrived.

Julia, of course, never dreamed of taking a taxi. She put things in order at the flat, enveloped herself in a voluminous green mackintosh, tied an oilskin pixie-hat over the ginger curls, added goloshes to the beetle-crusher shoes she invariably wore, and came very quietly out of the flat. She paused on the front doorstep, looking up and down at the unsympathetic rain. Then she unfurled her umbrella and stepped into the deluge. There was wind as well as water, so she had to proceed in an attitude that suggested a croquet hoop. So it was that, as she battled stormily down the street, she failed to see a man in the uniform of Civil Defence cross the road and proceed in the way she had come, and having consulted the list in his hand, march up the steps of 28, inhabited by Mrs. and Miss King.

Dorothea was waiting in the lobby. 'I've got the tickets.' she said. 'Shall we go up or down?'

'He that is down need fear no fall,' said Miss Carbery with unmistakable meaning, so down they went.

The film wasn't quite what Dorothea had anticipated. There were no gangsters in it and the only villain was the hero. The chief character was a lady who was always being proposed to for her money, and was perpetually evading marriage as Dorothea was always evading death, by the skin of her teeth. The girl was so pretty and the suitors, particularly the villain, so ardent that Dorothea's heart began to burn. Oh, to be young; oh, to be enchanting; oh, to have this girl's gaiety and poise. But if your hair has always been straight as water and your mother disapproves of waving or dyeing, on the ground that God knows best, what chance have you? Besides, this girl had a perfectly respectable background, whereas I, thought the unhappy spinster, am one of Those.

'Wake up,' said Miss Carbery presently. 'What's the use of paying to go to the pictures if you sleep through them? You can do that for nothing at home.'

'I wasn't asleep exactly,' said Dorothea in a guilty voice. 'It's only that I'm not really very interested in the life of the soya bean.'

For the authorities had decided that you mustn't have jam without powder, and so reproduced the pictorial progress of the soya bean from seed to stove. And after that came the news.

When the two ladies finally emerged the rain had stopped, though the streets still glistened with moisture. Miss Carbery paused in the vestibule to re-don the green mackintosh, re-tie the pixie-hood, replace the goloshes, and was rewarded by hearing a girl murmur to her companion: 'Do you see what I see? Where do you suppose they find them?'

'I know where you'd find that chit if I had my way,' said Miss Carbery in a loud clear voice. 'Over my knee. And it's a pity her mother hasn't got as much sense.'

Dorothea, embarrassed again, hurried her companion across the road. Luckily the rush hour was over and they got on to a bus without any difficulty. Miss Carbery was still brooding on the uneducated young. Dorothea thought about youth too, but her subject was the girl in the film. Her tense attitude relaxed, she smiled, and felt at ease. You might never meet such girls, but it was nice to know they existed.

If Mr. Crook could have seen her at that moment he would have shouted, ''Ware hounds,' but there was no one at hand to warn her what lay just ahead.

CHAPTER FIFTEEN

I

THE REVEREND CLIFTON BRYCE was standing on his front doorstep saying a prolonged good-bye to one of his most influential parishioners, when he caught sight of Dorothea rounding the corner of the street. He had been waiting for just this opportunity and, being a man after Mr. Crook's own heart, he resolved to make the most of it. Like every one else, he knew about Everard Hope's will, but unlike some of his neighbours, he didn't feel he could hustle round to see the fortunate heiress just because she was about to come into money. Still, as he liked to proclaim from the pulpit, Let patience have her perfect work—and he had given patience a long rope, and here was his chance. It wasn't that he wanted anything for himself—he did sincerely believe that clergymen should set an example in austere living, and he'd been talking about austerity long before Lord Woolton discovered the word—but they did need new hassocks for the Lady Chapel and the Fabric Fund was running low, too.

So he hastened to speed his parting guest. 'Good-bye,' he said with his famous smile,

297

holding out his hand. 'Mind you tell your husband to come and see me now he's on leave.'

'I'll do my best,' promised the I.P., 'but you know what these sailors are.'

'Tell him he must pay me a fleeting visit,' said the Vicar.

The I.P. laughed with delight. How witty! How—as dear Harold liked to say—on the spot. The Vicar backed into the hall, saw the blue delphiniums from the I.P.'s garden that she had brought for his delectation, and indicated them with another smile. He had better blooms in his own little patch, but naturally he didn't mention the fact. A stray taxi ambled past and the parishioner hailed it. The Vicar smiled with aching jaws, this time with relief. It wasn't often that taxis turned up just when you wanted them, not in the Bush, anyhow. The taxi drove off, its occupant smiling and waving as though she were going to the war, and the Vicar peeped out again. Miss Capper was quite near now, but his gratitude to Providence was checked a little when he saw that she was accompanied by what looked like a green rubber elephant. That, he concluded, must be the female who had come to stay with her. Dorothea hadn't told him about Miss Carbery, but he knew, just the same. Vicars always do. The authorities might do worse, when they want recruits for the Secret Service, than consult Crockfords. As he dodged back again, to make a strategic advance at the right moment, his eye fell on the delphiniums. He picked them up. He'd offer them to Miss Capper. What luck the I.P. had brought them. Certainly they weren't the equal of his, but Dorothea wouldn't mind that, even if she noticed it. For his purpose they'd have done practically as well if they'd been made of blue paper. Like Cecil, the Vicar knew it's the thought that counts.

Just as the two ladies were passing the Vicarage gate out popped Mr. Bryce like a jack-in-the-box, carrying the flowers. Dorothea was delighted. So, it appeared, was the Vicar.

'The very person I was hoping to see,' he said. 'Dreadful afternoon it's been, hasn't it?'

Dorothea introduced Miss Carbery and said they'd been to the pictures.

The Vicar said: 'How nice! Miss Capper, I wonder if I could persuade you to take over the secretaryship of the Solomon Islands Association. As you know, Miss Conder had it for years and she . . .'

Miss Capper knew. There had been a requiem for Miss Conder two months ago. The Vicar seemed to have some difficulty in filling her place. But Dorothea was delighted at his proposal. She had always longed to be approached in some such connection, for the Vicar had to a nicety the capacity to make people feel as though they'd been decorated when they agreed to spend whole mornings dusting the pews and cleaning the church brass.

The Vicar next extended the delphiniums. He was walking along with the two ladies in the most amiable manner. 'Just a few garden flowers,' he said. 'I wonder if you'd care to have them.'

'Beautiful,' breathed the ecstatic Dorothea. 'I was thinking, at the Dedication Festival party (which was always held in the little Vicarage garden) how beautiful your delphiniums were. Though, of course,' she added honestly, 'they weren't out then.'

The Vicar didn't undeceive her. He knew she would find the flowers twice as beautiful if she believed they came out of his 'little plot.' As they had now reached Dorothea's doorway she suggested the Vicar might like to come up for a drink.

'Don't tell me, Miss Capper, you've got anything alcoholic on the premises,' boomed the Vicar.

Dorothea looked startled. 'Oh—I didn't know you—it's only just some sherry I happened to have in.'

She didn't add that she had bought it at the grocer's about a year ago, when she had had dreams of being dashing and giving parties like other people. But the few she had invited had all been engaged and she had shrunk into her shell again. The sherry had cost 3/10 and was guaranteed full and sweet.

'I'm afraid Mr. Bryce will have to excuse the mess the flat's in,' said Miss Carbery. 'I had to come away in such a hurry.' You could see she didn't approve of Dorothea's emancipation.

Mr. Bryce pooh-poohed the idea that he minded a little clutter. He liked a place to look lived in, he explained. Dorothea opened the front door and the three of them came into the hall. Dorothea began telling the Vicar about the broken lock. 'Miss Carbery thinks we ought to be able to claim the expense from the Town Hall, seeing it was one of their employees who broke it. . . .'

The Vicar said he thought so too.

Dorothea said most likely they were both right, but the damage had occurred while the authorities were trying to safeguard her premises, and if there was an air-raid the Civil Defence would drag her from the ruins without charge, so really she did think, especially as this was the first time it had happened . . . Didn't the Vicar agree?

The Vicar said it did her credit.

Miss Carbery said she couldn't see there was any credit in being soft.

They reached the top floor, and Dorothea was about to push open the door of her flat when the Vicar, always the gentleman, stepped forward and did it for her, a smart military push, immediately afterwards stepping back for her to precede him. At the same instant there was a resounding crash and something came hurtling to the ground. Dorothea and Miss Carbery stood looking as though Lucifer had fallen out of Heaven into No. 30 Blakesley Avenue. The Vicar moved cautiously forward and stooped down. Then, in a voice free from all professional artifice, he exclaimed: 'Thank God, I was with you. Otherwise you'd have rushed in and . . .'

Dorothea was shaking. 'Yes,' she whispered, and even her words were unsteady, 'that's what I was meant to do, of course.'

They stood for a full minute without so much as a word between them, staring down at the heavy axe that had been balanced on the lintel of the door to strike down the first-comer who should enter the flat.

II

Miss Carbery recovered speech first. 'What a fool!' she exclaimed, striking her hands

302

together. 'What a blind damned fool!'

The Vicar looked rather startled.

'I thought it was extraordinary,' she went on. 'We've had Civil Defence men in the house before—that is, we had them at Fox Norton—and they never went round breaking everything up. Of course, that's why he came. So as to be able to get in again when the place was empty. He probably watched the house. You said you didn't know him,' she added, turning to Dorothea.

'I simply don't understand it,' said Miss Capper. 'It doesn't make sense.'

'It makes a lot of sense,' said Julia, 'if you couple it up with what's gone before. A railway truck doesn't make sense if there isn't an engine to draw it. Cast your mind back to this morning? Now do you see why he wanted to look at everything? And it's no use looking for finger-prints on the handle of the axe,' she added vigorously, 'because we've all touched it, so there's no help to be got there.'

She stooped as she spoke and picked it up.

'You must have a charmed life,' she observed grimly to Dorothea. 'It's up to you to make the most of it.'

The Vicar followed the two ladies slowly into the flat. He was badly shaken. So, it appeared, were the delphiniums. He wished he hadn't let Dorothea believe they came out of his garden. It is, of course, the nature of delphiniums to fall, but all the same the Vicar didn't like anyone to think his would. Dorothea paused instinctively on the mat to pull off her goloshes. Miss Carbery, who had preceded her, hadn't been so careful, and there were large damp footprints corresponding to what Crook would have called her great splay feet. Miss Capper didn't like to call attention to this at such a moment, but she was distressed all the same. Everyone had warned her it was madness to have a fawn carpet in the hall, but she had wanted something cheerful, and up to date it had kept wonderfully clean. And now Miss Carbery had spoilt it. There was mud as well as damp on the goloshes, and you can't get mud very well off a pile carpet. The Vicar rubbed his feet hard on the little mat for that purpose and offered to get in touch with the police. He said he knew one of the men at the station in connection with a theft from the Altar Flower Fund box some months previously. But Dorothea said: 'I think I'd better get in touch with Mr. Crook first.'

'Surely the police...' began the Vicar, but Dorothea said no, she trusted Mr. Crook even more than the police. The Vicar could hardly believe his ears. He hadn't been crossed by a woman since he got his first incumbency. Motherless, sisterless, wifeless, his word was law. And here was Dorothea flouting his offers of help. He could hardly believe it. Most likely she didn't realise the seriousness of the position.

'It's all right,' said Dorothea when he tried to explain, 'this isn't the first time. Oh, it's the first time they've used an axe, but . . .'

The Vicar laid the delphiniums down with a little bang that brought more of the blossoms fluttering to the floor. Of course an affair like this was enough to upset any one, but he hadn't suspected this strain of obstinacy. It was almost as though Dorothea wanted to keep the police out of it, as if she had something to hide. Naturally, he wouldn't go so far as to say she deserved to have axes falling on her head, but he did seriously wonder if she was the right person for the Solomon Islands Association. He thought, on his way back, he'd drop in on Miss Groves and sound her. It was a pity he hadn't kept the delphiniums for her also. It didn't look as though either Dorothea or Julia intended to put them in water or even remembered their existence.

III

'Why wouldn't you let him get the police?' demanded Miss Carbery after the Vicar had taken his leave, wearing a Christian look that at any other time would have driven Dorothea frantic.

'I think I should get in touch with Mr. Crook first,' said Dorothea. 'I promised him I'd do nothing without consulting him. Besides...'

'Well?' said Miss Carbery, looking like one of the three classical sisters waiting her turn to snatch the tooth and the eye.

'It might disarrange Mr. Crook's latest plan,' furnished Dorothea reluctantly. She was remembering Crook's last word of advice.

'Don't be proud, sugar. Give that horse of yours a rest now and then. Confide in this lady, keep her in touch. If you don't and things go wrong, well, you'll have no one but yourself to blame.'

Dorothea would have liked matters to be a complete secret between herself and Mr. Crook, springing her mine on Miss Carbery at the eleventh hour, but since there's no sense paying a lawyer if you don't do what he tells you, she unfolded the outline of Crook's latest notion. Miss Carbery listened, her eyes nearly popping out of her head. They were protuberant at any time, but now they were like a snail's, set on the ends of horns.

'Is the man mad?' she demanded, as Dorothea's voice faltered into silence. 'Doesn't he know all these people are your sworn enemies that he suggests your giving a dinner for them? It's the very chance they're all praying for.'

'That's what he says,' Dorothea explained. 'He says it's the chance he's praying for too. You see, with all the family there, they may think it's safe to run risks.'

'Remember, history repeats itself,' Julia reminded her grimly. 'They were all in the house when Mr. Hope fell downstairs and broke himself to bits. And no one's found out how that happened yet.'

'I think Mr. Crook has,' said Dorothea. 'I think that's one of the reasons why he wants to see us all together. He says this has stopped being a joke and it's time someone put an end to it.'

'So far as I'm concerned,' announced Julia, more grimly than ever, 'it was never a joke. I hope your man knows what he's doing, but don't forget he's a lawyer and you can never trust that bunch.'

'My trouble,' said Dorothea sadly, 'is that I don't know who is to be trusted.'

She went to the telephone to ring up Mr. Crook and inform him of the latest developments. But Crook had gone out.

'Where are you going to have this ridiculous party?' Miss Carbery demanded. 'Here?

You won't be able to swing a cat with eight of us round the table.'

'Nine,' murmured Dorothea. 'Mr. Crook's coming too?'

'We shall be so packed together we shall probably feed the wrong face,' said Julia ungraciously.

'Oh, I don't mean to have it here,' said Dorothea. 'There's a room you can hire at the Yellow Primrose. Quite a nice room, I think. And, of course, the Primrose is the sort of place where it's all right to hire a room.'

Her restrained voice and downward glance said volumes. Julia glanced at her with unconcealed contempt. 'No one's going to try any fun and games with you, my dear,' she thought.

'Is your friend planning to poison all the rest of the party?' she inquired with interest. 'That's your only hope, I should have thought.'

'I'm sure he won't do anything that'll get him into trouble,' returned Miss Capper. 'But, of course, he knows just how far it's safe to go.'

'The relations may smell a rat,' said Julia bluntly.

'I dare say they will, but Mr. Crook says they'll all come to see what it looks like—the rat, I mean. I promised I'd see about the room this evening. He thinks the sooner we arrange this the better.'

The Yellow Primrose was an inexpensive restaurant not far from Blakesley Avenue. It 'did' 2/- luncheons (everything palatable being marked 3d. extra) and 2/6 dinners. Inside it was rather dark and all the tables were bamboo; the chairs were painted primrose, and the china was yellow and so were the lampshades. The room that could be hired was upstairs. It was a fair size but an odd shape, and had the sort of furniture you might expect. The table was circular, the carpet looked like a vegetable hotchpotch, the ceiling was cracked and ornamental, and the china on the mantelpiece matched it.

'Hardly the right surroundings for an heiress,' said Miss Carbery candidly. 'What's behind those curtains?'

Long mustard-coloured plush curtains with tatty ball fringes hung from ceiling to floor on one wall, hiding dividing doors, painted the same cheerful yellow as the rest of the woodwork.

'I suppose there's another room there,' hazarded Miss Capper.

'It isn't what's behind there now that's important,' observed Julia, 'but what or who is behind there on the night of the party. There's nothing to prevent your friend buying up the proprietress and installing a private murderer for the occasion.'

'Nothing beyond the fact that he'd be out of pocket and might lose his reputation and even his liberty,' agreed Dorothea with the nearest approach to sarcasm she ever achieved.

'I wonder if they can manage the food all right.'

'Why couldn't your Mr. Hook or Crook call a business meeting at his office?'

'I think he thinks this would be more friendly,' returned Dorothea, after some consideration.

'About as friendly as a cageful of alligators. What's the menu to be? Soup—Crime. (She pronounced it French fashion.) Entree—Bones in Blood. Sweet—a bombe of some kind.' She was so pleased with her own wit that her good humour was restored.

'He says it will be the end of attempts on my life,' continued Dorothea.

'So long as he's sure it won't be the end of your life, too, well and good,' agreed Miss Carbery. 'I suppose you know that if anything should happen to any of your loving relatives you'll be held responsible.'

'But if I was innocent,' said the guileless Dorothea, 'they couldn't touch me.'

Even Crook might have given up hope of

her after that.

The invitations dispatched, Dorothea set about making preparations for the feast.

'Do it handsome,' Crook had said to her. 'It's the last time you're goin' to give any of them anythin'. I'll see to that.'

She was rather troubled about the question of wine, and tried to remember what Hugh had given her at luncheon. A good deal of nervous explanation at a wine merchant's resulted in her purchasing two bottles of 'special' burgundy at 11/6 a bottle, and some beer for Crook. She was also anxious to have Grand Guignols, but it proved impossible to get the recipe for these, and she decided to dedicate to the feast the one bottle of sherry that hadn't, after all, been opened on the Vicar's account last week.

She rang Crook up and told him about these arrangements. When she described the sherry he said: 'Grand, sugar. Now we can dispense with the arsenic.' After some consideration, Miss Capper decided this was a joke.

She and Julia pondered a good deal on the nature of the statement Crook said he intended to make after dinner. Julia said perhaps he'd discovered there wasn't any money, after all, but Dorothea told her very seriously that in that case she was sure her lawyer would not allow her to spend money she could ill afford on entertaining people whose sole interest in her to date had been to try and put her out of the way with as little delay as possible.

On the morning of the day itself Dorothea went to see Mr. Crook to make sure all the preparations were in order and to receive his final instructions.

'Now don't lose your head,' he told her. 'Granted you're in a spot, but remember I'm there at your side. That's the difference between you and Everard Hope. He had the family round him but no Arthur Crook. You hang on to that thought. I promise I shan't take my eye off you the whole evening.'

'I am not really very nervous,' Dorothea assured herself bravely, travelling home by bus, folding her hands tightly over one another. 'And of course he must know best.'

When evening came she had another good time wondering what to wear. Eventually she draped herself in a black velvet frock with a diamante girdle, and wore the black suede cavalier shoes bought to impress Hugh. She tried putting a diamante ornament in her hair, but it wouldn't stay straight but kept slipping over one eye, so, having tried the effect of applique-ing it on various parts of the velvet gown, she put it back in the drawer and fastened round her throat a little moon-stone locket on a silver chain that she had been given on her twelfth birthday. She had said Morning Dress on the invitations, and black velvet and diamante are not really morning wear, but she thought she, as hostess, might be allowed a little licence. Miss Carbery, on the other hand, adhered strictly to instructions. She put on a bright orange jumper and a mixture tweed skirt. She said there was a war on and she didn't intend to forget the fact. She didn't let anyone else forget it, either. The bright orange of her top fought fiercely with the green and red of the tweed throughout the evening. Crook had drawn up the invitations, that were so worded as to ensure the presence of all the people concerned. On second thoughts he told Dorothea not to worry about the food, so long as there was beer in abundance, as the visitors were coming to have their curiosity satisfied rather than their appetites. He came in good time and stood looking round the room in a proprietorial way. He wore the re-grettable brown suit that was his daily wear and had brought a small bag with him. Julia observed in an audible aside that they ought to have put 'Speeches' on the invitations, but Crook, overhearing her, said: 'Oh, why? No sense raisin' their hopes. No one's goin' to do

313

any talkin' but me.' Garth and Lucille were the first of the visitors to put in an appearance, Garth in a grey suit and Lucille in a black dress with pearls. When she saw her Dorothea realised how inadequate it was to say that any one wore 'black with pearls,' since such a description would apply to them both but with what a difference! Lucille would have ignored Dorothea if that had been possible, but since it wasn't she gave her the frostiest of greetings and ignored Julia instead. This took some doing, considering Julia's get-up, but Lucille achieved it. Cecil and Lilias came next, she, placid and friendly, saying: 'I'm glad we're meeting at last. I hope you didn't think we were all trying to rush you. I am afraid it must have looked rather like that.' Dorothea, wondering what she'd think if she knew the facts, said untruthfully: 'No, of course not.' She didn't know how to meet Cecil's eye, and he also was nervous. This might be a last chance—everything now depended on what the fellow, Crook, had to say. He didn't care for the chap's looks, but he did give an impression of power. The lawyer looked at Cecil in a way that seemed to admit that all forms of life had their place, but it was a little strange to find this particular manifestation at Dorothea's dinner-party. Cecil kept looking at his watch.

Perhaps, he thought, there was going to be some offer to divide the spoils. (It must be remembered that this was his first meeting with Crook, and though he was a novelist he did sometimes make mistakes about character.) He was as jumpy as a hop-toad, and when Garth inadvertently stepped backwards on to his toes, in natural reaction from his first taste of the sherry, he nearly came out of his skin. The brothers arrived together. Christopher looked as nearly aloof from the human scene as any living man can. The late edition of the *Record* told him that the lady who had been causing him so much anxiety had been run down in the dark by a bus the previous night and had since died of her injuries. He felt he'd like to decorate the driver, or at least reassure him that he'd done the world a good turn. It wasn't often that life palmed the ace like this. He was so pleased that he was charming to Dorothea, who instantly wondered how she had ever suspected him of sending her poisoned sweets. And indeed she did him a gross injury to imagine that such a thought had ever entered his mind. She had never been in any danger from Christopher.

Hugh was friendly and casual. 'Tried any more Grand Guignols?' he asked.

'I wanted them for to-night,' said Dorothea, responding eagerly, 'but I couldn't get the recipe. There's only sherry.'

Hugh took the sherry and responded rather as his hostess had done to the first of the Grand Guignols.

'Clever of you to get sherry these days,' he said, when he had come round from the first shock.

'I wanted to do the thing in style,' returned Dorothea, trying to sound *mondaine*.

She turned to speak to Julia, who had nudged her sharply, and Hugh skilfully tipped the rest of the sherry into a potted plant, to which he then transferred his complete attention, in the expectation of seeing the plant stagger off the table. The fern, however, seemed possessed of more resistance than Hugh and made no sign whatever. Dorothea turned to Crook and offered him some sherry, but he only whispered reproachfully: 'Want to do your best friend in before the curtain rises? I never saw such a girl.'

Dorothea offered the decanter to the rest of the party, but no one would take a second glass and they sat down to dinner. It wasn't much of a meal. Dorothea, who had begun the evening in a hopeful frame of mind, had to admit that she wasn't doing her guests very proud, but the company was so intent on what was to follow the food they didn't seem to notice what they ate or rejected. Dorothea had Crook on one side and Julia on the other. Julia had suggested this and Crook backed her up.

They passed from water in which the dish-cloths had been boiled, and a little macaroni added, to what Christopher supposed was that nameless part of a beast of the field not commonly offered on the market—anyway he couldn't identify it—and finished up with a savoury consisting of a prune wrapped in a fragment of salt bacon. The men were chival-rous enough to leave the burgundy to the women. Lucille took one sip and left the rest of hers, but the other three merely thought it tasted nasty but not nastier than wine always did taste. Towards the end of the meal Mr. Crook opened the bag and produced a bottle of sloe gin. This surprised even Christopher, who didn't realise that Crook could have pro-cured a whole ox to be roasted had occasion demanded it. When the gin had been the rounds Crook said he thought they ought to drink a toast— 'The Giver of the Feast.' Dorothea blushed and simpered and looked a bit silly, but she looked sillier still when Crook suggested: Everard Hope. Garth looked up sharply, thinking the speaker con-victed of appalling taste, Cecil was so much startled he upset some of his beer, Christopher and Hugh exchanged glances. Of the party they had by far the most common sense, and neither expected to hear that he was to profit by any chivalrous action on Miss Capper's part. If she had given the party herself they might have permitted themselves to hope, but when they set eyes on Crook they told one another the Minotaur had returned in human form. They didn't mind. Minotaurs made a pleasant change.

'If it hadn't been for Mr. Hope we couldn't have had this party at all,' Crook explained.

'People have to die sometime,' snapped Julia.

'But they should choose the right moment,' said Crook.

Garth opened his mouth to speak, but Hugh got in first. 'You think he didn't?'

'Obviously not, for one person.'

'Which one?' That was Cecil, barking out of sheer nervousness.

'Whoever would have benefited by the will Mr. Hope intended to make if he had lived another thirty-six hours.'

There was a slightly uncomfortable silence.

'Does anyone know who that was?' inquired Garth in a voice that was meant to strike Crook to the earth like a thunderbolt. But even the gods never tried to get Crook down. The odds were too heavy.

'I could make a good guess,' said he modestly. 'Only, as I'm tellin' my clients, what the soldier said ain't evidence.'

Cecil spoke again. 'None of us had any notion of Cousin Everard's intentions,' he said importantly. 'You can't involve us in his death.' He had two glasses of sloe gin and had no idea how potent it was.

'I'll say you hadn't,' agreed Crook. 'Anyway, I don't think he was goin' to the expense of havin' a lawyer down from London to benefit any of his dear cousins.'

Even the brothers registered curiosity here.

'No,' continued Crook, 'I don't think he took much interest in them really. I fancy there's only one person who could hold his int'rest at that stage, and that...' His leisurely bright eyes passed from face to face. The tension reminded Lucille of the night Everard Hope died. 'That,' wound up Crook coolly, 'was his wife.'

There was a moment of utter shock. Then a voice called out, another joined issue. The word Wife was heard in several accents, but before any one could pose a coherent question Crook made a sudden lunge towards Dorothea, who was leaning forward, absorbed, and cried out, 'Watch it, sugar,' in

a voice of extreme urgency.
At that instant all the lights went out.

CHAPTER SIXTEEN

I

IT WAS a macabre situation. A moment ago they had all been remembering the night of Everard Hope's death, the darkness, the clamour, the mystery. And here, all in an instant, most of the same features were repeated. Darkness, noise, a deep cry, a groan. Julia was heard shouting: 'Where's the damned switch?' She moved across the room and collided with Hugh, who had the same idea. Christopher had put his hand in his pocket and brought out a pocket-lighter. You could hear the scratch of it as it failed to work. Garth lighted a match and held it above his head. Something—a puff of wind? a human breath?—blew it out. As he tried to light another, someone knocked against him and the box fell out of his hand. It was a full minute before the lights were working again.

'That was a fool trick,' said Julia's rough voice. 'Who d'you suppose...?' And then she stopped.

Everyone had moved in some degree—everyone, that is, except Dorothea. She had only sunk more completely over the table, and in the glare of the electricity they all saw

the hilt of a great black knife sticking between her shoulder-blades.

There was a wild scream; that was Lucille,
who couldn't stand the sight of blood (though
actually there was none to be seen). There
was a sickening thud, and that was Cecil
swooning to the floor, because he couldn't
stand the thought of blood. There was a
fierce exclamation and that was Garth. 'What
the devil?' There was a mutter, 'God! That's
torn it!' and that was Christopher. A
woman's clear voice said: 'We must get a
doctor,' and that, of course, was Lilias. Hugh
went towards the door, saying superfluously,
'I'll go,' but he found his way barred by
Crook.

'I don't think so,' said Crook grimly. 'I
don't think anyone better leave the room till
we've had the police.'

Julia said hardly, 'This family has a predil-
ection for violent death'; and Crook rejoined,
'Almost looks like coincidence, don't it,
lady?' and opened the door a couple of
inches. They realised he must have attracted
someone or else their clamour had done it for
him, for they heard his voice speaking. He
gave a telephone number and then came the
word, 'Police.' After that he came back and
shut the door. Garth was standing at Lucille's
side, saying scornfully: 'There isn't any

blood. You needn't look like that.' Lilias said: 'It's more dangerous when the bleeding's internal.' Julia observed: 'She's still breathing. While there's life there's hope.' Cecil had had some of the burgundy dashed over his face by Christopher, who thought no fate too bad for some wine, and he was now sitting up, looking dishevelled and more demoralised than ever. Christopher was fingering his cigarette-case, not quite liking to light up. He also was thinking of the night Everard Hope died. No one liked to go near the prostrate Dorothea, though Julia would certainly have done so if Crook hadn't mounted guard and kept them all away.

'This is a job for the doctor and for me,' he said grimly. 'I promised her I'd keep an eye on her and preserve her from harm.' His big face looked dangerous for the first time that evening.

'Spoke a bit soon, didn't you?' asked Garth, and then there was the sound of feet at the door, and two men came in. The first was tall and dark with a black smudge of moustache and walked with a slight limp. He carried a doctor's small bag and went straight to Dorothea, without asking questions. The other wore a police sergeant's uniform and waved the little group of people away from the table. He said something to Crook, and

323

Crook said, 'I expect so,' and went towards the curtains.

'Door's locked,' he said, after a minute. 'But we can probably get the key from the proprietress.'

'What happened?' the man inquired. 'You in charge?'

'Actually the lady was. It was a dinner-party.'

They say it is as impossible to surprise the police as to shock a doctor, but the man's brows did lift a little.

'I see.' He looked as if he'd like to ask whether one of the guests had mistaken Dorothea for an old hen to be carved up, but he restrained himself and repeated his request for information.

'We can't tell you anything,' said Julia harshly. 'At least I can't. One minute we were all talking and the next the lights went out. When they went on again she was like that.'

Crook thought even he couldn't have improved on the account for terseness and accuracy.

'Who was nearest the lady?' the sergeant inquired.

'I was one side,' said Crook.

'And I was the other,' said Julia. 'Are you going to suggest I struck that knife into her?

324

And if so, what do I gain through her death?'

'Only a hundred thousand pounds,' said Crook gently. 'That's all. Just one hundred thousand pounds.'

II

For an instant the assembly was like Canute's sea when he commanded it to retreat and it refused. The voices were rather like waves, all washing over one another, all mingling and incoherent, so that one voice repeated what another had just said, like part-singing. In the middle of it someone appeared with the key of the dividing doors, and the sergeant unlocked them and swept everybody into the inner room.

The doctor said sharply, 'Sergeant,' and he went across and helped to lift the unfortunate Dorothea on to a couch that stood against the wall. The knife was still in her back. When Garth, glancing over his shoulder, looked at the floor, he saw a little trail of dark spots on the carpet. The sergeant said something about an ambulance and shut the doors. An uneasy silence fell on the waiting group. It was Lucille who broke it.

'Mr. Crook,' she said, 'what did you mean by that last remark—about the wife, I mean?'

'Just what I said,' returned Crook. 'I told you Mr. Hope's next-of-kin was his wife.

And I said that if Miss Capper died this lady,'
he indicated Julia, 'would inherit a hundred
thousand pounds. How does that add up to
you?'

The voices began to clamour again. Out of
them came Christopher's, saying: 'But what
gave you the idea in the first place?'

'When you get a chap as mean as Everard
Hope—and he was meaner than the meanest
flower that blows—and you find him paying a
salary for sixteen years to a lady he doesn't
particularly want in his household, well, then
I begin to smell round for rats. I believe that
fellow would rather have eaten stewed boot
than spend good money on food. He lived in
a ruin and looked like a scarecrow, but he
kept a secretary-housekeeper, though he
practically never wrote letters and his larder
looked like one of the European countries
when Hitler had gone through it. Why?
Because Miss Carbery meant to stay. She was
the only one who could make Everard Hope
put down any money at all. When she turned
up at Miss Capper's flat she had some money,
because she offered to lend it to Dorothea,
and she hadn't inherited it because she said
not. Of course, if Dorothea had been a bit
quicker in the uptake she'd have jumped to
the truth a bit sooner. You told her that you
(he turned to Julia) were one of the poor re-

lations, too. Well, if you weren't a wife, where did the relationship come in? Anyway, once I got the idea I toddled off to Blackpool and looked up the registers, and there it was.'

'How long ago was this?' demanded Garth.

Crook told him airily: 'Just about sixteen years.'

'You mean, the year Cousin William died?'

'I mean, the month Cousin William died. Now do you see light?'

The shock was so great they all looked mistrustfully at one another, suspecting a leg-pull, thinking that Crook had no respect for anything, not even sudden death. Before any of the cousins could speak, Julia had leaped up and marched over to Crook, her face as glowing as her jumper.

'What put you on to the marriage?' she demanded.

'Rule of thumb,' said Crook modestly. 'Couldn't find any other key that opened all the locks.'

'Why on earth she didn't tell us after my cousin died,' began Garth stiffly, but Crook interrupted with his usual rudeness.

'Be your age. First thing you'd have wanted to know was when the wedding took place, and when you heard that she and the lucky heir got triced up directly after the funeral, well, you might have thought it a bit odd. No, I don't think either of them could afford to do much talking.'

'Meaning there was something fishy about Cousin William's death?' deduced Hugh.

'Plain as the nose on my face,' returned Crook, 'and I can't say fairer than that. Well, why should anyone want to marry Cousin Everard?'

'He had a hundred thousand pounds,' said Garth.

'Precisely. And why should a man with a hundred thousand pounds want to marry Miss Carbery? No offence meant,' he added quickly. 'Besides, I'm all for givin' coincidence a good run, but it's a bit thick to suggest that on an icy March day that big landing window would have been open at the bottom. And if Cousin William had come in a bit mops and brooms the odds are he'd have collapsed into a chair to sleep it off. And even if he had wanted fresh air, why choose the heaviest window in the house to open?'

'Meaning,' said Hugh, 'that Cousin Everard opened it for him? But—he was out.'

'Who says so?'

'He found the body on the way back.'

'Well, if I dropped something out of a window, what's there to prevent me goin' out by the back door and pickin' it up? And what was he doin' comin' in by the back-door anyway? No, no, you take your Uncle Arthur's words for it, Everard Hope didn't go walking in snow and blizzards just for fun.'

'Do you suppose, then, that William was so bottled he couldn't tell whether a window was open or shut?'

'Remember, they always had curtains across that window. With the curtains drawn, who's to tell if the window's open or not? And it wouldn't be too hard to give a reeling man a push. You know they said he clutched the curtains as he went over. But if he'd opened the window himself he'd have drawn back the curtains first, and they wouldn't have been there to be clutched at.'

'I suppose you realise,' said Garth, 'that you've no proof?'

'I don't need it,' said Crook, sturdily. 'It's not my job to show how William Hope died, any more than I have to bring a case against anyone for the death of his brother. And if I had, so far as he's concerned, I wouldn't quarrel with the verdict—Death by Misadventure.'

'I'm glad you don't consider I pushed him downstairs,' said Julia raspingly.

'I didn't say that,' Crook corrected her. 'I said I didn't quarrel with the verdict. Not quite the same thing.'

'Any relation to Maskelyne and Devant, Mr. Crook?' asked Hugh. 'Mean to say, he pushed him down, but it wasn't murder.'

'No,' agreed Crook. 'Not murder. I'd be more inclined to call it self-defence. You see,' he went on comfortably, oblivious to poor Dorothea in the next room, 'I see it this way. I think Everard had got to the end of his tether. He'd been pretty sick about the way William was wasting an inheritance that he regarded as his own, and was beginning to wonder how much, bar the house, would be left when his turn came. Besides, I dare say it looked as though William might outlast his brother. And then I fancy William must have talked of getting married. That cut Everard out altogether.'

'Not necessarily,' said Garth in his cold way. 'Only if there were legitimate issue.'

'Well, there wouldn't have been any difficulty about that,' Crook assured him heartily. 'If half the yarns you hear are true there were probably three or four ladies with a right to demand marriage lines. And that was too much for Everard. Think of it. He'd lived in penurious righteousness for years, and now it looked as though he wasn't going to have any reward. Mind you, as my colleague points out, I've no proof, but I did go to school when I was a kid, though not the sort of school you'd think a whole lot of,' he added, nodding in friendly fashion towards the Lacey brothers. 'Still, they taught us arithmetic. Two and two make four, and a lot of the classy colleges don't teach you that much. Now I have to do a bit of hedge-hopping here, because the next fact we have is his marriage to Miss Carbery almost immediately afterwards, a marriage they both kept secret.'

'You mean, she saw him, she threatened to give him away,' said Lucille.

'It could be, lady, it could be.' He looked at Julia. 'Don't care to make a statement, I suppose?'

'Why should I?' said Julia. 'Oh, it's no use denyin' the facts. We did get married. It suited us both. He got a housekeeper and I got a home.'

'Well, well,' said Crook, 'let it go at that. I ain't the Recording Angel. Still, most people's idea of a home wouldn't be The Brakes. Now we jump sixteen years and Cousin Everard dies too.'

'Perhaps you've a theory to account for that,' suggested Garth sarcastically.

Crook went to the dividing doors, peeped into the other room. There had been voices and footsteps for the past few minutes.

'All right,' he said. 'They've got her away. We may as well wait till that bobby comes back.'

'Has he gone with them?' asked Lucille.

'She might come round enough to make a statement,' Crook explained. 'The police haven't got where they are to-day by takin' chances. Still, we've all the time there is. No, I don't think Miss Carbery meant to shove the old man downstairs. No motive, see? If the accident had taken place after Midleton's visit, that 'ud be quite a different pair of pumps. Because Midleton was comin' to alter the will, and I don't think Everard Hope was payin' his expenses from town just to do any of his cousins a bit of good,' he said again.

'You mean, he was being blackmailed into action by his wife?'

'No hard words,' said Crook. 'But—yes. I think the idea was that he should draw up a new will and leave all the money to Mrs. Hope—Mrs. Everard Hope. That's how she saw it anyhow. She made him send for the lawyer and he was comin' on Friday. The old man put the visit after the annual party, because he thought, like everyone else, that there's safety in numbers. If there should be an accident while the house was full of people—well, anyone might escape scotfree.'

'God!' said Christopher. 'You mean, he never meant to make that will.'

'He didn't mean it to be necessary,' agreed

332

Crook. 'You know, there was some queer things about the night he died. He was terrified of fire. Well, that's all right. Nothing strange about that. But a man who's as alarmed as he was don't stop to put on his trousers and put in his teeth when he hears the call. He just bolts out of bed and lugs his dressing-gown with him. Everard Hope wasn't only wearin' his dressing-gown, he'd got it nicely tied round his waist. He had his stick and—his bed hadn't been slept in. Maggie told me that, and I guess you knew it too.' He nodded to Julia.

Julia scowled scornfully. 'The old fool! He botched everything he put his hand to. I suppose he thought it was brilliant to give the alarm and then station himself at the head of the stairs ready to trip me up as I came dashin' by. But as a matter of fact, if he'd really thought it was a fire he wouldn't have been on that staircase at all. He'd have gone shuffling down by his private stair, and the rest of us could have roasted for all he cared.'

'So you see what happened,' wound up Crook. 'His little plan went wrong. It's always the way with amateurs. They fall foul of the timing.'

'It wasn't that,' said Julia shortly, 'but I had a torch and I saw just in time and—well, it wasn't me that went rolling down the stairs.

Take that into court, if you like, but they'll only tell you to laugh your silly fat head off.'

'You know a lot,' said Crook admiringly. 'If you'd known just a little bit more I dare say you wouldn't have taken so many risks. About puttin' poor Dorothea Capper under the sod, I mean.'

Julia laughed rustily. 'So I've murdered her, too, have I.'

'If you haven't it's not from want of trying. You see, when I do a jigsaw puzzle I like to make all the pieces fit. When you came up to "protect" Miss Capper and all sorts of things began to happen—the sort of things that had never happened before—I began to look for Cause. Cause and Effect, see. No effect without a cause. There were three actual attempts on Miss Capper's life. I discount the other two, but I'm convinced of three. The poisoned sugar. The poisoned chocolates. The axe over the door. Another thing I learnt at my school,' he went on pleasantly, 'was a thing called Lowest Common Multiple.' (Actually he meant Greatest Common Factor, but no one liked to contradict him.) 'You take a lot of numbers and find one that's common to them all, and that's what you're looking for. Well, I took these three attempts, and I found one common factor, and that was Miss Carbery. You,' he nodded

334

to Hugh, 'might have poisoned the sugar, though I don't see how you could have known Miss Capper liked her things sweet, and you might even have sent the chocolates, but I don't see how you could have fixed the axe over the door. Any of you might have sent the chocolates, though I can't see how any one, except Captain Lacey, could have known Miss Capper was a sugar fiend, and then—why not send them to her direct?'

'Because they knew I liked Dubois' chocolate peppermints and always had them,' snapped Julia.

'And that's another thing,' continued Crook. 'Dubois don't operate through agencies, you have to buy them direct, which means they keep tabs on their customers. Well, it's a funny thing that they've never heard of any Mr. Hope or Mr. Tempest or Mr. Lacey, but they sold Miss Carbery a half-pound box of peppermints a day or two before Cousin Everard died. Since then there's been a dearth of peppermints and they've only just got going again. So, you see, it doesn't look as though any one could have packed those sweets except Miss Carbery.'

'And I suppose I sent them to myself?' suggested Julia.

'Oh, I don't think they came by post,' said Crook.

'What are you getting at?'

'Well, you didn't take them in, did you?'

'Certainly not,' said Miss Carbery, perceiving the trap and avoiding it. 'I found the parcel, as I told her, outside the inner door when I came back from doing a bit of shopping.'

'Didn't occur to you to wonder how it got there, I suppose?' suggested Crook.

This time Miss Carbery did not perceive the trap. 'The postman left it there, I suppose.'

'First time I've heard of a postman walking through a solid door. They don't deliver letters to the flat, remember. There are boxes nailed on the front door, one for each flat, and the tenants do their own collecting. You should know. And don't tell me he rang the bell and one of the other tenants let him in, because they're out all day.'

Miss Carbery said sullenly: 'Perhaps there was a charwoman. I don't know...'

'Perhaps the same mythical Belinda let in the A.R.P. man, too,' suggested Crook. 'I mean, you shut the door behind you, didn't you, when you went out? And there's another thing. How the hell did that chap, that careless hulking chap, who broke up half the house just by walking through it, come in on a pouring afternoon and not leave a single footprint on the hall carpet? The nice clean fawn carpet. He hadn't, you know. Miss Capper told me, saying more than she knew, that she and the Vicar stopped to wipe their shoes but you clumped right in. There was mud as well as wet, and those carpets keep their impressions. Well, your impressions are there, but no one else's. That takes a bit of explaining away, too, don't it?'

Garth spoke. 'I think Miss Carbery—Mrs. Hope—should be warned that she doesn't have to answer any questions unless she likes.'

'Sure she don't,' agreed Crook warmly. 'Anyway, I ain't the police, so nothing she tells me holds good in a court of law. But— it's a damn' funny thing that Mr. Hollins never wrote about those chocolates. Sure you didn't forget to send 'em?'

'I'm not responsible for the deficiencies of the Post Office,' said Julia swiftly. 'I can only tell you I did send them.'

'Registered post?'

'Of course not. It only holds things up twenty-four hours.'

'Neat,' commented Mr. Crook. 'No proof either way. Still, the lost property office don't know anything about them either. As a matter of fact, I'll tell you why I don't believe they ever left this flat, and that is I don't

think there was anything wrong with them—
bar the one in the top row that was left for
Miss Capper to take. One or two of my clients
have experimented with pumpin' poison into
chocolates, and they tell me it's a damn difficult thing to do. I think the first two chocolates were taken out—p'raps they were even
eaten, while Miss Carbery had the flat to
herself—and when she heard Miss Capper
comin' in she just locked herself in the what-
you-may-call-it and waited to give Miss
Capper a chance to digest the dose of death.
Only—like her husband—she didn't time it
quite right. Out she came, and there was
Miss Capper with the chocolate in her
pocket. So you had another shot. I will say
one thing for you, sister,' he continued,
admiringly, 'you've got what it takes. You're
a fast worker. Pity you aren't on my side
instead of the other. You saw your chance—
you wouldn't know the feller was goin' to
break down the lock, but when he did you
went to it like a member of the Secret Service. But you know what they say—
Providence looks after fools and
children—and Providence popped up with
the Vicar as a trump card, and there was
another good opportunity gone down the
drain. I figured you must be gettin' a bit
warmed up by this time, so I took the bull by

338

the horns and suggested this party. I guessed there'd be an attempt on Miss Capper's life, and I thought it was time we called a halt.'

'You've done that all right,' said Garth, colourlessly.

'And I suppose,' said Julia breathing through her nose like a hippopotamus, 'I waited till the lights went out and then stuck that knife in Dorothea's back.'

Crook looked quite surprised, but he looked pretty satisfied too.

'Oh no,' he said. 'It was I who did that.'

CHAPTER SEVENTEEN

I

A CLASSIC SILENCE followed this confession. Even the sophisticated Laceys seemed aghast. Before any one could speak the door opened and the policeman came in, followed by the doctor who had given his name as Martin.

'It's all right,' said the sergeant.

'All right to leave her?' said Crook.

The sergeant said: 'I guess so. You've got all the parties here, haven't you?'

'That being so,' said Crook, 'you can take off that moustache, Bill. It don't look real anyhow.'

The doctor put his hand to his face, and when he took it away he was clean-shaven.

'Meet Bill Parsons,' offered Crook. 'Bill and me are a team. And that's Watkins.' He indicated the sergeant. 'Just part of the Arthur Crook service.'

The company was still in the dumb-founded stage. Only Garth was capable of speech, and it was at once clear that he was in a towering fury. 'There's a law against imper-sonating the police,' he said in a thick choked voice.

'Be your age,' said Crook. 'It's being done on half a dozen London stages this very minute. If there are any fancy dress dances going on anywhere, you'll probably find two or three policemen among them. I should worry.'

'Look here,' said Hugh in so quiet a voice that every one turned to look at him. 'I think you owe us an explanation. You say you stabbed Miss Capper?'

Crook turned to the sergeant. 'Got the knife? Thanks.' He held it up before the eyes of them all. 'Now watch.' He turned to Bill with a sudden vicious plunge of the arm. The knife sank into the shoulder up to the hilt.

'Theatrical property,' explained Crook. 'You asked me if I had anything to do with Maskelyne and Devant. Well, I don't say they ever used a contraption of this kind—I wouldn't know—but I know damn' well a lot of play-acting chaps do. You can buy 'em for spoof parties, or you could before the Government stopped most of our innocent fun. The blade just folds up into the handle when it touches anything solid, and it's so contrived that the knife will stay fixed so long as no one monkeys about with it. All perfectly simple when you know.'

But Hugh Lacey's face showed no lightening. 'I suppose this practical joke was necessary,' he said in tones of extreme distaste.

Crook turned in a flash. 'What do you think I am?' he demanded. 'I told Miss Capper she was runnin' one hell of a risk, but I'd keep an eye on her and keep her safe. And she is safe. And she's safe because I got her out of the way in time.'

'You mean, you believe someone would have attempted her life?' cried Cecil in his thin indignant voice.

'I'm damn' sure they would. It was too good a chance to miss. I don't quite know what method was goin' to be used, but we'll soon find out.' And before any one could anticipate his action he had stepped forward and snatched Miss Carbery's bag. With a furious exclamation she tried to grab it back, but Crook moved out of reach, and at the same time his two allies caught Julia by the arms.

'Game's up,' said Crook laconically. He opened the bag and began to rummage inside. After a moment he held up something small and shining.

'Neat,' he said. 'That's a hypodermic syringe. I suppose it was to be used on Dorothea at an appropriate moment, and the odds are you,' and he nodded towards Cecil, 'would have been held responsible. By Miss Capper at all events.'

'The woman must be mad,' stammered Cecil furiously. 'I wouldn't even know how to use such a thing.'

'Quite simple,' said Crook. 'You must let me show you sometime.'

'And why on earth should she pick on me?'

'Because she thinks you tried to put out her light with one of these the day of the Alexandra Hall concert.'

'I never heard anything so infamous. Of course, I realised then she wasn't normal—the way she suddenly fought me like a tiger and went rushing down the stairs—she ought to be shut up. . . .'

'In a nice box six foot long,' agreed Crook. 'You know, I don't believe you'd be quite your own bright self if you had people popping up trying to rub you out at every turn. No, she's not a fool, but she's got the wind up pretty badly, and you can't blame her.' He looked soberly at the glittering toy in his hand. 'Queer the shapes death can assume,' he said. 'One little dig and—I suppose it would have been found in someone else's coat-pocket when the ball was over. Y'know. I think the police better have a look at this.'

'Velly clever man,' shouted Julia with such rage that they were all staggered. 'And if I say that isn't mine and I never set eyes on it before and it was slipped into my bag when my attention was distracted—why, you might have done it yourself.'

'Well, I might,' agreed Crook. 'But how about the poison in the flat? Oh yes, while we were havin' boiled block ornament here a chap was goin' through No. 30 Blakesley Avenue with a tooth-comb, and he found a lot of int'restin' things. Didn't you, Watkins?'

Watkins said expressionlessly: 'I dare say the lady can explain.'

'Item,' said Crook, who seemed to have the situation in the palm of his hand, 'a neat little instrument for drillin' holes, specially useful for delicate work like fillin' up chocolate creams. I wonder what else you used that for. But, you know, you made one bad blunder. *What made you keep this?*'

He thrust out his big hand, on the centre of which lay something round and brown and gleaming, something not quite perfect all the same, because of certain marks on the surface.

'Recognise it?' asked Crook. 'That's the chocolate Miss Capper put into her mouth and just didn't eat. That's the worst of amateurs. They always trip up over some trifle. You should have burnt this thing pretty damn' quick if you wanted to keep out of trouble.'

'What kind of fool do you suppose I am?' shouted Julia, beside herself with fury and humiliation. 'Of course I burnt it. I didn't keep it in the house another hour. It's a plant. You've done another one, and you...' She stopped dead and something—some physical change—took place that only Crook could watch unmoved. It was as though life itself began to ebb out of the big vital form. The great ruddy face fell into folds, her limbs sagged.

'For God's sake get your policeman,' said Christopher. 'We've had enough of this. This isn't the gladiators' ring in ancient Rome.'

'We've got the police,' said Crook mildly. 'I'm not quite a fool either.'

'But you said...' exclaimed Cecil.

'Didn't you hear your cousin tell you it's illegal to impersonate the law? There's been enough illegality about this affair, one way and another. It's up to you now, sergeant. I don't have to find you proof or sketch a case. All I had to do was prevent Miss Capper comin' to a sticky end before her time, and I've done it.'

II

'What will happen to her?' asked a shrinking Dorothea, some time later. 'They—they won't hang her, will they?'

345

Crook stared. 'What for? She hasn't killed anyone, has she? She hasn't committed sedition or looted bombed premises or struck a superior officer.'

'If she hasn't killed anyone it isn't for want of trying,' said Dorothea, with more spirit.

'What's that got to do with it?' Crook demanded. 'If I handle a case for a client and we lose it, the fact that I did my best don't help him, do it?'

'No,' said Dorothea thoughtfully. 'I suppose not.'

'Still, you don't have to bother about her,' Crook went on. 'She'll be out of your picture for some time, and when she comes back it won't make any difference to her if you're alive or dead.'

Dorothea shuddered. 'That horrible money!'

'I always told you you couldn't expect to get a fortune for nothing,' said Crook mildly.

'I shan't touch a penny of it,' said Dorothea. 'I shall send it all to Mr. Churchill for the expenses of the war, the whole hundred thousand pounds.'

'Well, not the whole of it,' said Mr. Crook temperately, 'because you won't get it all.'

Dorothea reddened. 'I mean, naturally, when I've settled my debts.'

'Don't forget Mrs. Hope's share,' murmured Crook.

'Mrs. Hope?' Miss Capper seemed utterly at sea.

'Julia to you.'

'But she doesn't—she isn't—I mean, it's not her money.'

'Well,' observed Crook mildly, 'she was the old boy's wife, and if she likes to claim maintenance, she *can* be awarded up to one-third of the income of the estate. After all, she was technically supported by him.'

'She was working for her living,' said Dorothea warmly.

'That's what I said. She was the old man's wife. Mind you, I don't say she'll claim it. I don't say she'd get it if she did, but you have to bear the possibility in mind.'

'She can have it all for all I care,' cried Dorothea wildly. 'I never asked for the money and I don't want it.'

'Now, now sugar,' Crook soothed her. 'That's no way to talk.'

But Dorothea refused to be soothed. 'I mean it—I won't keep a penny. I was much happier without it.'

Crook saw with horror that she was in earnest. Dorothea was thinking she couldn't understand why people envied the rich. The responsibilities involved far outweighed the advantages. To handle money required a

347

fund of energy, enterprise, and courage she didn't possess. Far better, far more safe to live like a mouse in its hole, unenvied, unnoticed, than run the tremendous risks of 'being someone.' Having money, she had thought, meant a wider and fuller life. She had expected, for instance, that she would establish a new and far more intimate relation with the Vicar—but it hadn't worked out like that. She had simply been pursued by people who wanted to deprive her of her inheritance and didn't much mind how far they went, so long as they achieved their objective. Like a great many uncourageous people, Miss Capper was able to persuade herself that there was a definite virtue about poverty. All the virtues, she believed, involved this quality. To her, meekness meant poverty of spirit; humility poverty of pride. The meek and the humble were permitted to remain obscure—and safe. Not for them the danger and the heat of the sun. 'I am content to dwell in the shadow,' murmured Dorothea's shrinking spirit.

So she said again: 'There's no need for any one to go to law. I relinquish all claims. I'm sure it's what my mother would have wished.'

Crook felt much the same Hugh had done when Dorothea announced that she preferred an ice to crepes suzettes. People like that deserved to be murdered.

'Well,' he told her, not attempting to disguise his disgust. 'I can't think why you've been beefin' about all the attempts on your life. A coffin seems to be all you want.'

All she was fit for, he thought. Once his account was paid she couldn't lie there too soon for him.

III

It was Sunday morning. The Vicar came down the chancel steps and marched into the pulpit. His eye that, like the poet's, could roll in a fine frenzy, took in the whole of the congregation waiting with such meek intensity for his message. All the familiar faces were there and he had ceased to expect novelty. He noticed Miss Capper in her usual pew, wearing her usual Sunday uniform of nice brown æolian dress (cleaned), shiny brown straw boater (re-blocked), brown lace-up shoes (re-heeled), neat rayon stockings efficiently darned, suede fabric gloves (one coupon and home-washed) lying beside her. She wore a flat contented look. Her brief fling over, she was glad, she told herself, to be back where she belonged. Other people might be called to be wild birds of Heaven, but her vocation, she was sure, was that of the little brown domestic hen. One of her favourite romantic authors had said there is no loneliness like the loneliness of the open sky. Experience had taught Miss Capper that, in spite of the high-brows, the romantics do frequently tell the truth.

'The Book of Job, 19th chapter and the 20th verse,' intoned the Vicar. 'I am escaped by the skin of my teeth.'

The twins in the pew behind Dorothea sighed and closed their Bible. They'd lost, as usual.

'Do you ever think, my brethren,' inquired the Vicar, leaning over the edge of the pulpit and putting the question in a You-are-the-one-I'm-talking to voice that enchanted his congregation, 'of the vast importance of the insignificant?'

There was a noticeable quickening and thrill all through the church. This was what they called a promising beginning. Insignificant but important. It was a pleasant cud to chew.

'For instance,' continued Mr. Bryce, 'what would Job have done if his teeth had had no skin?'